Plato's Promise

A Woodland Tale

Plato's Promise

A Woodland Tale

James G. Tauber

iUniverse, Inc.
New York   Bloomington

Plato's Promise
A Woodland Tale

This is a work of fiction. All of the characters, names, incidents, organizations, and dialogue in this novel are either the products of the author's imagination or are used fictitiously.

iUniverse books may be ordered through booksellers or by contacting:

iUniverse
1663 Liberty Drive
Bloomington, IN 47403
www.iuniverse.com
1-800-Authors (1-800-288-4677)

Because of the dynamic nature of the Internet, any Web addresses or links contained in this book may have changed since publication and may no longer be valid. The views expressed in this work are solely those of the author and do not necessarily reflect the views of the publisher, and the publisher hereby disclaims any responsibility for them.

ISBN: 978-1-4502-3341-5 (sc)
ISBN: 978-1-4502-3342-2 (dj)
ISBN: 978-1-4502-3343-9 (ebook)

Library of Congress Control Number: 2010907560

Printed in the United States of America

iUniverse rev. date: 07/14/2010

Acknowledgments

I am deeply grateful to the following people:

My father, Edward E. Tauber, for providing me with many great life lessons and raising me to live right.

My mother, Wilmet A. Tauber, for her love and patience. She took a job in my high school and tracked my attendance in an effort to ensure I came to school often enough to graduate. She succeeded.

To my sisters, Cookie, Amy, Sally, and my brother, Bob, for their role in making our childhood a wonderful, loving time in our lives.

The late Dr. Robert V. Rentschler, Jr. for providing me the inspiration to stop thinking about writing and to actually write.

The Greek and Roman Stoic philosophers whose writings, notably Plato's *Republic*, inspired elements of this book.

The staff of iUniverse for their patience, assistance, and encouragement.

To Jeannie: thank you for all your support and for believing in me.

But I have promises to keep,
And miles to go before I sleep ...
—Robert Frost

Chapter 1

A promise is a pledge, an oath. A promise represents one's word, and keeping it, or failing to keep it, serves as a reflection of one's character. A promise made by a son to a father on his deathbed must be kept, without fail, regardless of the cost. Plato knew this. He fully understood that failure to honor such a promise could have serious consequences, to him and to his father's good name. He knew. He willingly made a solemn deathbed promise to his father, a promise he had every intention of keeping. But years passed without Plato fulfilling his commitment.

Plato, a wise old duck, was now in the twilight of his life. Against all odds he had survived. His advanced years were apparent. His multicolored feathers had lost some of their youthful shine. Yet in spite of his age, he was vital and vibrant. But Plato knew he would not survive another winter.

Plato held his head high and wore a solemn, dignified expression on his face as he sat alone at the edge of a small lake. The lake was located in the heart of a woodlot no more than three hundred acres in size. The trees—oak, hickory, elm, and poplar—had recently taken on the darker hues of summer, replacing the brighter and lighter colored greens of spring. The woodland floor was open and covered with moss and occasional patches of ferns. Saplings grew in the few areas where sufficient sunlight penetrated the forest canopy. Small animals easily moved along the woodlot floor, scratching and scattering last autumn's fallen leaves.

It was growing dark, and the setting sun painted the landscape with a hot blush of color. The surface of the lake burned with shades of red and orange. Small fish occasionally breached the surface of the lake as they attempted to escape the gnashing teeth of larger fish, the splashes flickering like jets of flame in the evening light.

Plato had been sitting on a sparse patch of grass. He liked to float alone in the evening and listen to the melody of frogs and insects as they sang songs of love to potential mates. Tonight it was silent; there were no love songs in the air. Plato rose and waddled to the edge of the lake, passing dozens of stalagmite crayfish mounds glowing yellow in the fading sunlight like tiny fumaroles along the bank. His movements made a rhythmic squishing and popping sound as he stepped into and then raised his webbed feet from the ash-colored mud that lined the shore. As he entered the water, he could smell the pungent, sulfurous odor of dead and decomposing plant life that had been pushed up on one side of the lake by the prevailing breeze.

The lake was dark and deep. No one, not even the deepest diving ducks, had ever reached the bottom. Most of the birds in the woodlot believed the lake to be bottomless. All about the body of dark water, bubbles boiled up from the depths and rippled the surface. As Plato paddled farther out into the lake, he caught a strong scent of death, which caused him to recoil and stop paddling. An animal or bird had died nearby and was in a state of decay.

It was late spring, and as the sun began to sink below the horizon, the lake took on an eerie, unearthly appearance. Fog formed over the surface, ascending high over the center of the lake, joining with the clouds overhead. Plato strained his neck and stared at the column but was unable to see the top. The last rays of sunlight merged with the fog, creating a blend of gray, tinged with various shades of red and orange. Plato paddled farther out into the blazing lake and mingled with the smoky mist. An orange wake rose and spread behind him and then slowly rolled away in small, undulating waves like molten lava.

Lost in thought, the old duck appeared serene, yet there was also an air of melancholy in his demeanor. Plato floated quietly toward a labyrinth of reeds and cattails at the far side of the lake. As he neared the maze, he felt a change. The water was no longer cool. It grew warm and then hot. His legs burned as though they were on fire. The fog was stifling, and Plato found breathing difficult. Filled with apprehension, he paused, looked, and listened in an effort to discover any danger lurking nearby. Detecting none, he slowly and cautiously approached the confusion of reeds and cattails.

Plato would float among the reeds at night. He felt protected there. But tonight the reeds were threatening. He sensed something ominous within. He stopped, unwilling to enter. It was then he saw it. Unrecognizable at first, it slowly materialized before his eyes. Plato gasped and back-paddled. His breathing quickened and then came in spasms and racked his body. Shivers of fear raced along his spine and caused his feathers to stand on end. Was it real or just an apparition? Was his eyesight or imagination playing tricks on him in the fading light and mist? No, it was clearly there. It was real. It must be. There before him, in the lake of fire and smoky fog, was what appeared to be the figure of his dead father.

Plato stared at the specter, blinked several times, and then spoke, his voice breathless and weak. "Father? Father, is that you?"

"Yes," answered the spirit.

"I've missed you, Father. What are you—"

"You promised."

"I've tried but I haven't been able—"

"You didn't promise to try. You promised to do it. You've not kept your promise to me."

"I've tried, Father."

"Don't try, Plato. Do it. There's no peace unless you do it. There will be no peace for you unless you keep the promise you made to me. No peace; only endless suffering. Now promise me again, right now, that you will do it."

"I'll do it, Father. I don't know how but I'll find a way. I promise," said Plato. Hanging his head, Plato could see, in his reflection in the dark water, the guilt and shame he wore on his face.

"Keep your promise, Plato. Keep your promise. Keep your promise ..." The voice faded and then was gone.

Plato looked up; and his father, the ghost of his father, the apparition, the specter, whatever it was, faded from sight and disappeared into the mist.

Chapter 2

The first light of day illuminated the lake. The forest bustled with the sounds of life. Birds greeted the morning with song. Squirrels left the safety of their homes and started their ritual pursuit of food. Plato floated motionless in the lake, lost in thought. He had not slept but instead had spent the entire night with his mind in conflict, one moment focused on a possible solution so he could keep his promise and the next filled with distress over the vision he had seen and the words he had exchanged with his father.

His father; had that really been his father? Had any of it really taken place? Plato glanced around. The lake and forest were no longer threatening. Dawn had brought peace to the lake and the woodland, and it had brought peace to Plato's mind. It didn't matter if the events of the night were real or imagined. Plato was resolute in purpose. He would do all he could to find a way to keep the promise he had made to his father.

Chilled by a night spent in the water, Plato took flight. Up into the warmth of the sunlight he flew, circling the woodlot and enjoying the view of the shadows cast by clouds upon the forest and by his own shadow moving across the tops of the trees. The combination of the exertion of flying and the warming rays of the sun soon removed the chill. Plato searched for a good place to land where he could relax, think, and stay warm. He would eat later. Finally, he selected a tree not far from the edge of the forest and landed.

He was just getting settled when he noticed activity in a nest not far from where he was perched. It was a family of ducks, and it appeared that the parents were awake and had started their day while the youngsters still slept.

Plato watched the activity from time to time while he turned over thoughts in his mind about how he could keep his promise.

The forest around the nest beckoned with the sounds of life waking from the previous night's rest. These sounds indicated food was available for those stealthy and resourceful enough to seek and catch it. The mother and father ducks had begun their morning routine of gathering food for themselves and their youngsters. They would fly off and soon return with some healthy morsel. Each would then take flight again, searching, finding, and obtaining food, sometimes eating it on the spot. Then they would collect something for the children and return to the nest. This process would play out repeatedly until there was sufficient food in the nest for everyone.

The activity eventually wakened the children from their slumber. Hardy and Laslo struggled to their feet and blinked repeatedly in an effort to adjust their eyes to the light of day. Hardy remembered today he would get his final lesson. Tomorrow he was going to fly. Suddenly, he was wide awake and filled with nervous energy. Laslo, on the other hand, staggered around the nest in a daze trying to shake the effects of the long sleep from his little body.

"Where did you go last night?" asked Laslo. "I nearly froze to death." He stopped and looked down. "I ... I can't feel my feet."

"I slept with Mommy and Daddy last night."

"Are you still afraid? What a little sissy. You run off to sleep with Mom and Dad because you're afraid and you leave me alone to freeze? The only thing you're good for is to be my foot warmer at night. And you can't even get that right."

"Leave me alone, Laslo. You're just jealous because I'm going to fly tomorrow and you're not. You don't need to feel your feet anyway. You walk funny even when your feet are warm." Hardy smiled a smug little smile at the thought that Laslo was jealous.

"Jealous? I'm jealous? Jealous of who? You? Don't make me laugh. You're going to make a complete fool of yourself tomorrow when you ..., no, *if* you jump out of the nest. I'm betting you won't fly. I'm betting you won't even leave the nest. And if you don't jump, I'm going to ask Dad to let me fly. I'm not afraid. No, I'm not afraid. Anyway, I know how to fly already. I can feel it in my bones."

"You can't fly. Mommy and Daddy both say I'm ready and you're not. So just accept it. And how can you feel it in your bones? You said you can't even feel your feet. Remember?"

"I can't feel my feet because of you. The feeling is coming back into my feet but that head of yours will always be numb." Most of the feeling had returned to Laslo's feet and he was doing his best to strut around the nest. "I can outwalk, outtalk, outthink, and outfly you, Hardy. On my worst day I'm better than you on your best. Don't you ever forget that; do you hear me? Don't you ever forget that."

"You think you're the best at everything. But you know what? I can't remember anything that you've ever done except talk." Hardy decided to go for what he knew would really bother Laslo. "You don't look like a duck and you don't walk like a duck. So why do you think you can fly like a duck? Maybe you're not really a duck after all. It's just possible you were left here, abandoned. Mommy and Daddy probably just take care of you because they know no one else would have you. You know, I was here before you, and I don't remember seeing an egg. I bet you don't remember seeing any pieces of eggshell in the nest, do you? Yeah, I'm pretty sure you were just dropped off here." Hardy had a big grin on his face and was giggling to himself.

Laslo stared at Hardy, speechless. Hardy added, "I doubt Mommy and Daddy will let you fly this week. Even I can see you're not ready. And what's the story with those silly-looking feathers sticking up on the top of your head? No. You're not really a duck and there's no way you're ready to fly."

"I'm gonna fly upside your head," said Laslo, squinting. Laslo spoke slowly and deliberately. He lowered his voice in an attempt to sound as menacing as possible. "Then you'll know if I'm ready or not."

Plato overheard every word and struggled not to laugh out loud. He had now focused his full attention on the two young ducks.

"Oh, I'm really scared. Maybe I should just shove you out of the nest right now and then we'll see if you really can fly. I can do it. You know I can," said Hardy.

"That's it. I'm going to give you what you've needed ever since you were born."

"Since I was born? That was what, about two, maybe three days before you were left here, young fellow? And what is it you think I need anyway?" Hardy paused but spoke again just as Laslo was about to reply. "I'll tell you what I need. I need a real brother who is actually a duck and not some orphaned, wild-haired thing that was dumped on this family."

"Hardy, you're such a—"

Caw! Caw! Caw!

"What was that?" asked Hardy, the tone in his voice now one of concern.

"I don't know. I thought I heard that sound several times before but it was never that loud."

"You don't think it's a hawk, do you? Daddy told us about hawks and he said they're dangerous." Hardy put his wing on Laslo's back and hugged him. "I think we should lie still on the bottom of the nest like Daddy told us to do."

"I'm not hiding like some scared little baby just because we heard a noise. We don't even know if that was a hawk. And get your wing off me." *Laslo's always trying to show how fearless he is*, thought Hardy. "You can go ahead and hide if you want to. I'm not gonna hide. I'm not scared. No, I'm not scared at all."

"What's that?" cried Hardy, pointing with his wing. A large bird was approaching the nest. "It's a hawk. I told you we should do what Daddy said."

"That's Mom, you idiot. It's not a hawk. And here comes Dad. I can't believe what a sissy you are."

Plato had abandoned his thoughts and was watching and listening to the two young ducks. Their innocence and childlike naivety brought joy to him. It also caused him to reflect on how far he had strayed from that innocence. He wished he could still look at the world with the open mind of these two young ducks. The challenges of life had taken a toll on him.

Mother and Father landed in the nest and dropped the last of the morning's food they had collected. Hardy was relieved to have his parents back in the nest. He was really scared. He had never seen a hawk. In fact, he wasn't even sure he knew what a hawk actually was. But he knew it was something even his father was afraid of.

"Daddy, I think we heard a hawk. It was real loud and it sounded like it was really close by," announced Hardy.

Father looked at Hardy and then at Laslo. "Did you see it?"

"No. We just heard a loud noise and it was scary."

13

"Hardy was scared. I wasn't," claimed Laslo.

"Well, a hawk is something you'd better respect. There's good reason to be scared of a hawk. But your mother and I were nearby and we didn't see or hear anything. I'm sure there was no hawk nearby."

"I told you, Hardy," teased Laslo.

"Did you boys lie in the bottom of the nest like I told you to?"

"I told Laslo we should but he didn't want to. He said it was just a noise."

"Hardy was right. If you even think there might be a hawk in the area, you need to do what I told you to do. Is that clear?"

"Yes, sir," said Hardy.

"Dad, it was just a noise. We didn't see anything. I don't want to be a scared sissy like Hardy. If we'd seen a hawk, I would've hid in the bottom of the nest. But there was no hawk," reasoned Laslo.

"Well, son, hawks can see much better than we can. If you wait until you see it before you hide, there's a good chance it probably has already seen you. Then it's too late. The next time you lie in the bottom of the nest. Do you understand?"

"Yes, sir," said Laslo, disappointed that Father had not agreed with him or praised him for being brave.

Father could see the disappointment on Laslo's face. "Son, being brave doesn't mean being foolish. You need to think before you act. Sometimes it's best to hide."

"Yes, sir. But I still don't want to be a sissy like Hardy. He's afraid of everything. The other day I just farted and it scared him so bad he nearly threw himself out of the nest."

"That's not completely accurate," said Hardy. "Laslo farted—that's true. The noise was almost deafening and, I admit, it startled me a little and I flinched. But it didn't scare me. It was the smell that made me almost throw myself from the nest."

"Hardy, that wasn't nice," scolded Mother playfully.

"No, it wasn't nice. It wasn't nice at all. It was totally disgusting. The truth is if there hadn't been a stiff breeze blowing I would have thrown myself from the nest. In fact it was so bad, at one point, I'm pretty sure Laslo was considering throwing himself over the side, too."

Laslo wasn't saying a thing. He just stood there with a silly grin on his face looking both pleased and proud. The little feathers sticking up on his head gave him an enhanced appearance of mischievousness.

"I think there's something wrong with Laslo. It's my opinion that you need to be very careful what you feed him. I don't know for sure but I think it's those big, shiny yellow beetles that cause him to fart like that. If he were to get a hold of two of them, it could be a disaster for this family. You know, I'm not exaggerating when I say we could lose the nest. If he does that again with two beetles in him, we would probably have to abandon this nest permanently."

"That's enough," said Mother.

"Mommy, it's one of those things that you can't fully appreciate unless you experience it firsthand. It was bad. It was really bad. There are no words to describe it."

"Hardy, I said that's enough."

"All right, but if it does happen don't say I didn't warn you." Hardy was grinning as wide as possible. He was full of the dickens and was finding it difficult to stop. "Have you noticed that each day it's warmer than the day before? I know it doesn't make any sense but I think Laslo's farting has something to do with it. Somehow he's making the world get hotter."

"Do you hear this?" Mother asked Father. She looked in Father's direction and saw that he was standing at the edge of the nest with his back to the group, shaking with quiet laughter. "You see? This is your fault. You encourage these boys."

"I'm sorry. But you've got to admit it. That's funny."

Hardy glanced at Laslo with a mischievous look on his face. "Daddy, Laslo thinks he can fly. He said he can feel it in his bones." Laslo glared at Hardy and then quickly looked at his father with as innocent a look on his face as he could portray.

"Laslo is not ready to fly. He's not ready until your mother and I say he's ready. Tomorrow is your day to fly. Laslo will get his chance in a few days," said Father. "Laslo, you'd better not try to fly until your mother and I say it's time."

"Yes, sir." Laslo wanted to get his wings on Hardy's throat so badly he could taste it.

"Daddy, I think if we gave Laslo three of those beetles he could probably outfly *you* in a race." Hardy was still wound up and was giggling nonstop.

"Okay. That's enough. You boys get your breakfast and then we'll do your final lesson. Tomorrow you fly."

"Oh, boy," said Hardy. "Are you sure you don't want go through that stack of food one last time just to be sure there are none of those yellow beetles in there?"

"Enough," said Father. His tone made it clear that he was serious now.

Hardy and Laslo each started their meal while Mother and Father straightened up in the nest and talked quietly to each other. The two boys had settled down and were no longer taunting and teasing each other.

Laslo checked to make sure his parents weren't watching and then leaned over and whispered to Hardy, "I just ate one of those big yellow beetles. Now you're gonna pay. I'm feeling rather gassy already."

"You'd better not, Laslo. I'm serious. I can't take that. I'm going to fly tomorrow and I don't need to go through that again. That last fart of yours drained half the life out of me. I get a bit lightheaded and woozy, not to mention sick to my stomach, just thinking about it."

Laslo checked again to be sure his parents weren't looking in their direction. Then he stood directly in front of Hardy, pushed his little backside right in Hardy's face, and strained with all his might. He looked back at Hardy and, adopting an expression with an exaggerated grimace, began to flap his little wings as rapidly as he could. Hardy squealed and scrambled away. The commotion caught the attention of his parents, who turned and looked in the direction of the two boys. Laslo immediately adopted a pose of stretching out his wings and yawning, covering what he had really been doing.

Seeing his parents staring at him, Laslo stopped stretching and looked back at his parents with a quizzical expression. "What? Is there something wrong?" asked Laslo.

"Is everything all right, boys?" asked Mother, looking at Hardy. Father didn't say anything but stared at them both with what appeared to be a knowing look on his face.

"Yes, Mom," answered Laslo, looking in Hardy's direction.

"Yes, Mommy, everything's fine," Hardy replied. He looked over at Laslo, who nodded at him and grinned, the little feathers on top of his head appearing to stick up more than usual.

"I don't know what you boys were up to but I'm sure it was pure nonsense," said Mother with a suspicious expression on her face.

"We weren't doing anything, Mom. We weren't doing anything at all," replied Laslo.

"I'm sure you weren't, Laslo," said Mother.

"Who's that?" asked Hardy, pointing with his wing toward a large old duck sitting in a nearby tree.

"Yeah, who's that and what's he doing watching us?" Laslo took several steps across the nest in the direction of the duck and then puffed himself up trying to look big. Hardy raised a wing and waved hesitantly to the old duck. The old duck shook his head, smiled, waved back, and then flew off.

Mother and Father watched as the old duck flew away and then looked at each other, their eyes wide with surprise.

"Why would Plato be here?" whispered Mother.

"I have no idea," said Father. "That was strange."

Chapter 3

Plato decided he would meet with the birds in the woodlot. He would speak to them and see if he could convince them it was time for change. He wasn't confident of success. The injustice had existed for years and most of the woodlot residents were more than satisfied with the way things were. It was a small step, a desperate step, but Plato could think of no better way to proceed. Anyway, he had to do something, so why not try this?

Plato sent word out that a meeting would take place the following evening at the lake two hours before sunset. The word spread and at once conversations started all over the woodlot. Everyone had the same questions. What did Plato want to tell them? What was wrong? Plato was their leader, but he spent most of his time alone, occasionally speaking with some birds individually. Few could remember Plato ever calling a meeting before. There was that one time just before the big storm when Plato had warned them the storm would be severe, more violent than any storm they had ever known, and would last for days. He told them they should prepare themselves for the worst. His warning saved many lives. If Plato wanted to meet and say something to them, it must be important.

The next evening, everyone was assembled at the lake. Meetings were for the adult males only. The young were not allowed to attend. The right to attend meetings had to be earned by surviving two winters. Many had arrived early so they could greet friends and see if they could learn what Plato planned to speak with them about. The trees adjacent to the lake were filled with many varieties of birds, and the lake itself was filled with ducks. Everyone had assembled at this location, the primary location for all meetings. There was a large log just offshore where a speaker could address all assembled and easily be heard.

Plato circled overhead and then landed on the log. He paused briefly and looked about to determine if everyone had arrived. He also needed to catch his breath before speaking. The chatter on the lake and in the surrounding trees had gone silent. Everyone stared at Plato in anticipation.

Plato waddled to the center of the log and faced the assembly of birds. "Good evening. Thank you for responding to my request. I'm sure you're wondering why I have asked you here so I'll get right to the point." Plato paced the length of the log as he formed his thoughts. "I want to talk with you about the crows. In particular, I want to talk about the living situation. The crows have been banned from living in the forest. They are not even permitted to come here for water. We imposed this on the crows and they accepted it. But it's wrong. I think it's time for a change, and I wanted to hear your thoughts on the subject." Everyone was silent. Plato stood facing them, expecting an outcry of protests, but not a word was said. "Well, doesn't anyone have anything to say?" asked Plato with a smile. "I can't believe no one has an opinion they want to express."

"I'm in shock," said a large, young duck resting in the water just in front of Plato. "We thought something was wrong. We thought you had something important to talk with us about." The crowd murmured, with most agreeing they were also surprised by the subject.

"This is important," said Plato.

"Well, I have something to say," said a blue jay. "I'm confident that practically everyone here but you will agree with what I'm going to say. We don't want any crows in the woodlot, period. Not to live, not to drink. We like things just the way they are. We've all made that clear to you before when you've brought this up individually."

"I agree," yelled a robin. "We don't need any crows here. They live in the pine grove because they can't behave. If they had behaved, they would still be living in the woods with us. This situation is their doing." A loud chorus of voices echoed their agreement.

"Only a handful of crows misbehaved. There is no reason why—"

"You're wrong," yelled the blue jay. "There are good reasons crows need to stay in the pines. They attacked us. They're dangerous. This arrangement has worked for years. We haven't had any problems since crows were confined to the pines. They need to stay there."

"We know your views. What about the rest of you? Is there anyone who agrees this is wrong? Speak up." There was only silence. "If any are treated unjustly," said Plato, "then all of us are at risk of the same injustice. It's time we at least looked at this again and talked about it with open minds."

"No crows," yelled the blue jay. "No crows, no crows!" The assembled crowd joined in. "No crows. No crows," they chanted as a group. One by one and then in groups the birds left. All had departed with the exception of one lone duck.

"And you, Glaucus. Don't you see the wrong in this?" asked Plato.

The duck swam over the log and looked up at Plato. "I don't know if it's right or wrong. I haven't given it any thought. I don't like crows. I don't want them here. But I am curious why you think this must be changed now. Why now? Why is this so important to you?"

"My reasons are my reasons. Anyway, you know why it's important to me. It's obvious that no one here is even willing to discuss it. Even you; I don't think even you want to give it any serious consideration either. Am I right?"

"You are. I do have one more question. You were sitting in a tree the other day watching my boys. Why?"

"Those were your boys?"

"You saw their mother and me."

"Oh? My eyesight isn't good anymore. I'm sorry, but I didn't recognize you. I wasn't there to watch your boys. I had gone there to do some thinking. I was tired and didn't notice your home at first. Once those boys got going, I got such a kick out of them I couldn't help watching and listening. I apologize if I invaded your privacy or caused you any concern."

"I was a little concerned. It's unusual to see you, much less to see you near my home watching my children. If you get a kick out of children, you could have visited and gotten involved with them at any time. After all, you are their uncle. Well, I just want to be sure my boys are not in any danger. So, there's no problem then? There's not anything you're keeping from me?"

"No; my presence was purely coincidental. I know of no danger to your boys. That one boy of yours is really something; he appears to have no fear. He's really full of it."

"That's Laslo. He's fearless all right. I think maybe too fearless. I worry about him. He's gonna get into trouble for sure. Hardy has better judgment. He appears a little timid at times, but I think he's just, uh, deliberate."

"Well, we could use more courage around here; especially more moral courage. Glaucus, if you think about the crows and change your mind, let me know." Plato laughed. "I could use—"

"Not gonna happen. Don't like crows. Good-bye."

"Don't leave yet. I really could use your help. Isn't there any way I can convince you to talk with some of your friends? If we could get a few to just think about this, maybe we could start the process for change."

"I've got kids to raise. I don't have time to take on your life's mission. Plus, as I said, I don't like crows."

"It's not about liking crows. It's about what's right. It's about living right. The crows know it's unfair even if they agreed to the arrangement. I'm convinced it's just a matter of time before this becomes a problem."

"We'll deal with it then. We outnumber them three or four to one. What are they going to do?"

"I'm not saying they are going to do anything now. But there is growing distrust and resentment between us and the crows. There's really no good reason for it. It's going to eventually bring serious problems. You have to admit crows have skills that could keep us all safer and more secure if we were all just one community. What do you say? Help me out with this."

Glaucus stared at Plato, turning an idea over in his mind. After a few moments, he smiled and nodded. "I may help, if you agree to help me with the kids."

"I don't know anything about kids. I like them but I know nothing about raising them. You know that."

"If you want me to help you, I'm going to need your help. They're learning to fly and before long they'll be going out on their own. Normally, I'd follow them, without their knowledge of course, just to make sure they're safe. Once I know they're skilled at looking out for themselves, they won't need watching. You could keep an eye on them when they go out and I could use that time to talk with some of the fathers and see if I can get any of them to consider listening to your foolish ideas. So, what do you think? The more you watch the kids the more time I'll have to try and help you."

Plato smiled and shook his head. "What choice do I have? Give me a few days to take care of some things and then I'll do it."

"They won't be ready to go out on their own for another two weeks. You have plenty of time. Thanks, Plato. This'll be good for you."

"Right."

"It will, really. Good-bye." Glaucus turned and flew off, leaving Plato alone in the lake.

Chapter 4

Today was the day Hardy would fly for the first time. As the time for his first flight drew near, Hardy became increasingly nervous. He would sit quietly, thinking for a few moments and then get up and pace about the nest. Laslo watched Hardy closely, and whenever Hardy glanced in his direction, Laslo would just shake his head and grin. Laslo's expression communicated his feelings clearly. He considered Hardy a scared sissy, so he was somewhat disgusted with Hardy's display of nervousness.

Father and Mother had been sitting on opposite sides of the nest staring at the ground and into the trees. They were looking for any potential signs of danger in the area. They wanted to be sure Hardy's first flight was as safe as possible. They were certain Hardy was ready to fly, but first flights are unpredictable. Hardy was to fly to another tree not far from the nest. He could, however, fail to fly and end up on the ground. There's always danger there since ducks are nearly defenseless; their primary mode of survival is to fly away from danger. And there is always the chance a predator could be sitting in the trees just waiting for an opportunity to capture a young duckling. With no warning, Father left the nest and flew high into the air. He circled the area several times, making sure there were no hawks or other dangers nearby. When he was satisfied, he signaled to Mother it was time for Hardy to fly.

"Hardy, it's time for you to fly. Hurry, let's go. No delays," said Mother.

Hardy started waddling over to the edge of the nest. Laslo stepped in front of Hardy and spoke. "I just want to wish you luck on your flight, Hardy." Then he hugged Hardy and placed his cheek against Hardy's cheek. Laslo's head was on the side of Hardy opposite from where his mother was standing.

Laslo whispered to Hardy, "You're going to need all the luck in the world. Like I said, you're going to make a complete fool of yourself today." Then Laslo backed away from Hardy, smiled, and said, "Go for it, Hardy." Mother looked on with watery eyes, touched by the display of affection from Laslo.

"Thanks. Thanks a lot. Your support means a great deal to me." Hardy then waddled over to the edge of the nest, climbed into the opening, and perched right on the edge. He looked down. It was a long way to the ground. He was really high. Then he looked over to the branch he was to fly to. It seemed too far away. He was not sure he could do this.

"It's okay, Hardy. You can do it. Just step off and do what you already know how to do," said Mother.

Hardy's little heart was pounding so hard he could hear it in his head. His breathing rate had increased, and he felt like he couldn't catch his breath. He was feeling dizzy and everything seemed to be spinning. His mind was clouded; he was unable to focus his thoughts. What was the first thing he was supposed to do? Fall. That's right, fall. Gain speed. His heart raced even faster with that thought. Then Hardy looked up and saw his father circling overhead. He wanted to show his daddy he was brave.

"Here I go, Mommy." Hardy leaned forward and was about to leap.

Caw! Caw! Caw!

The sound startled Hardy. He lost his balance and nearly fell from the nest. Overcompensating in his efforts to not fall out, Hardy fell over backward into the nest. "Was that a hawk, Mommy?" cried Hardy.

"No. That was a crow. You don't need to be afraid. It's okay. Climb back up there and fly, sweetie," answered Mother.

Laslo was lying on his back laughing. "That was great. What did I tell you?" Laslo's little feet were kicking as he laughed.

"That's enough, Laslo," said Mother. "Come on now, Hardy. Let's get going."

Hardy climbed back up into the opening. He looked around briefly and then jumped from the nest. Immediately he began to fall. He felt out of control and his speed was increasing. Hardy began to flap his wings furiously, but he didn't fly. What was wrong? He was still falling. Hardy was beginning to panic. He saw the ground getting closer. He wasn't going to fly after all. Then he turned his wings slightly. He felt the air begin to slow his fall. He began to move forward and was no longer falling. Hardy flapped his wings as hard as he could and began to gain altitude. He looked for the branch he was supposed to land on. He was too low. There was no way he was going to get high enough to reach that branch. Hardy picked a lower limb to land on. He realized the tree was getting closer much more quickly than he expected. He was going too fast. Hardy dropped the feathers on the back of his wings and raised the front edge of his wings. He immediately slowed down and then his feet were on the branch but he had gained too much speed and fell on his face. He thought he was going to fall from the tree but struggled and was able to stay on the branch.

He was excited. He had flown. He looked over at the nest and was surprised how close it appeared to be. Mother was standing in the nest with a big smile on her face. And there was Laslo, doubled over in laughter. Hardy couldn't wait until Laslo got what was coming to him.

"Great job, Hardy. Stay there and wait until I come over to you," hollered Mother.

"Yeah, great job," yelled Laslo, laughing.

I sure would like to slap that silly grin off his face, thought Hardy. Hardy was breathless. *Flying is hard work*, he thought. *How do Mom and Dad fly so high and so far and not return to the nest exhausted? Who cares?* He had flown and that was all that mattered at the moment.

Mother flew over and landed on the branch next to Hardy. "Hardy, you were wonderful. I'm so proud of you. Did you like flying?"

"That was amazing, Mommy. I was really scared at first but then I started to fly. Things happen really fast when you're flying." Hardy was out of breath. "Flying wears you out quickly, too."

"You'll get stronger in no time. And as you practice you'll learn to relax when you fly. Then you'll find it gets much easier. But you're right. Flying does take a lot of energy," said Mother.

The two just stood there for several minutes while Hardy caught his breath. Hardy was still excited from the thrill of his first flight. He kept reliving the flight over and over again in his mind.

"Have you thought about the flight back?" asked Mother. "You'll need to get much higher to get back to the nest."

"I have thought about it and I don't think I can go up fast enough to get back to the nest."

"So what do you think you should do?"

"I need more room. The nest is too close." Hardy knew from his first flight that he could gain altitude, but not quickly enough to get back to the nest. He was also surprised he was now thinking the nest was too close.

"How do you suggest you get more room?"

"Maybe if I flew in a sort of circle back to the nest I would have room to get high enough. But I don't think I can fly very far before I'll get too tired. And I don't know if I can make the turns."

"Why not fly over to that tree over there? Do you see the branch that is sticking out a little farther than the others? It's a little higher than we are now."

"I see it, Mommy."

"Okay, you can fly over there and then rest and catch your breath. And when you're ready you can fly from there back to the nest. You can do that, can't you?" asked Mother.

"That's a great plan. Of course I can do that."

"I'm going back to the nest so I can keep an eye on you. Wait until I get there and then I'll let you know when it's time for you to fly again. Then you fly over to that tree."

"All right; I'll do it."

"You did a great job on your first flight. Now you know you can fly. So, relax a little and enjoy the feeling. Experiment a little with your wing strokes. And think about your landing well in advance." Mother was smiling at Hardy, and he could see how proud she was.

"I'm going to land perfectly this time. I just hope I get up high enough to land on that limb."

"You'll be fine." Mother then flew off and landed in the nest. Hardy was amazed at how easy she made flying look. Flying was not easy. Hardy's mother took a long look around the area. She stared into the trees and at the ground. She then checked with Father and got an all-clear signal. "All right, you can go now."

This time Hardy didn't hesitate. He leaped off the branch, and again he fell. This time it wasn't as frightening, and he kept his wings to his sides for a moment or two to gain speed. Then he spread his wings and immediately began to glide. Hardy started flapping his wings, changed the angle of his wings, and slightly raised his tail. He gained altitude and was now a little higher than the branch. Hardy timed his arrival this time and spread his wings, lifting the front edges. He slowed and landed almost perfectly on the limb. He still had a little too much speed, which caused him to have to run several steps before he could stop.

"Not bad," yelled Laslo. "Not bad at all, considering it was you flying."

"Thanks, I guess."

Hardy heard his mother call to him. "That was wonderful." Hardy looked over at the nest and Mother was giving Laslo a good talking-to. Hardy noticed he was not nearly as out of breath this time. He stood on the limb for a few minutes, reliving the last flight until he caught his breath. "I'm ready to come back now."

"Wait just a second." Mother checked the area again and got another all-clear from Father. "Go ahead. Fly over here."

Hardy jumped from the branch and began to glide. He flapped his wings as hard as he needed to and was able to get the needed height to make it back to the nest. As he neared the nest, the opening didn't appear to be large enough. He panicked slightly as he approached the opening. Then he realized it was large enough. Of course it was. Mommy and Daddy fly into that opening. Hardy landed on the edge of the nest and struggled to get his balance. Mother reached out and gave him a slight pull with her bill. Hardy was back in the nest.

"That was great. Flying is fun," Hardy squealed, elated by his experience.

"You should be proud of yourself. I sure am proud of you and so is Laslo. Aren't you, Laslo?"

Laslo immediately answered, "Yes, Momma, Hardy did a good job." Laslo looked at Hardy, slightly shrugged, and rolled his eyes a little.

Then Father returned to the nest. He had a big smile on his face. "Good job, son. What do you think about your first flight?"

"It was great, Dad. I was really worried at first after I jumped out of the nest. I thought I was going to fall all the way to the ground. But then I started to fly. Everything worked just the way you said it would. But it all happened much faster than I expected." Hardy was so excited he was practically yelling.

"You did great," said Father. "What was the delay at the beginning?"

"I thought I heard a hawk and got scared," replied Hardy.

"He nearly fell out of the nest. Then he fell over backward into the nest. Dad, it was priceless. Maybe the funniest thing I ever saw," said Laslo.

"What did I tell you?" said Mother with a stern tone and an even sterner look on her face.

"I'm sorry, Momma. It's just that—"

"Enough," said Father. "I'm proud of you, Hardy. Do you have any questions?"

"What? Am I the only member of this family with a sense of humor? If you see something funny, you should laugh at it and enjoy it. And that was funny," mumbled Laslo.

"Not another word from you, young man; do you hear me?" Father's voice was raised, and he gave Laslo a look that definitely got his attention.

"Yes, sir."

"Hardy, do you have any questions about your flight?" asked Father.

"No, sir.

"Did you learn anything you would like to share with your family?"

"Does that include ... that?" asked Hardy, pointing at his brother.

"Yes, it includes Laslo, even if his behavior leaves a lot to be desired," said Mother.

"That's too bad. Are you sure he's really one of us?" asked Hardy. Laslo immediately looked at his mother, anxious to hear her answer.

"Hardy, I'll have no more of that. Are you going to share what you've learned or not?" Laslo was disappointed with the response from Mother.

"Yes. Well, landing is much more difficult than I thought it would be. And everything looks different when you're flying. And you have to think about things well before you think you do or else you don't have time to get ready to do it right."

"Well, this certainly was a big day for our family, wasn't it?" said Mother.

"Yes, it was," answered Father. "Laslo, didn't I say you would enjoy watching Hardy fly? Was I right?"

"Yes, sir, I really enjoyed that. I mean, I really enjoyed it. It was funny."

"Well, in a few days Hardy will get a chance to watch you fly for the first time. Hardy, trust me; you're going to enjoy watching that."

"You bet I'll enjoy watching that," said Hardy. "Then we'll get to see just how good Laslo really is."

"Don't get too excited," said Laslo. "I'm going to make it to the right limb on my first try. And, I'm going to stick my landing. Like I told you earlier, I can outwalk, outtalk, outthink, and outfly you on any day." Laslo was so confident he could fly better than Hardy he seemed cocky, almost arrogant.

"We'll see," said Hardy.

"Yes, you will see," said Laslo. "Yes, you will. Oh yeah, and there won't be any hesitation by me jumping from the nest. What were you thinking about for so long?"

"I was just trying to remember everything Dad told me."

"You were scared. Admit it."

"I was not," said Hardy, his voice now raised.

"That's enough, boys," said Father. "Laslo, you may want to save your bragging until after you've accomplished the feat. And if you do accomplish it, why brag? It won't be necessary. We'll all see what you do. Hardy, you were very brave and you did a fantastic job."

Laslo checked to be sure his parents weren't looking and shook his head at Hardy, indicating his father was just being nice. Hardy paid no attention to Laslo and just tried to reflect on what he had just done.

I can fly! thought Hardy. *I can fly.*

Chapter 5

Plato decided he would talk with the crow leaders and see if there was any interest on their part to try and resolve the living arrangements. He knew the crows had accepted the situation and kept to themselves, but he had also seen the resentment in their eyes. They didn't like the arrangement; how could they? The pine grove was in serious decline and didn't offer the shelter it once had. And getting water wasn't convenient for them. They had to fly three, maybe four times the distance than it was to the woodland lake. And the young birds from the woodlot would tease and harass the young crows for no reason. But Plato wasn't confident the crow leaders would entertain any proposals on his part. Crows are honorable birds. They accepted the situation simply because a group of young crows had misbehaved and caused the problem that led to their being banned from the woodlot.

Plato flew out of the woodlot, across the old orchard, and over the cornfields. He looked for an older crow, one he recognized, so he could tell him he wanted to speak with the crow leaders. Plato was surprised to find no crows in the area. After searching for an hour, he turned and headed toward the pine grove. He circled the pine grove several times and yelled numerous greetings during each trip around. Finally, three crows came out to greet him. Plato recognized one of the crows.

"Greetings, old friend, how have you been?" said Plato.

"I'm good. It's been a long time, Plato. Is there something wrong?" asked the crow.

"Nothing's wrong, Dion. Well, there's nothing new that's wrong. I was hoping to speak with the elders and the younger leaders. I want—"

"Not again. It's never going to work, Plato. Why don't you just give it up?"

"I can't do that. It's wrong and you know it. I know it. I'm convinced everyone knows it. And I know it can be fixed. We just need to get everyone talking. It's all about eliminating distrust."

"Well, we aren't interested in changing anything. It's obvious by the way we're treated that no one but you is interested in your cause." He stared at Plato, who stared back with a slight smile on his face. "Okay, I'll set up a meeting because you, old friend, asked. But it won't do any good. How have you been? You look well."

"I am well, thank you."

"Come back tomorrow at midday. We'll meet at that old tree where we've met with you and with your father before that."

"Thank you. I'll be there. It's been good seeing you again."

"It's been good for me too, Plato. Tomorrow." The three crows then banked and flew back to the pine grove.

Chapter 6

The next day Plato flew to the designated location to meet with the crows. The tree where the meeting was to be held was enormous, dominating the landscape. It had probably been there for well more than a hundred years, maybe two hundred years. The trunk was broad with roots that spread out from its base, the tops visible above ground. The lower limbs were massive and spread so wide they sagged under their own weight. The upper limbs grew shorter with height and gave the tree a somewhat regular tapered appearance, terminating more than a hundred feet above ground. The old tree was still healthy with a thick growth of dark green leaves on all the branches.

Plato flew a wide circle around the tree, closing the distance as he flew. He heard crows in the tree and saw Dion fly out to greet him.

"Good morning. Everyone's here. Most are only here because they have great respect for you. There doesn't seem to be much support for change. But there are a few, well, at least one among the group who may be interested in what you're going to propose."

"Good morning, Dion. If I can change one mind, then that's progress— one step closer to making things right. Are we ready?"

"Let's go."

The two completed a lap around the tree and glided in on the wind for a landing. Dion landed on the end of a large lower limb and Plato landed next to him. They walked in toward the center of the tree. As they walked, the leaves blocked out much of the direct sunlight and created a shield from the outside world. Soon they found themselves among the assembled crows. All were quiet.

An old crow stepped forward. "Greetings, Plato. How are you?"

"It's good to see you again, Aris. You look well. I was not sure I would live long enough to ever see you again. Nature's been merciful to give me this opportunity to be with my old friend again."

"Your words are kind, Plato. Everyone, this is Plato. Some of you know him personally and some only by reputation. He's our friend, and he's here to speak with us. Please give him your full attention. Plato, you have their attention."

Plato slowly waddled to the center of the assembly of crows. There were probably thirty crows present. He took his time and looked at all of them, making eye contact with as many as possible. He detected friendship in some, skepticism in others, and resentment in several. His eyes locked on the eyes of one crow who only glared. Plato saw hatred burning in those eyes.

Plato bowed his head, cleared his voice, and then lifted his head and spoke. "I have spoken to some of you before. I don't give up easily when something is wrong and needs correcting. I despise injustice. For years you have had to live in the pine grove while the other birds live in the forest. You've been prohibited from entering the forest even to get water at the lake. This may have been necessary and considered acceptable in the past. It seems it may have been the only option at the time it was imposed. But I think it's time for a change. I believe the present living arrangement needs to be changed. I think there are mutual advantages to all of us living in the forest together. So I am here to propose that together we try to fix things. Are you willing to begin discussions on how we can do that?"

The assembly sat quietly for a moment and then there were individual discussions among many of the crows. Plato watched, looking for any positive sign.

"What about the birds in the woodlot, Plato?" asked Aris. "Have you spoken with them? How do they feel?" The assembly of crows nodded in agreement and looked at Plato, waiting for his answer.

"I have spoken with them. Unfortunately, there's little support for change. They prefer the status quo. But my brother is going to help me work on changing some minds. I'm seeking a starting point. I don't expect this to happen overnight."

"Well, if there is no support among them, you'll find very little here. We don't want to live where we're not wanted."

"I'm willing to hear more of your thoughts," said a large spectacular-looking crow.

"I don't believe I've had the pleasure of meeting you," said Plato.

"His name is Alexander. He's the leader of our army."

"You have an army?"

"Of course we have an army. Relax, it's purely for defense. We are very good at running off hawks and owls. But we need to be much better. The pine grove doesn't offer the shelter it once did. We're a little more vulnerable."

"Well, Alexander, I am pleased. Is there anyone else willing to listen to what I have to say and then talk about this?" The question was greeted with silence. Some crows turned their backs on Plato, indicating they had no interest at all in his proposal.

"I hef something to siy." It was the crow Plato had seen earlier with hatred in his eyes.

"You're to remain silent," boomed Alexander.

"I'll listen," said Plato. "Let him speak."

"We don't need no duck coming here en offering us inything. We er strong. If we wint eh plece in the forest, we er fully kepible of tiking it."

"Antus! No more. I'll deal with you later. Plato, I apologize for his behavior," said Alexander.

"Cowards," said Antus. "Stind up for yourselves. Er you crows or not?"

"I said no more. Paris, escort him out of here and use whatever force is necessary." A large stern-looking crow shouted orders, and he and several other crows removed Antus from the meeting. Antus was protesting and arguing with his escorts but left without further incident.

"I apologize again for that. It's uncalled for," said Alexander.

Aris then walked down and joined Plato and stood next to him. "You're our friend, Plato. We appreciate what you're trying to do. But we have accepted this situation. You have our approval to converse with Alexander, but we don't see how anything can come of it. Alexander is wise, and he is the leader of our army. But he doesn't speak for us. I think we are done here."

The crows began departing, some taking a moment to exchange pleasantries with Plato and to thank him for his concern. After all had left, Plato was alone with Alexander. Plato waddled over to Alexander and stood directly in front of him.

They stared at each other briefly and then Alexander spoke. "I appreciate your coming here and trying to find support and a way to correct the living situation. You are correct in saying it's unjust. There are many crows who think so. In fact, most feel that way. But they're too proud to admit they would like to live among the other birds in the woodlot."

"Thank you for sharing that, Alexander. It's actually encouraging; it means we may be able to get some to work with us."

"I'm not so sure. Like I said, most are too proud. And don't be fooled by the elders' attitude. There's a great deal of resentment building among the younger crows. You saw how Antus behaved. He's the worst. I'm doing my best to keep him under control. But he's trouble."

"It appears he's very angry. How would you like to proceed? Do you have any ideas or proposals?"

"Why don't we meet again here tomorrow? Maybe we can find a starting point. And feel free to bring others with you."

"I'll come alone. It was a pleasure meeting you, Alexander. I have hope we can find a way to make things right."

"It was an honor meeting you. Tomorrow at midday, I'll come alone. And I think it best if no one else knows we're meeting. Take care." Alexander turned and flew away.

Plato left and returned to the woodlot.

Chapter 7

Hardy and Laslo had made great progress in their flight training over the previous week. They had also learned to swim and dive and visited the lake every day. Both Hardy and Laslo had taken their first flights and numerous flights since then, building skill and endurance. The two had learned how to look for potential dangers and how to find food. Learning to navigate was the most challenging part of their training, but at last they were ready for their first solo flights—Hardy first and then Laslo, which didn't sit well with Laslo, who was convinced he was the better flyer.

Laslo's first flight went pretty much as he predicted, with one exception. In his mind, he was a graceful and skilled flying machine and believed he demonstrated that on his first flight. He wasn't. However, his first flight was a success. He walked to the edge of the nest, turned, looked at Hardy, and smiled.

"This is how it's done," he said and off he went, fearlessly, without any hesitation. Laslo immediately began to flap his wings furiously but not out of fear. He wanted to reach the limb that had been set as his goal. He wanted to show Hardy he was the better flyer. Laslo didn't fall as far as Hardy had fallen before finding the proper glide angle for his wings. Therefore, he was able to reach the designated limb and his landing was nearly perfect except for two steps he took which were necessary to catch his balance. He took a brief rest and then flew back to the nest. He made another good landing and was able to enter the nest with no assistance from Mother. After completing his flight, he strutted to the rear of the nest and sat next to Hardy.

Smiling victoriously at Hardy for a full thirty seconds, he finally spoke. "Nothing to it; I told you I knew how to fly."

"You looked ridiculous. You made it to the limb and back: so what? You were flapping harder than any bird I've ever seen. You were rocking back and forth, completely out of control in the air. I thought something terrible had happened to you, like maybe you had injured yourself or something." Hardy was disappointed Laslo had been so successful and was not going to give Laslo any break at all.

"Yeah right; like I said, I can outfly you any time and I just proved it. Deal with it."

Hardy was not too happy about Laslo's natural flying abilities, but what really bothered him was Laslo's lack of fear. Hardy had been scared, and it was all he could do to leap from the nest. Laslo didn't even hesitate and smiled confidently before jumping out.

Over the next week it became obvious that Laslo was a better natural flyer than Hardy. Hardy struggled with learning new maneuvers, always fearing he would lose all control and fall from the sky. Laslo would listen to Father's instructions and then attempt the maneuver without a concern in the world. Occasionally, he would experience a problem and once, on a left turn and climb maneuver, he tried to climb much too quickly and lost complete control. It took him nearly ten seconds to regain control as he fell. He then laughed about it as if it were nothing and went right back and tried it again, nailing it. But Hardy was diligent, and while more cautious and at times even timid, he steadily improved.

Father had taken the boys out one day and taught them how to land in water. He explained that it was similar to landing on a branch. However, as they touched down they had to paddle their feet. This would help move them forward as they settled on the water's surface. If they failed to paddle hard enough, their forward momentum would cause them to fall facedown in the water. It wouldn't hurt, but it was not the sign of a masterful duck to take a "face dive," as Father called it. Father demonstrated the technique and landed flawlessly, making it look simple.

Hardy watched closely and imprinted the foot-paddle rate in his brain. Then it was his turn. He executed an excellent landing, but his little legs were not as strong as his father's and his feet had not grown enough to give him sufficient propulsion at the paddle rate he used. *Splash!* Hardy took a perfect face dive and came up coughing for air. As he cleared his lungs, the first thing he heard was Laslo laughing so loudly it could be heard all over the forest.

"I'm embarrassed to call you my brother. Maybe you're not really a duck; what do you think?"

Hardy committed himself to a simple goal. Somehow, someway he was going to get even with Laslo. Laslo had to get his and it had to be soon.

Now it was Laslo's turn to attempt a water landing. Of course Laslo had seen what happened to Hardy and so he paddled his feet like mad. His little feet were really going as he came in for a landing. He was paddling hard but not hard enough. He tipped forward and came close, but no face dive. He looked at Hardy and then took his wing and tossed some water into his own face.

"Don't worry, Hardy. I'll make it look like we both took a face dive so the others won't tease you. After all, what are brothers for?" Laslo then laughed and shook his head at Hardy.

The next day Laslo and Hardy were in the nest alone. Mother and Father had gone foraging for food. They wanted to have some time alone together so they left the boys at home by themselves. While they sat in the nest discussing navigation methods, Laslo broke wind. Actually he passed gas twice in quick succession. The first was fairly impressive even by Laslo's standards and it took him by surprise. But the next one that followed about five seconds later could only be described as colossal. It started innocently enough, under low pressure, but it kept building pressure and continued for so long that Laslo began to get concerned for his own safety. It caused a burning sensation so severe that Laslo snuck a quick peek just to be sure he hadn't set fire to the nest or his tail feathers. These two made the previous one Hardy had described to his parents seem like an experiment. These were the real deal and both were silent. Laslo gave Hardy no warning, waiting for his reaction. And that didn't take long.

Hardy was in midsentence when he was blasted with the first wave. It immediately took his breath. Hardy gasped for air as expressions of surprise, followed by shock and disbelief, and then revulsion were clearly visible on his face. Hardy began to flap his wings in front of his face while circling the nest, seeking respite from the choking cloud of gas that had enveloped him.

Just as Hardy started to think he was a goner, he got a breath of fresh air and then another. He had just begun to relax when the next wave struck. This time there was no escape. Hardy tried everything he could think of to find relief and finally hung over the side of the nest as far as he could. Any fear of falling was gone. Hardy would have welcomed a fall to the ground if there was clear air to be found there. But Hardy didn't believe at that moment there was clear air left anywhere in the world. Not anymore. Hardy staggered to the center of the nest, gagged several times, appeared to convulse, and then went limp. Laslo was sure Hardy was pretending, but the ruse, if it was one, lasted so long he started to have doubts. What Laslo did not know was that Hardy had seen Mother returning to the nest.

As Mother approached, she saw Laslo sitting with his back against the side of the nest and his wings resting on the nest rim. And there was Hardy lying motionless in the bottom of the nest. A jolt of fear went through her. What had happened to her Hardy?

Hardy had soaked his wing tip in his mouth and rubbed saliva around his eyes. The result was perfect. Mother landed in the nest.

"Hardy, what's the matter, sweetie?" she asked. Hardy didn't answer. He didn't move a single muscle. He even held his breath so it would appear he had stopped breathing. "Laslo, what's wrong with your brother? What happened?" Mother was screaming she was so upset.

"There's nothing wrong with him, Mom. He's just faking," answered Laslo.

Hardy moaned slightly and began to stir. He raised himself up, leaned on one wing, slowly raised his head, and looked up at his mother. Hardy attempted to show the most pitiful face he could manage.

"Have you been crying? What's wrong, baby?" asked Mother.

"It was him," said Hardy weakly, slowly raising his wing and pointing at Laslo.

"What did you do to your brother, Laslo?" asked Mother. "Goodness, what's that odor?"

"I didn't do anything to him," said Laslo. "He's faking."

"Mom, he farted again. This time it was worse. You've gotta do something, please," pleaded Hardy.

Just then Father flew in and landed in the nest. "What's wrong? What's going on? And my god, what is that smell?"

"Everything's okay," answered Mother.

"What's wrong with Hardy?" asked Father. "Good Lord, that smell. What is it? Did some of those carrion-eating crows crap in this nest? They'll do that, you know. Sons of—"

"Father, please," said Mother sharply. "No crows have been here. Apparently Laslo is suffering from a little flatulence, that's all."

"A little flatulence? Did you say a little flatulence?" asked Father. "Look at the size of him. There's no way a little flatulence did this. I'm surprised the little fellow's still in one piece."

Mother gave Father a look that could stop a hawk in a full attack dive. "Hardy, are you okay? I think it's time you stop pretending," said Mother.

"I'm not pretending, Momma. You have no idea what I've been through," said Hardy weakly as he struggled to sit up. "I tried to tell you; there's something wrong with Laslo."

"I think I have some idea what you've been going through, son," said Father, blinking rapidly, trying to clear the tears that had formed in his eyes. "This nest is rank."

"There's a lingering odor but let's not exaggerate, okay?" said Mother.

"Hardy's always exaggerating, Momma," Laslo replied.

"Ooohwee! Good night, Irene, but this nest stinks," said Father. "Laslo, are you sure you're okay?"

"What are you worried about Laslo for?" protested Hardy. "Try to imagine what I've had to deal with. This nest smells as sweet as dogwood flowers on a spring morning after a light rain compared to what it was like in here just a few minutes ago." Hardy finally got to his feet and walked slowly around the nest, taking deep breaths, filling his lungs with fresh air. He eventually sat down. It was more like a collapse, really. He sat with his back against the side of the nest directly opposite Laslo.

Hardy began to tell his story to his parents. "We were just sitting in the nest talking. You know, we were talking about navigation, so we would be ready for our solo flights. Dad, you have to move my solo flight up. I need the ability to escape from the nest when he does that again. And he will do it again. He's rotten I tell you."

"I'm with you, son. We'll do it later today if you feel up to it. Go on, tell us what happened." Father sounded breathless. He, Mother, and Hardy were all breathing through their mouths as if they had just flown a long distance into a strong headwind. Laslo was the only one breathing normally.

"I was talking to Laslo and it just came out of nowhere. There was no sound, no warning. Nothing. One second I was fine and the next I couldn't breathe and my eyes were burning. It was that bad." Hardy was looking right into his father's eyes as he told his tale.

"Dad, he's exaggerating. He always does that," said Laslo.

"Let him finish. Go ahead, son," said Father.

"It seemed to last forever but then it started to clear. I was able to get two, maybe three fairly decent breaths, and then it was back, this time with a real vengeance. There was no way to get away from it. I felt myself getting weak so I hung over the side of the nest. But that didn't work either. It had somehow surrounded the entire nest."

"Stop exaggerating, Hardy," yelled Laslo.

"I'm not exaggerating! Mom, Dad, as I hung over the side of the nest, that fart cloud began to spread out and move through the trees. It started to rain and I thought to myself, *Thank God. I'm saved.* But then I realized it wasn't raining. Bugs were falling from the trees by the hundreds. But it didn't kill them. They would hit the ground, lie there and shake for a while, and then they'd stagger around blindly. Be careful. We can't eat anything from that direction for at least a month," said Hardy, pointing downwind. Hardy paused and then continued his description of the events. "Do you remember that dead possum that's been over there for the past ten days? You know, when the wind is just right it makes living here difficult?"

"We know the one you're talking about, dear," said Mother.

"You're not buying this story, are you?" asked Laslo incredulously.

"Laslo, let Hardy finish," said Father. "I want to hear this."

"Well, there was a buzzard there eating that possum. It seemed like he was enjoying it, too. I don't know how they can do that. It's disgusting. Anyway, apparently Laslo's fart cloud reached him because suddenly he looked right up at the nest. He had a look of shock and pain on his face and then his face turned bright red. I knew what he was going through. I actually felt a little sorry for him."

"Really, Hardy," said Mother. "I think you're taking this too far now."

Hardy didn't hesitate for a second to respond. "No, Momma. You need to hear this. As I was saying, that buzzard turned bright red and then almost immediately he went pale and broke out into a sweat. I mean the sweat was just pouring off him. Then he turned his head and vomited. When he had finished vomiting he dry-heaved for a least a full minute. A couple of times

I thought he'd stopped but then I guess he got another whiff, and he heaved some more. Maybe he didn't get another whiff. Maybe he just remembered the smell. I mean, the thought of it right now makes me want to gag. Like I said earlier, I actually felt sorry for him. Daddy, he had just been eating a ten-day dead possum, and he liked it. But he couldn't handle Laslo's farts. Nobody can. The last I saw of that buzzard he was in a daze, staggering up that small rise over there, and then he disappeared into the woods." Hardy shook his head and paused. "I'm not sure he's going to make it. He didn't look like he was doing very well." A sad expression spread across his face. "That's sure no way to go." Hardy paused again briefly. "That's pretty much it. Then Momma and you showed up."

"Well, that's some story. But I think Laslo's right. You may have exaggerated a bit with some of the details," said Mother, relieved that the story was finally complete.

"Okay. I admit it. I exaggerated just a little. But I had to so you would fully understand what it was like. You can't underestimate Laslo and just how disgusting he really is. He's nothing more than a web-footed, feather-covered, bubbling cauldron of rotting beetles and stinking gas," replied Hardy. "Daddy, I was serious about moving my solo up. I need the ability to escape the nest when necessary."

"We'll do your solo in about an hour, Hardy. One thing's for sure. Based on the way this nest smells, if only 10 percent of Hardy's story was accurate, then that was a fart for the ages. One I can brag to the other dads about for a long time to come. What're we going to do with you, Laslo?"

"Nothing, Dad, it's just a natural thing and it wasn't that bad."

Hardy laughed out loud in derision. "There was nothing natural about it. Everything about it was completely unnatural. And yes, it was that bad."

"Well, I don't understand it. We've been careful not to bring any of those yellow beetles back to the nest since your last complaint," said Mother.

"Maybe I was wrong about the beetles. Maybe it's something else he eats, or maybe he just has a rotten spot in him." Hardy paused. A look of revelation crossed his face. "No. Wait a minute. This only happens when you and Daddy aren't here. He knows exactly what he's doing. And I don't think I was wrong about the beetles either. He's hiding them." Hardy paused briefly, lost in intense thought. "He has a stash," yelled Hardy. "It's gotta be right here in the nest. We need to turn this nest upside down, tear it apart if necessary until we find them." There was a note of determination mixed with desperation in Hardy's voice.

"Mom, Dad, that's the most ridiculous thing Hardy's ever said. I'm not hiding anything in the nest, especially big yellow beetles. Don't believe him. You've already seen how he exaggerates."

"Hardy, I think you need to drop it. We're not going to tear this nest apart looking for beetles just because you suspect Laslo has hidden some here. You have no evidence he's done that," said Mother.

"The 'evidence' nearly choked me to death earlier. And it may have killed that poor buzzard," exclaimed Hardy.

"That's enough. We're not searching the nest," said Father. Laslo looked at Hardy with that smug look of victory he always has when he prevails.

"Do I get to do my solo today, Dad?" asked Laslo.

"There won't be time today. You'll go out first thing in the morning. We need to be sure you can leave the nest when necessary also." Father looked at Hardy and winked.

"That's not fair. Hardy tells a ridiculous story and he gets rewarded by having his solo moved up?"

"Yours is moved up, too. It just can't be done today," said Father. "Now drop it or yours won't be moved up." Hardy gave Laslo that same victorious look just for spite.

"Dad, do crows really crap in other bird's nests? Why would they do that?" Hardy asked.

"No one knows why they do it. I guess they think it's funny. Yes. Crows have been known to do that."

Mother couldn't stand it anymore. "I don't like this conversation. It's vulgar and that's not the kind of thing you should be sharing with the children. Anyway, that's just a rumor about crows from years ago. We don't know if it's even true. We've never had any problems with the crows." Mother wanted her children to grow up with an open mind and not be prejudiced by unconfirmed stories.

"I understand your concern, Mother. But it's not a rumor anymore. I was talking to some of the other fathers down at the lake earlier. Apparently several nests were visited by a group of crows yesterday. They left a heck of a mess in some of those nests. In one case, it was so bad the family just moved out." Father's revelation surprised Mother. The children were listening intently and hanging on Father's every word as he continued. "It seems a group of ten to fifteen young crows were caught in the act. They were led by an average-size crow who's called Antus by the others. Rumors have existed for years that something like this happened before to our grandparents. I guess those rumors were really true." Father paused briefly. "Hardy, grab a quick bite to eat, if you think you can get anything down, and we'll go do your solo."

"I can get it down, Daddy. I just don't know if I can keep it down," said Hardy, glaring at Laslo. Hardy was pleased with how things had turned out. He had finally convinced his parents that Laslo wasn't so perfect after all. And there was a chink in Laslo's armor. Hardy had noticed a look of concern on Laslo's face as Mother and Father had listened to his story. Hardy finally had seized the initiative, but he needed to follow up with something else and soon. But what? Hardy had to quickly come up with something good, something really good.

Chapter 8

Plato was floating alone in the dark, listening to the sounds of the frogs and insects. He loved their music and could listen to them for hours on end. Plato had been thinking about his upcoming meeting and what he could propose to Alexander. Unfortunately, he had come up with nothing new, just the same arguments he had been making for years. But Alexander agreed the situation was unjust. So they already had agreement on that—a good starting point. Maybe they could come up with some ideas on how to proceed.

The pond had grown quiet. The frogs and insects had stopped singing. Plato glanced to his left and saw, just above the tree line, a crescent moon barely visible through the mist. He began to struggle to breathe. He inhaled as deeply as he could, but it didn't seem he was getting the air he needed. The water grew warm and then hot. A small unfortunate creature, apparently caught by a predator and condemned to a painful end, wailed, its cries of anguish wafting across the lake. In the distance, the lonely hooting of an owl hinted at more suffering to come that night.

Plato felt confined in the reeds. He wanted out. His heart started to race and his breathing now came in gasps. He began paddling his feet in an attempt to escape into open water. There it was ahead, open water. Just as he saw the escape path, it began to vanish. Plato stopped paddling and stared. The open water was visible one moment and gone the next. Now it was visible again, now gone. His vision was blurred as the air now seemed to move and ripple before him. Then Plato understood. He relaxed and waited a moment. The figure of his father formed in front of him.

Plato spoke.

"Father."

"Your promise, Plato. What have you done?"

"I've met with the birds and the crows. No one wants to change. I've tried to convince them."

"There's little time, Plato. Little time."

"I'm meeting with a crow who's interested in helping. Maybe something will come from that. But the elders don't—"

"Forget the elders."

"Forget the elders? They're the leaders. Nothing can happen without the elders. How can I forget the elders?" asked Plato.

"Think, Plato. Think."

"But, Father—"

"Think!"

The figure dissolved before Plato's eyes and disappeared. The water felt cool again and the frogs and insects were singing their melodies. The reeds and cattails were again comforting in the dark. Plato bowed, tucked his head under his wing, and slept.

Chapter 9

The next morning Plato woke feeling rested and energetic. He was excited and hopeful about his meeting with Alexander. If they could come up with an idea, maybe they could develop a plan for changing everyone's minds.

Plato grabbed a bite to eat and then waddled onto the shore. He sat quietly and warmed himself in a spot where a shaft of sunlight penetrated the trees. As he basked in the warmth of the sun, Plato reflected on the events of the night. The visit by his father, or whatever or whoever that was, had not frightened him as much as it had the first time. This time it seemed less frightening, but it also seemed more real. That was puzzling. What had his father meant when he said, "There is little time"? And why would he say, "Forget the elders"? It made no sense. But then neither did a visit from his dead father.

It was time to leave and meet Alexander. Plato took flight and, after gaining sufficient altitude, took a circuitous path to the tree where they were to meet. He made certain no one saw him enter the tree. He landed on the same limb he'd rested on the day before. He was early, but Alexander was already there.

"Good morning. Am I late?" asked Plato.

"Good morning. No, I've been here for about an hour. I made an excuse so I could get away from my duties with the army. I came here early in a rather roundabout way so I wouldn't be detected. That way we're not likely to be interrupted."

"Great. So do you have any ideas on what we can do? I haven't come up with anything that I am confident will work."

"Well, I've thought about this a lot also but have nothing exciting to offer. I think we should just exchange thoughts and ideas and see if we can get anywhere that way. Who knows, maybe one of us will come up with something."

"That works for me," said Plato.

Alexander and Plato talked for the next hour exchanging thoughts and ideas. Occasionally they would take an idea and debate its merits or discuss related options. On one occasion, Alexander grew frustrated and, with raised voice, threatened to use force if necessary. But it was just rhetoric born of frustration as he and Plato had not been able to hit upon any ideas they believed would succeed.

"Do you believe this? The best we can come up with is to go back to our homes and try to convince others, one bird at a time, to work with us. This is unacceptable," said Alexander.

"Gaining support one friend at a time may be the only workable option. Of course, there is one other possibility."

Alexander looked surprised. "What's that?"

"Maybe we're just not smart enough."

Alexander straightened up suddenly and glared at Plato. Then almost immediately he began to laugh. Plato joined in and they had a good time poking fun at each other's respective intelligence level.

"I suppose you're right, Plato. Maybe we're not smart enough. Who's the smartest bird in the woodlot?"

"Most would say that would be me," said Plato with a grin, causing them both to break out into laughter again.

"We're done for," said Alexander.

"Probably," said Plato, laughing. "Who would be the smartest crow around? Would that be you?"

"No. It's not me. Not me by a long shot."

"Aris?"

"No. There's a young crow, first year. His name is Nestor. I've never met him but everyone, including Aris, says he is by far the smartest crow anyone has ever known. Some say they don't believe any crow has ever lived who is as smart as Nestor. I'm sure he's smart but that may be an exaggeration," said Alexander.

"Nestor. I'd like to meet him. Would that be possible?"

"Not likely. He's too young. It wouldn't be allowed. He's just learning to get along in the world. Maybe you'll cross paths. He's young but big for his age. He looks a little ruffled, feathers sticking out at all kinds of wild angles. He has bowed legs and big eyes. He also has a sister and they're inseparable. That may help you recognize him. Oh, if you cross paths, watch out for her. The word is she's a real handful: outspoken and confrontational. Won't stand for even the slightest thing she perceives as insulting or disrespectful."

"I like her already," said Plato. "Why don't you speak with him?"

"Not a good idea. The general of the army could not go to a first-year crow. The elders would have a fit. But if I cross paths with him, I'll see what I can do."

"Okay. Well, I think we should try to stay in touch and report back to each other on any progress we're making. And maybe my brother can make some progress."

"We should. I've enjoyed getting to know you, Plato. Your good reputation is well deserved."

"Thank you, Alexander. It's been an honor spending time with you. And I appreciate your effort to find a solution to this mess. If we don't find a way, it's just a matter of time before peace will be threatened."

Alexander stood tall. His expression changed and became stern, his face like stone. "You can be sure of that. No question. I'll be going now. Good-bye, Plato." Alexander turned and flew off.

"Good-bye," said Plato as Alexander departed.

Chapter 10

Nestor and Justine had learned to fly, and both were growing anxious to go out together on their own. Both wanted the freedom to come and go as they chose, but Justine was the less patient of the two. They had taken progressively longer flights with their parents, building strength and stamina. They had learned a great deal: how to find food, how to watch for predators and other potential dangers, the locations of staging areas, how to avoid leading predators such as owls and hawks back to the roost, and how to communicate a variety of signals to other crows. Those signals included locating calls, greeting calls, assembly calls, and alarm calls. They learned how to safely chase off predators and how to work in conjunction with other crows to mob an invader and escort them away from the roost.

Most importantly, at least to Nestor and Justine, they had become proficient with their navigation skills. The two had taken numerous instructional flights with their parents where they were required to play an increasingly larger role in navigating for the family group. Nestor would navigate for part of the flight and then Justine would take over.

Finally, each was sent out alone with instructions to fly a particular route away from the nest. This was a complex route and they were expected to fly out and return using different routes. They were not aware of it, but Father would fly high above and behind each of them, keeping an eye on them to ensure they stayed safe and did not get lost. Both Justine and Nestor had successfully completed all the tasks placed before them by their parents. They would now be allowed to go out alone together. They would also be expected to stay together and take full responsibility for feeding themselves and for their individual and collective safety.

Nestor and Justine were both thrilled about their first trip together without their parents' supervision. In fact, Justine was ecstatic. During the past week, they had discussed how they would share time so each could pursue their respective interests. It was actually a very simple compromise they had reached. Justine wanted to meet other crows, so they needed to visit common feeding areas like the cornfields and resting areas where crows would gather during the day. Safety in numbers was the primary reason for the group gathering but it was also an opportunity to socialize.

Nestor was satisfied with practicing advanced navigation methods while they flew and with exploring interesting things he spotted. That was fine with Justine as long as it didn't dominate too much of their time. Anyway, Nestor thought it might be enlightening to observe the behavior of other crows in different settings while Justine got to know some of them. Nestor didn't really care to socialize much.

Before leaving on their flight together, Nestor and Justine received some final instructions from their parents. First and foremost, they must tell their parents what route they were taking and where they were going. Secondly, they were to return no later than three hours before the sunset. That way they didn't have to sit in the staging areas and return in the dark to avoid attracting owls to the roosting area. They had enough to learn, and flying in the dark was something they had not done yet. Finally, Father had one more bit of advice and instruction.

"Nestor and Justine, do you remember our discussions about how you can feel changes in your head and bones as we change how high we are flying? I hope you two have been paying attention to that during the past week or so."

"Yes, sir, we have. In fact I've noticed a change today which is strange. It feels like it does when we are gaining altitude." Nestor had a rather puzzled look on his face.

"I've noticed the same thing, Papa," said Justine.

"Well, I want to talk to you about that. Sometimes this happens and when the change is not great nothing comes of it. But when you notice a big change or if the change is rapid, it usually means a storm is coming. Don't ask me why this happens, Nestor, because I don't know. It just does." Father was a little embarrassed that he didn't know. "In any case, it's important that you pay attention to any change and be sure you watch the wind and clouds. Any sign of an approaching storm and I want you to return to the cornfield just on the other side of the apple grove. That way you will be within minutes of home if the wind suddenly picks up. Flying in strong winds is not easy and you're not really up to that. If it starts to get windy or if you see storm clouds approaching, I want you back to the nest. Understood?"

"Yes, sir," answered Nestor. Father looked at Justine. He had a look of concern on his face.

"Of course, Papa," said Justine.

"It's very important that you do this, so don't get distracted while you're out. Now, one more thing: it's also important that you get plenty to eat. You need to eat more than normal. Eat more even if you're full. If a storm comes, it can last for days and we'll be confined to the nest. While you're gone, we'll put a few things in the nest to eat but it won't be enough if we have a big storm."

"Yes, sir," replied Nestor.

"Sure, Papa. And don't worry. We'll do what you told us to do." Justine didn't want her father to worry about them.

"Okay. Tell your mother good-bye and have fun. And be careful. Nestor, you look out for your sister, do you hear?"

"I will, Father."

"I can take care of myself," said Justine.

"I know you can. Let me finish what I was going to say," said Father. "And, Justine, you look out for Nestor, do you hear me?"

"Yes, Papa."

Justine and Nestor said good-bye to their mother. After surveying the area to make sure it was safe, they took off on their adventure. They flew straight out of the nest with the sun directly behind them, using a large old oak tree in the distance as a marker beacon. As they neared the oak tree, a road was visible just beyond. They reached the road and made a left turn and followed for about a mile until the road intersected with another road. At the intersection, they made another left turn and soon the old orchard was on their left and a large cornfield was on their right. There was a lone tree ahead, just inside the fence line next to the cornfield. The tree did not have many leaves, the canopy being rather bare. There were at least fifteen crows sitting in the tree chattering. Justine signaled to Nestor she wanted to go meet the group of crows, so they descended and landed on the fence near the group of trees.

Justine took a moment to preen her feathers. She was still young but had matured physically and was, as far as crows go, gorgeous. Realizing all the young male crows were watching her every move, she took her time. While preening, she turned completely around so they could get a good look at her. Her feathers fit her body like a fine robe; the feathers were shiny black with shades of purple when the light reflected just right. Nestor was observing Justine and the reactions of the young male crows. He also noticed a group of five female crows who appeared to be rather annoyed with what they were seeing. They would alternate between watching and then talking quietly amongst themselves.

Finally, Justine was finished preening and she turned and faced the group of crows. She held her head up high and spoke. "Hello. My name's Justine and this is my brother, Nestor. What are you all doing?" She spoke in a soft but confident voice, clearly enunciating her words.

"Oh, we're just taking a break and talking. We've been in the cornfield eating; some more than others," said one of the crows, glancing over at a crow that was definitely overweight. "We think a storm's coming. My name is Damien, that little guy there is Clyde, that's Benito, and that fat one over there is Buddy. What are you two up to?"

"We're just out exploring the area. We saw you down here and thought we'd drop in and introduce ourselves. You don't mind, do you?" asked Justine.

"Heck no," answered several of the crows in unison.

Nestor saw that the females had turned their backs on the group and were engaged in their own private conversation. One of the male crows was off to one side and appeared to be sound asleep.

"Does the scriggly one speak?" asked one of the crows in a husky, hoarse-sounding voice. It was Antus. Antus, for some reason had trouble making some a sounds. He was an average-size crow. Nestor had jokingly mentioned earlier to Justine that Antus did not seem to be the brightest crow in the roost. But Antus was a crow who wanted to control things around him.

"Who do you think you are speaking like that about? Nestor?" Justine's voice was now slightly raised. "I've warned you before about that." The young female crows had stopped talking and were now watching the events closely.

Antus walked along a limb above the group of crows that had been speaking with Justine. He stopped, turned, and faced Justine. "You, Justine, er welcome to stey. I think the boys en I would enjoy spending some quility time with you," laughed Antus, and the other male crows chuckled. Antus then looked directly at Nestor. "But thit hiss to go. He's not henging with this group. He's not welcome here."

"Who died and left you in charge?" asked Justine, now visibly angry.

"I'm Intus. I'm the leader of this group, duly ippointed. Isn't thit right, guys?"

"That's right," said the crows in unison.

"Well, it's a free world and I choose to stay right here. And Nestor is staying here also."

"It's okay, Justine. Let's just go. There are other things we can do," said Nestor.

"Listen to him, Justine. He's the smirtest crow iround or hiven't you heard. If he's not gone in the next minute he is going to get hurt en hurt bid. Thit's for certain." Antus fluffed his feathers and flapped his wings slightly in a threatening manner.

"If you so much as touch him, I'll take you apart, Antus, right here in front of this entire group. How would you like that?"

"Ooooh, I'm terrified. Miybe I should leave right now while I've got the chince," laughed Antus. His comment garnered more chuckles from his group.

"Let's go, Justine." Nestor moved beside her and bumped her a little. "Let's go now." Nestor then turned and flew from the fence.

Justine looked at all the crows and shook her head. "You are all despicable. You should be ashamed of yourselves. Anyone that would have him as their leader must be a real idiot. None of you are worth wasting one more minute of my time." Justine then turned and flew off to catch up with Nestor, who had circled back and was close by. Nestor and Justine could hear the laughs and the insults being directed toward them as they flew away.

Antus could be heard above the rest of the crows. "You two think you're so smirt. You're nothing special. Do you hear me? You're nothing."

"I can't believe that just happened; who does Antus think he is?" screamed Justine. She was angry but also stunned and confused by what had just taken place.

"He's a sad, angry, pathetic crow. He obviously needs to feel important; that's how he does it. Just forget about it, Justine. We'll find a different group to hang out with. We don't need to associate with that kind of group anyway.

They're headed for trouble and quickly." Nestor seemed slightly annoyed but not that upset.

"Forget about it? No way. Antus and his group are going to get theirs and I'm going to see to it."

"And just how are you going to do that?" asked Nestor.

"I'm not sure yet. But I am going to get even with him. You can bet on that."

"Don't let them bother you."

"Oh, they bother me. They have no right to treat others that way. What they just did was wrong and it was definitely not fair. It needs to be put right and I'm going to see that it is." Justine was calming down and now focusing her thoughts on revenge. She would get even with Antus. "You didn't do or say anything and he started in on you. Why? And how can you just take that? Why don't you stand up for yourself?"

"Justine, I've told you before. It's my opinions and thoughts that determine how I feel; what someone like Antus thinks of me is of no importance whatsoever. Do you think I need him or any of that group to like me? Please."

"Are you afraid of him? Nestor, is that it?" asked Justine. "You don't have to be afraid of him. I think I could whip him in a fight."

"Look at the size of me. I'm nearly full grown. Do you think I'm afraid of Antus? No way. There was nothing to fight over; nothing to be gained. It was better to just leave and avoid trouble. Like I said, we don't need that group as friends."

"That's not the point. You have to stand up for yourself, Nestor. Sometimes you have to just fight. When something's wrong, sometimes you have to fight to make it right." Justine was dumbstruck that Nestor wasn't as angry as she was.

"True, but I don't think it's true in this case. Even if it is, that wasn't the time or place. There were at least ten male crows there. You don't think Antus would take me on by himself, do you? The others would have helped him. You can be sure of that."

"Any other crow that tried would have had to deal with me, and I am more than handful," yelled Justine.

"Yes, you are. There's no question about that. But this may come as a surprise to you; those girl crows would have jumped all over you. They didn't like you being there. You can bet they would have jumped at the chance to make sure you didn't come back around that group of boys."

"Why didn't they like us, Nestor? What did I do wrong?"

"You did nothing wrong. Let's review what happened. You were polite. You greeted them. You introduced yourself. You asked what they were doing. Right?"

"Right; so why didn't they like us?"

"Antus was the only one that had seemed to have a real problem with us. He's the one that started all that nonsense. I think Antus feels threatened by us," said Nestor.

"Threatened? But we didn't do anything."

"Look, didn't you notice how concerned he looked when you and the other crows were speaking to each other? They seemed to like you. I think that scared him. I also noticed the group of girls seemed to be annoyed that the boys were paying such close attention to you. I think they're just an insecure group of crows. Maybe you should be more understanding."

"Understanding? After the way they treated us? I don't think so," said Justine.

"We'll just find another group to hang out with. Why do you want to be friends with that group?"

"I don't want to be friends with them. Not anymore."

"Then just forget about it and let's find another group to be friends with. Come on, what do you think?"

Justine didn't answer right away. She was deep in thought. "Oh, all right. It is sort of silly to let that stupid Antus ruin my day. We don't need them, do we?"

"No, we don't. There are plenty of other crows out there and each with more brains than that whole group put together." Nestor laughed out loud, which was rare for him.

"Okay, Nessy. Let's find some new friends."

"It's Nestor, Justine. My name is Nestor."

Chapter 11

Nestor and Justine spent the next two days exploring and looking for another group of crows they could make friends with. The storm didn't materialize; however, it had gotten a little cooler so they now had excellent weather for traveling about. The exploring part went well, and Nestor found plenty of things that sparked his curiosity and commanded his attention. Justine even found a few things that intrigued her, but she was more interested in finding a group of new potential friends. They avoided the area where they had encountered Antus and his group. Nestor and Justine flew around all day and covered a lot of ground but found no groups of young crows. They did see some isolated young crows about their age alone or two at a time leaving or returning to the roosting area but were unable to make any friends. They both found it rather strange that after two full days of searching they were unable to find any young crows in the area.

Justine decided that she and Nestor should follow one of the young crows in the morning to find out where he was going. Maybe one crow would lead them to a group, and then they could make some new friends. Justine suggested to Nestor that they follow a crow surreptitiously. Nestor didn't really care for that idea, believing it unnecessary. He preferred to approach a crow, befriend that crow, and ask to join him in his travels. But Justine insisted and Nestor agreed.

So the next morning, Nestor and Justine left the roosting area and flew out to the road. However, this time they turned right and flew only a short distance before securing themselves in the braches of a large oak tree where they talked while waiting for a crow to come along. They had only been there about ten minutes when a lone young crow approached and flew past their location. They waited briefly and then took wing and followed, making sure to stay far behind, occasionally changing their altitudes in an effort to avoid detection.

The crow they were following changed directions occasionally and on two occasions circled and retraced his flight path briefly. Nestor and Justine would increase their altitude and fly off briefly in a different direction in an effort to ensure the young crow did not discover that they were following. The young crow resumed his flight and Nestor and Justine fell in and followed above at a good distance. However, two other crows had also been following, noticed them, and concluded they were following the first young crow. The two crows intercepted Nestor and Justine and directed them to land so they could speak. One of the crows called out to the crow Nestor and Justine had been following, and that crow circled back. The five of them landed on the large lower limbs of a hickory tree with the three crows facing Justine and Nestor.

"Why were you following him?" demanded one of the crows.

His head lowered, as was his habit when interacting with others, Nestor looked up at the three crows. He stared, his eyes appearing larger than normal, for a full ten seconds. Justine was looking at Nestor, waiting for him to answer. Several more seconds passed. "What makes you think we were following him?" asked Nestor.

"We've watched you for the past ten minutes. It's obvious you were following him. Now answer my question: why were you following him?"

Nestor didn't answer immediately, thinking about how he should answer. Again, Nestor let several seconds pass before answering. Finally he responded. "We were hoping he would lead us to a group of crows so we could introduce ourselves. We just wanted to make new friends."

The three crows stared intently at Nestor and Justine.

"Why didn't you just speak to me and ask to go with me? Why would you follow me without my knowledge?" asked the crow they had been following.

Nestor turned and briefly looked Justine in the eye, giving her an *I told you so* look. He then said, "We've had a little trouble making friends. We haven't seen any groups around. We don't know where everyone goes each day. We just thought it would be better if we found a group and approached them rather than approaching just one at a time. We shouldn't have had any trouble finding crows but we did. The few we've seen seem aloof and secretive and ... so why are you three so concerned about this anyway? What are you all up to?"

"We need to be sure you're not spies," answered one of the crows. Nestor and Justine quickly exchanged glances. They noticed the three crows staring as if they were trying to detect any sign that Nestor and Justine were not being truthful with them.

"Spies? Are you serious? Spies for whom and for what purpose?" asked Justine.

"Are you two friends with a crow named Antus?"

"Good Lord, no," answered Justine. "He's the most despicable creature I've ever encountered. I wouldn't have anything to do with him if he were the last living thing left in the whole world."

"Why are you all worried about Antus?" asked Nestor. "Do you think we are spying for him? Why would he want us to spy on you? What are you all up to?"

"Wait here." The three crows flew off to a nearby tree and began to talk. The discussion appeared to be very lively, with one of the crows waving his wings around animatedly. Justine and Nestor just watched.

"What do you think this is all about, Nessy? This all seems very strange." Justine wore a puzzled expression, and there was a note of concern in her voice.

"I don't know," answered Nestor. "Here they come."

The three crows returned and stood on the limb opposite Justine and Nestor. "My name is Hector," said the largest of the three crows. "This is Frederick and this is Marshall. What are your names?"

"Well, it's nice to meet each of you. This is Justine. I'm her brother, Nestor. I apologize for our behavior, Marshall. We should not have followed you like that."

"It was my fault. It was all my idea. Nestor didn't want to but I talked him into it," said Justine, looking a little embarrassed.

"I think you two should come with us. You need to meet Alexander. He's our leader. Maybe you can join our group," said Hector.

"What does your group do?" asked Nestor.

"We'll answer no questions. Alexander will decide what, if anything, you can know about our group. Follow us." The three crows took flight. Nestor nodded at Justine and they followed.

"What do you think this is all about, Nessy?"

"Again, Justine, I don't know. But I have every intention of finding out. This is interesting; most interesting."

Chapter 12

Hardy had taken his solo flight and satisfied his father that he was sufficiently skilled to go out on his own. The flight took nearly four hours from start to finish. Father had instructed Hardy to fly out from the nest in any direction he chose for at least a half hour. Then he was to turn and fly cross-country for at least one hour. He was then to return directly to the nest but must not retrace his flight path. Hardy was permitted to explore, rest, and take nourishment as needed but must be back at the nest before dark. Hardy said good-bye to his mother and father, and after glaring at Laslo for a full thirty seconds, he smiled, turned, and took off on his solo flight. Unbeknownst to Hardy, his father left about five minutes later and kept Hardy in sight during his entire solo, taking care to keep Hardy from noticing he was being followed.

Hardy flew from the nest, passing near the crows' roosting area, taking care not to invade their airspace. Hardy was excited and confident in his ability to successfully complete this solo flight. He had worked hard and was proud of what he had accomplished in recent weeks. Hardy felt free and enjoyed the feel of the air passing under his wings and the warmth of the sun on his back. He remembered to maintain an awareness of his surroundings and where he was at all times in relation to the nest while keeping a wary eye out for danger. Occasionally, he would change wing angles, raise his tail, dive, and climb. In short, he practiced a number of different skills his father had taught him. He had been taught well and was a skilled and strong flyer.

After flying south for about a half hour, Hardy turned to the east and headed for the farm country. His flight so far had taken him over wooded areas.

Hardy had enjoyed his flight so far but he especially had a fondness for flying over the farmlands. There was so much to see and he always saw something new and fascinating. About an hour had passed when Hardy decided it was time for a short break. He thought he would look for a body of water to land in where he could get a drink and maybe find a little food. He would also get a chance to practice his water landings. As he looked about the landscape, he saw several glistening lakes ahead in the distance.

As he neared the lakes, Hardy began his decent. He picked a small lake and began adjusting his flight path so he could approach the landing flying into the slight breeze that was blowing. As he descended, he noticed something strange about the lake. The sunlight reflected from it in an unnatural way. Hardy wasn't sure exactly what was amiss, but his instincts told him to stop his descent and circle the lake until he could determine what was wrong. As he circled around the lake, he noticed a man near one of the other small lakes. The man bent down near the edge of the lake and in an instant he began to lift the lake off the ground. This obviously startled Hardy and so he gained altitude and watched from a safe distance. The man folded the lake into a small square shape and then placed it in the back of a truck. The man got in the truck and drove away, leaving Hardy puzzled.

What Hardy had witnessed was a farmer collecting some polyethylene sheeting from the ground, set there earlier to prevent weed growth from areas prepared for planting. The sheeting looked like water from the air, and had Hardy not been alert and paying close attention he could easily have attempted a landing. And what a surprise that would have been. Hardy landed near one of the strange lakes and examined it. After satisfying his curiosity, he took to the air again.

Hardy continued his flight and soon found a real lake. He made a pretty good landing, although he had still not completely mastered water landings. Hardy rested for a brief time, drank water, and fed on some insects he found on the water's surface. Soon he was off again for the final leg of his solo flight. However, after getting airborne, he decided to practice his water landings and made about a dozen landings before he was satisfied. He then continued on his solo.

Hardy had been flying for nearly ten minutes when he noticed a group of crows resting in an old tree near a fence line. The crows were an interesting mix of various shapes and sizes. One was very large—fat, actually. He was so large Hardy wondered if he could even fly. Another crow seemed to be sleeping soundly in the same tree but away from the others. As Hardy flew overhead, one of the crows began to yell at him. A few of the other crows started yelling, taking their cue from the first crow, but Hardy couldn't understand what they were saying. The sleeping crow didn't wake and the fat crow just sat there, appearing not interested in wasting any energy just to yell at a passing duck.

Hardy continued on his flight back to the nest. He had paid close attention to the terrain, the angle of the sun, and used other navigational tools he had been taught. Right on schedule he returned to the nest and was congratulated by his mother. Not long after he landed, Father arrived and feigned surprise that Hardy had already returned to the nest, and he too offered his congratulations. Hardy had passed his solo flight test and was now cleared to venture out on his own. However, he was to wait until Laslo had also been cleared, and they were to take their first few flights together. Laslo successfully completed his solo flight the next day. That evening they planned their first trip alone and agreed they would revisit the farmlands area as it was a favorite flight area for both of them.

After dark Hardy and Laslo rested in the nest and soon Laslo was sound asleep. Hardy lay in the nest deep in thought, contemplating the next day's flight. Slowly an idea formed in his mind. A smile spread across Hardy's face as he took a brief look at Laslo resting peacefully. "Laslo actually looks like a sweet, innocent young duck-thing when he's asleep," said Hardy quietly. Tomorrow was going to be a good day, a very good day, indeed.

Chapter 13

Nestor and Justine followed the crows and circled a field near a wooded area. There was a small stand of trees in the field about fifty yards from the forest. Circling the area Nestor and Justine observed no sign of activity. They wondered if this was their final destination or an interim stop to determine if anyone had followed them. Frederick began to glide and, tipping his wings from side to side, called out, "Caw! Caw! Caw!" There was a slight pause and then again he called out in quick succession. "Caw! Caw!"

As they continued to circle, Nestor noticed several crows flying in from the east and another small group from the north. As he glanced around, he saw two more groups flying in, one from the west and one from the south. Soon they were in the midst of fifteen to twenty crows.

Justine called out to Nestor in a low voice to get his attention. She directed his attention to the small group of trees in the opening. Nestor was surprised to see the tree filled with at least another thirty crows. Hector flew in close to Nestor and Justine and advised them to follow. He told them they would land in the field next to the small group of trees. Hector led the way followed by Frederick and Marshall. They were flanked on each side and from the rear by the remaining crows, all of whom followed them to the landing place. As the group landed, Nestor and Justine found themselves in the midst of at least seventy crows, all strangers to them. The entire group of crows had their attention focused upon them, causing them both to feel a little uneasy.

"What's going on, Nessy?" asked Justine.

"I'm not sure but I think we're about to meet Alexander."

As they stood there and waited, Hector flew up into the group of trees and disappeared among the limbs and leaves. Several minutes elapsed. Nestor found it rather odd that all of these crows were so interested in them and that there was complete silence. He looked overhead and saw at least five groups of crows, five per group, flying overhead in what appeared to be a structured formation intended to patrol the area.

Suddenly, Hector reappeared in the trees, flew down, and landed next to Nestor and Justine. He turned and looked back at the group of trees and as he did, all the other crows looked in the same direction. A large majestic-looking crow walked out on a limb and looked down at the group. The crow's feathers were as shiny as any Nestor and Justine had ever seen and lay perfectly against his body. He held his head high and looked down upon the group where Nestor and Justine stood.

"Is that Alexander?" asked Justine in a low voice.

"Shh. Quiet," said Hector, also in a low voice.

The large crow flew down and landed nearby. He walked over and stood in front of Nestor and Justine. He said nothing but stood there and stared into Nestor's eyes for nearly a full minute. Nestor lowered his head and peered back at him. Then the crow turned his attention to Justine, staring into her eyes.

He continued to stare for about fifteen seconds when Justine spoke. "Staring is rude. I don't appreciate the way you're behaving. Stop staring and introduce yourself."

The crow continued to stare for about five seconds and then spoke. "You're a spirited young lady, not easily intimidated. That's good." The crow spoke with a soft voice. He then turned to Nestor and spoke in a powerful voice. "You are Nestor. I've heard of you. I'm told you're very smart. I'm told you're the smartest crow there is. Is that true?"

"I guess it's true, relatively speaking. I don't know if I'm the smartest crow there is. But I am smarter than the crows I've met to date."

The large crow smiled. "Great answer. I'm Paris. I'm second in command here. Welcome to our training grounds, both of you. I understand your name's Justine?"

"That's correct," answered Justine. "I have to say this morning has been very strange and to tell the truth this whole … thing … is a mystery to me. Would you mind explaining what this is all about?"

Paris stared directly at Justine with a look of surprise and then turned to Hector and shrugged. "I guess second in command doesn't impress her." Turning back to Justine he said, "You get directly to the point, don't you?"

"I do," answered Justine. "Now, would you please do likewise?"

"Justine, be patient. They're trying to evaluate us and determine if they can trust us," said Nestor.

"Can we? Can we trust you?" asked Paris.

"Trust us with what? How?" exclaimed Justine, a note of frustration in her voice. "We don't have a clue what this is all about."

Paris turned and walked away. He stood with his back to them for about thirty seconds and then abruptly turned and walked back. "Tell me about your relationship with Antus. How do you know him?"

Justine blurted out a response in a loud voice laced with indignation. "Relationship? Are you kidding? I have no relationship with Antus. Good Lord. And neither does Nestor. I doubt anyone with any reasonable level of intelligence and civility would have a relationship with anyone the likes of Antus."

"We've had only several brief encounters with Antus. All but the last were when he flew by our nest and yelled what he thought were compliments to Justine and insults to me." Nestor had the full attention of all the crows, especially Paris. "The last encounter was face-to-face. Justine wanted to make new friends and we saw a group of crows; maybe fifteen. We landed and Justine spoke to them. Initially things seemed okay but then Antus spoke. He threatened me and, of course, Justine, and he had words. We left and have done our best to avoid him ever since."

"Antus is an ignorant, self-absorbed, miserable excuse for a crow. It's difficult to understand how those other crows could consider him their leader," said Justine.

"So, that experience led to your thinking that you had to secretly follow Marshall?" asked Paris.

"Yes. At least partially," answered Nestor. "That was wrong but we were having a difficult time finding any young crows to befriend. We were having trouble finding *any* young crows. Now we know why; it looks like most, if not all, are here."

"Well, don't underestimate Antus. He's dangerous. He's a threat to the stability of our lives here." Paris spoke with a serious tone. "And Justine, you may think he's despicable. He is. But don't think for a minute he's stupid.

He may seem stupid but he's not. Antus is very intelligent. That makes him extremely dangerous because he's also a really troubled crow."

"Why are you so worried about Antus? What can he do that could be of concern to all of you?" asked Justine.

"I think it's time you met Alexander. He will decide whether to trust you, and he will decide if you will get an answer to that question." Paris looked at Justine and then at Nestor. "Come. Follow me."

Paris turned and flew toward the small group of trees in the clearing, landing among its branches. Nestor and Justine followed and landed next to him. Paris walked along the branches with Nestor and Justine following closely behind. The leaf cover was dense and it was rather dark inside them. They entered an opening where the leaves had been removed from the limbs and there, in the center of the opening, were ten magnificent crows. These crows were the most powerful, glorious crows Nestor and Justine had ever seen. Soon they were among them, and before they realized what was happening the crows had flanked them. They were in effect surrounded in a circle of beautiful, powerful, splendid crows. The circle began to part before them and there stood the largest, most perfectly formed crow in the world; at least that's what Justine thought. He was powerful and had an air of confidence that was immediately apparent. Justine took one look and felt like she couldn't catch her breath.

"Who is that?" whispered Justine.

"I am Alexander. I've been told about your questionable behavior, following one of us without their knowledge or consent. Are you sneaks? Are you spies? What have you to say in your defense?" Alexander's voice was strong and commanding. Nestor and Justine just stood there, unable to answer.

"Are you mute? I asked you to say something in your defense. It would be in your best interest to answer," boomed Alexander. "I've been told you two show great promise. So, prove my advisor wise. Nestor, speak up."

"We've already explained ourselves and explained why we did what we did. We've admitted it was wrong," said Nestor, calculating that it was important to stand his ground. "You've said your advisor told you about us. I would think he would have provided you with our explanation also."

"I'd appreciate your explaining it again to me."

"We will not," answered Justine. "We're not prisoners, are we?" Justine paused but got no response. "Well, are we?"

"No, you're not prisoners," responded Alexander.

"Well, we're not spies either. We're just two crows who were trying to make new friends. As Nestor said, we've already explained our behavior and we've apologized for it. We will not explain it again. You may be the leader of this group but neither Nestor nor I have accepted you as our leader. In fact, we haven't accepted you in any capacity whatsoever. Where do you get the authority to demand anything from us?"

Alexander was surprised by the conviction and power of Justine's response. His immediate reaction was one of anger as he felt that his authority had been challenged. But quickly his reaction changed to one of admiration and respect. Justine was correct; he wasn't their leader. He had become accustomed to unquestioning obedience. Justine's response was a good wake-up call.

"You're absolutely correct. You are guests here and my behavior is out of line. I offer you both my sincere apology. But please indulge me and allow one more question you may also find offensive."

"Ask," responded Nestor.

"We'll decide after we hear the question whether we'll answer or not," Justine added.

"Justine, let him ask. We've given him good reason to be suspicious of us." Turning to Alexander, Nestor continued. "If we elect to answer, it'll be the truth. We don't lie."

"Really? That touches on the essence of my question. You followed Marshall without his knowledge. You invaded his privacy. You violated his freedom to go where he pleases without being spied upon, uh, excuse me, Justine, extensively observed. That was dishonest, was it not? And is not that type of dishonesty in and of itself a form of lying?"

"It is. I understand why you may think we are not trustworthy. That was out of character for us and it has taught Justine and me a valuable lesson. But we weren't spying on Marshall, and we'll never do anything like that again," said Nestor in a quiet, subdued voice.

"Oh, I think you may do something like that again. But it'll be okay the next time," answered Alexander. "I understand you hate Antus. Is that true?"

"Yes. We despise him," answered Justine.

"We hate no one," said Nestor. "We just don't care for his kind and have decided to have nothing to do with him or his group. That's all."

Justine looked at Nestor with fire in her eyes. "Speak for yourself."

"Well, Justine, I'm wondering: are you always so confrontational?" asked Alexander.

"Not always; only when it is warranted. I don't like to be wronged and I don't like to see others treated wrongly. So far I see little of your behavior that would qualify as right."

"That's good," answered Alexander. "What I have to share with you is about just that. It's about righting a serious wrong. Would you care to hear what I have to say?"

"Yes. Absolutely," said Nestor. Justine didn't answer.

"And you, Justine. Are you interested in hearing about a great injustice that needs correcting?"

"I'm listening."

"Let's move to where we can be more comfortable. Paris, make sure everyone gets back to their posts." Alexander led the way to a more remote spot near an edge of the area that had been cleared. "Please sit. Would you care for something to eat?"

"No, thank you," answered Justine.

"Thank you, no," said Nestor.

"I'm sure the two of you have noticed that crows live in the pine groves while all the other birds live among the nicer areas of the forest."

"Nicer areas? I hadn't thought of the other areas of the forest as being nicer," said Justine.

"The pine grove meets all our needs and provides us with more than adequate shelter," added Nestor.

"Well, have you ever wondered why we crows live in the pines, many of which are dead and many of which have fallen over, while the other birds live in the more sheltered and safer parts of the forest?" asked Alexander. Nestor and Justine looked at each other inquisitively but neither answered. "Have you ever wondered why we have to travel a significant distance to get water when there is a lake right there in the forest no more than a minute's flight from the pine grove?" Again, there was no response from Nestor or Justine.

"No? Well, the reason is because crows were forced out of the woodlot years ago by the other birds. We live in the pines not by choice but because the other birds require it. So, what do you think of that? Is that right?" Alexander leaned forward and stared at both of them.

"Well, it raises a number of questions in my mind," said Nestor. "The most obvious is why would the other birds force us from the forest if we once lived there among them?"

"Exactly," said Justine. "And why would our parents stand for it unless there were good reasons?"

"Let me explain. A small group of crows decided that the forest should belong exclusively to the crows. This small group was led by a single mean-spirited crow. That crow really didn't have a good reason for wanting to take the forest from the other birds. He just didn't want the other birds to have it because it appeared to him they were happy there. Being unhappy himself, their happiness annoyed him. Does that sound like any crow we know?"

"Antus; it sounds exactly like Antus," said Justine.

"There's one major difference between Antus and the crow I just spoke about. That other crow was a near idiot. Antus is smart. He may not seem smart but he is. Smart and cunning and just as mean-spirited, unhappy, and jealous as the other crow I spoke about," explained Alexander.

"I always assumed we chose to live away from the other birds," said Justine.

"Why would you assume that?" asked Alexander.

"Well, the elder crows, and our parents, occasionally talk about the other birds in a very critical manner. So, I thought that the elder crows just didn't want to live near the other birds."

"I can understand your assumptions but they're not accurate."

"So, what happened? Did that group of crows do something that caused the other birds to ban crows from the forest?" inquired Nestor.

"That's an excellent question. The answer is yes. That coldhearted crow had a plan. He thought that if he could make life miserable for the other birds they would eventually turn on the crows. He thought that would lead to conflict and most certainly the crows, whom he believed to be far superior to all other birds, would prevail. He assumed the other birds would eventually leave the area and the forest would then belong to the crows." Justine and Nestor were listening intently as Alexander spoke. "So, this crow and his small band decided to start trouble. They conducted raids on the nests of the other birds. They would destroy the nests, tearing them to pieces. In some cases they just made the nests unlivable by defecating in them."

"That's disgusting," shrieked Justine. "I can't believe any crow would behave like that. He should have been banished from the flock by the others, him and his entire gang."

"That's precisely what happened. The other birds began to defend their nests but were unable to do it with complete success. The rogue crows were always able to sneak in and find an unguarded nest. Later they took to harassing any birds they found alone or in small groups. They made it impossible for them to eat in peace. In short, life became nearly intolerable for the birds. At least they decided they were not going to tolerate it any longer."

"What happened? Was there a war?" asked Nestor.

"The birds were prepared to go to war but decided to confront the crows in an effort to resolve the crisis peacefully. They spoke to the elder crows, and the elders, not surprisingly, were shocked and embarrassed by what they heard. You see, they had no idea what had been taking place. They asked the other birds for time to talk amongst themselves. They promised the other birds they would ensure the raids would stop and that they would deal with the renegades."

Alexander paused briefly and walked over and said something to Paris. Paris nodded and immediately left. "I have asked that some food be brought to us. I know you declined earlier but please have something to eat."

"We will. Thank you," said Nestor. Justine nodded.

"To continue, the elders met and discussed what had happened. There was a great debate. The families and close friends of the young crows that started the trouble wanted to go to war. They argued that they could easily expel the other birds from the forest. However, the elders would not agree and ultimately they banished the small group of crows. In most cases the other members of the banished crows' families left also."

Several crows arrived with some food and left it for the three.

"Thank you," said Alexander.

"Please continue. How did the crisis end?" asked Justine.

"The elders met with representatives of the birds of the forest. The elders were so ashamed of what had happened they offered to leave the forest and never return. The other birds expressed agreement, concluding that would be the only way to avoid conflict. A young but wise duck spoke on behalf of the crows and suggested the crows be given the pine forest area to live in. The crows could not use the woodland lake but must get their water elsewhere. That wise duck was opposed by many, but he argued that this arrangement was best for everyone. The crows would have a home in an area they were familiar with, and since they were effective at chasing off hawks and owls, everyone would be safer as a result of their staying in the area. The crows were to police themselves and take steps to ensure there was no repeat of the kind of behavior that started the crisis." Alexander paused and took a bite of food. Nestor and Justine took some food also and allowed Alexander to finish his snack before completing his story.

"So, it was agreed and that's how we came to live in the pine forest. Many crows think enough time has passed. The pine forest has been heavily damaged in storms and no longer offers good shelter. It's growing increasingly less safe to live there. Many think we should reenter the forest with or without the consent of the other birds."

"I think we got what we deserved," said Justine. "It seems to me the elders did the right thing. The arrangement was just. That young duck was very wise and gracious."

"I agree with Justine," said Nestor. Turning to Justine, Nestor continued. "However, I think Alexander may have a point. While it was probably a just and appropriate solution then, it may be time for a change. The pine grove is in decline and probably doesn't offer the shelter it once did."

"There may be something to what you say, Nestor, but I don't see how anything can be done to change the arrangement, except maybe seeking a new place to live," said Justine.

"The crows will not move to a new location. This is our home and this is where we'll stay. And we will get out of the pine grove and into the forest one way or another."

"What do you mean by 'one way or another'?" Nestor asked.

"Well, I, excuse me, we have a plan. It's simple and brilliant if executed properly."

"What is this 'brilliant plan'?" asked Justine with a note of concern mixed with skepticism.

"The plan is to wait until the nesting is completed so the other birds are not in need of their nests for their young. Then a small number of crows will begin roosting within the woodlot, next to the pine grove. We'll see how the other birds react. When the time is right, some crows will establish homes in the area; a small number at first. If we do this slowly and incrementally, we can have all the crows out of the pine grove and into the woodlot within a few years. There will likely be a crisis or two, but the confrontations will probably not amount to much. We'll reassure the other birds we just want a little space on the edge since the pine grove is no longer safe. We'll appeal to their reason and mix that with subtle displays of force. I'm sure we can avoid conflict if we proceed at the right pace."

"I think the plan is deceitful," said Justine. "I think it much preferable, if you want to move back into the woodlot, that a group of crows just meet with representative of the other birds and present the proper and logical arguments."

"And if they say no, then what? Any action on our part after that to move into the woodlot would be considered an act of aggression, and we would certainly have conflict then."

"Not if you don't move into the woodlot. Our situation was caused by crows, not by the other birds. If they won't permit our return, we'll need to find a new home elsewhere. That's the fair and right thing to do."

"Unacceptable," answered Alexander. "We will move into the woodlot. We have as much right as any other bird to make homes there."

"So, what if your plan doesn't work out as you envision? What if the other birds confront you with resistance?"

"That's what this training ground was established for. We have a formidable, well-trained force. The other birds cannot stand against us. We can either blockade the woodlot, preventing the birds from leaving to seek food, or we can invade and take the area we need and then defend that space. In either case, we'll prevail."

"At what price?" asked Nestor, "Lives will be lost on both sides."

"That's the price that may have to be paid. But that's up to them. In any case, if we execute the plan properly and are flexible in our pace, we'll likely avoid any conflict."

"So, how does Antus fit into this?" inquired Nestor. "You seemed very concerned about him for some reason."

"Yes, Antus is a concern. He's impatient and doesn't like the plan. He wants the entire woodland and he wants it right now. He thinks crows have been treated unjustly and that we now have a right to take the woodlot for ourselves. He believes it's owed to us. We think he'll start trouble before we have a chance to implement our plan. If he does, he could destroy the opportunity of achieving our goals peacefully."

"What makes you think Antus will do anything? He's a troublemaker but he's also a coward. I doubt he has the guts to start anything with that group of misfits he has with him." Justine was both unable and unwilling to hide her contempt for Antus.

"Antus knows the history. He's argued for immediate action. He thinks raids on nests like those done in the past will work. He's for harassment, vandalism, terror, and open conflict if necessary. He has even said he would kill to accomplish his goals. He's convinced if he starts something the elders will rally to his cause. He believes if the elders support him, this army we have assembled will be used to achieve the ends he has in sight. Finally, he believes that once the crows are established in the woodlot, everyone will be so pleased that he will be considered a hero and will be asked to be the leader of us all."

"You've got to be kidding. There is no way anyone in their right mind would choose Antus to be leader of all of us," said Justine.

"Don't be so sure," said Nestor. "If the enterprise were a success and Antus can arrange to be given the credit, we may all be surprised by what the elders may do. Antus could be placed in a key position of authority."

"Well, if that happens, I'll be living somewhere else," said Justine.

"Well, if that situation comes to pass, you could only leave if Antus allowed you to leave," said Alexander. "That's the kind of power Antus seeks."

"What makes you think Antus would do this?" asked Nestor.

"He's said so. I've already told you he argued for that course of action months ago. When he was overruled and we decided on our plan, he and his followers left. He promised us we would never be able to implement our plan; he would see to it. And he absolutely hates ducks, and any crow who doesn't hate ducks is, in his opinion, a traitor. He believes what he's doing is right and he's totally committed to his cause."

"Why is he so mean? And why hate ducks?" asked Justine.

"One of those banished years ago was the brother of Antus's father. His father became angry and resentful. He would've caused trouble a long time ago, but he was careless one evening while harassing a duck and, in his anger, didn't pay attention to what he was doing. An owl killed him. Antus's mother moved away, leaving Antus to fend for himself. He wrongly blames ducks for his misfortune."

"Now I understand why you're so concerned about him," said Nestor.

"Well, we need someone to keep an eye on him. He knows all of us. But you two could do it. I don't think Antus would have any idea you would be working with us." Alexander looked intently at both Nestor and Justine, hoping to see a positive reaction.

"Spies — you want us to be spies?" asked Justine.

"Well, sort of. I want you to get out in the area like you normally do. You don't have to infiltrate Antus's group; that wouldn't work. But you can keep an eye on his movements and activities. If you see anything that indicates he might be preparing to enter the woodlot or harass the birds in any way, you can report that to us. We just want reliable intelligence. It will be much better for everyone if we know what he's up to while he thinks we're in the dark." Alexander paused, trying to assess Justine and Nestor's reaction. "So, what do you think, will you do it?"

"We'll give it some thought. Give us a day or two and then we'll let you know," said Nestor.

Justine looked at Nestor, her eyes opened wide in shock and surprise. "We should be leaving now."

"Okay," said Alexander. "I look forward to hearing back from you. Remember, there's a lot at stake here."

Alexander spoke with Paris, who left briefly and returned with a group of five crows.

"They'll escort you out of the area," said Paris.

Justine and Nestor returned home in silence. They had a difficult decision to make and both understood the other's silence. They would talk about it and make their decision tomorrow.

Chapter 14

Hardy and Laslo woke early, anxious to get started on their first flight alone. This was going to be an exciting adventure and they were filled with nervous energy. Hardy seemed happier than normal, almost gleeful. Laslo was his typical self, a mixture of relaxed confidence and cockiness. He wasn't attempting to act cocky or doing anything that could be construed as cocky. It was just his whole mannerism and appearance. Normally, it really got on Hardy's nerves but today was different. Hardy was not annoyed by Laslo at all today.

"Do you want to eat before we go or just find something to eat while we're out?" asked Hardy.

"I think we—" Laslo was cut off in midsentence.

"Don't you two boys even think about it; you're going to eat something right here before you leave. I want both of you full of energy and alert on your first day out together," said Mother.

"No problem," answered Laslo. "That's exactly what I was going to suggest." Laslo then gave Hardy one of those looks with that grin that normally drove Hardy nearly crazy.

"Sure you were," said Hardy with a giggle.

The boys ate a good breakfast. Hardy paid close attention to be sure Laslo ate no yellow beetles.

"Mom, we're off," said Hardy.

"Okay. Now you boys be careful. Enjoy your day but pay attention to what you're doing at all times. Remember what your father and I have taught you about spotting danger," said Mother.

"The boys will do just fine," said Father. "If I even hear so much as a word about you two being careless, you'll have me to deal with. Better off you meet your fate out there than have to contend with me. Now that you're grown I'll deal with you differently than when you were kids. Have fun, be careful, and be back well before it gets dark."

"We'll be careful. I'll keep an eye on Hardy so you don't have to worry."

"Actually, it's not Hardy we're most worried about. You just take care of Laslo; don't you do anything foolish." Father gave them both a serious *dad means it* look. "Hardy, you keep your wits about you if there's any sign of trouble. And don't let Laslo get you into any trouble."

Laslo had a surprised look and started to speak. "What— "

"I will. I mean I'll keep my wits about me and I won't let Laslo get us into any trouble. Bye. We'll see you later. Don't worry, Mom. We'll be careful," responded Hardy. "I have a feeling this is going to be a day to remember for both Laslo and me."

Hardy and Laslo then turned and flew from the nest. They took a low glide path to gather speed and then, with a series of strong stokes from their wings, began to climb high while keeping the sun on their left sides. The two brothers flew side by side for about five minutes, all the while keeping an eye out for danger and maintaining a constant awareness of their location.

Plato had been sitting in a nearby tree, and after Hardy and Laslo passed by, he took flight to follow them. Plato was careful to keep sufficient distance so he would not be detected by the two young ducks.

Laslo suddenly began to play. He glided up close to Hardy and bumped him, causing him to fall from his flight path and struggle to recover. Before Hardy could say a word, Laslo banked left and went into a sudden dive and then turned and made a steep climb back to the same altitude as Hardy. The two were now separated by nearly one hundred yards.

Laslo's always showing off, thought Hardy. *Well, maybe he'll feel less like showing off before this day is over.* Hardy began to slip sideways and quickly closed the distance between them.

"You'd better pay closer attention to what's going on around you. Don't play around like that. You never know; there could be a hawk around."

"You and your fear of hawks; we've never even seen a hawk on any of our flights. You need to relax and quit worrying so much."

"You're gonna be sorry one day. Your carelessness is going to get you into big trouble."

"Wonderful. Advice from the great Hardy. That's just what I needed on our first day out together."

Hardy gave Laslo a dirty look and then went back to focusing on the business of flying. The two continued flying side by side without speaking. Another ten minutes passed.

"Hey, Laslo," yelled Hardy, "the other day on my solo I did a bunch of water landings in a pond. It was great. I think I have that whole thing really figured out. My last two landings were perfect."

"Really. I doubt that," answered Laslo.

"Yes, really. We have to go a lot faster than we have been. We were slowing down too much. Then it's all about leg speed and power. We haven't been paddling our feet fast enough. And when your feet just touch the water you have to immediately use more force with your legs. I'll show you if you want. I can help you improve your landings so you can do it is good as me."

"Hardy, you can't show me anything. I've told you a thousand times, I can do anything better than you. As soon as we see the first lake, I'll show *you* how to land."

"Well, you better make it a good landing because I'm gonna come in right after you and I guarantee you my landing will be better than yours," said Hardy. Hardy knew he had dangled the bait, Laslo had bitten, and he had set the hook. Hardy's little heart was pounding with excitement, and he was trying his best to not giggle. Laslo suspected nothing and Hardy wanted it to stay that way. The stage was perfectly set. Another minute or two passed when Hardy saw a pond shining in the distance.

"There's a pond right there. Can you see it?" asked Hardy.

"Of course I can see it. I saw it first, maybe a minute ago."

"Well then, go ahead and make your landing. And then turn around and watch me show you how it's done."

Laslo glared briefly at Hardy and then smiled that little smile. "Watch this," yelled Laslo, and down he went. Laslo banked, taking a steep glide path while arcing around the pond so he could approach into the slight breeze that was blowing. His movements were confident and effortless. Hardy had to admit to himself that Laslo was really skilled at flying.

Plato watched as Laslo banked and entered his descent path to land. "What is that fool kid up to?" whispered Plato. "He can't land there."

Hardy watched as Laslo started in for his landing. Then Hardy saw what he was looking for; Laslo was gliding in much faster than normal. He was so intent on bettering Hardy that Laslo had taken the bait without hesitation or thought. He had been focusing so much on his flying that he hadn't paid much attention to the pond.

Laslo was just about ready to touch down when he realized something wasn't quite right. But it was too late. Laslo was paddling his legs for all he was worth. When his feet touched the surface of the polyethylene sheeting, he was propelled roughly forward onto his face. He skidded briefly, and then a wing or foot must have caught and he began to somersault. He rolled over at least four times and then slid to a stop.

Hardy was beside himself. He knew immediately that this was the funniest thing he had ever seen. And probably the funniest thing he would ever see. And it was a victory. He had tricked Laslo and finally got even with the little monster. Hardy watched to be sure Laslo was okay. He saw Laslo struggle to his feet and look up. Hardy flew over, tipped his wings from side to side, and then flew off. Laslo was dazed but could hear that sound as clearly as if it was emanating right there next to him. Hardy's laughter seemed louder than anything he had ever heard before. He was sure everyone around for miles could hear it.

"I'll get you, Hardy!" yelled Laslo.

Plato laughed out loud. In fact he found it so funny he was having trouble flying. Finally, he recovered himself and ascended. He wanted to get high enough to keep Hardy in sight and still keep an eye on Laslo. He flew hard and got into a position where he was able to see both boys.

Hardy flew in a straight path so Laslo could find him without too much difficulty. He flew at a fast pace for a good ten minutes. This would give Hardy maybe ten or fifteen minutes before Laslo could locate him—time to cool off a little. Hardy spotted a tree near a fence at the edge of a pasture and decided it was a good place to land. He landed on the fence about fifty yards from the tree. Hardy kept a wary eye on the tree, trying to detect any presence of danger. A hawk could easily be hiding among the branches. Hardy had a plan, having remembered something his father told him. If a hawk came out of the tree, or for that matter another direction, Hardy would wait until just the last moment and then drop off the opposite side of the fence, which would shield him from the attack. He would then fly as quickly as he could along the fence line to get as much separation from the hawk as possible and then climb high, ensuring that the hawk would be unable to attack again.

After a few minutes, Hardy felt safer and started to move slowly toward the tree, which would provide Hardy with additional cover he could use if danger should come from above. He kept an eye out for danger from above but focused most of his attention on the tree. He moved to within twenty yards of it when he saw a large bird nesting in the tree. Hardy's heart skipped and began to pound. Was it a hawk? No. It was a crow; a beautiful crow. The crow was watching him and noticed that Hardy was startled.

"It's okay. You're safe. There's no danger near," said the crow. It was a female and Hardy thought her voice was confident with a pleasing tone. "My name is Justine."

Hardy took a deep breath and let out a sigh of relief. "Wow. What a surprise. I can't believe I didn't see you sooner. I thought for sure you were a hawk and that I was in big trouble." Hardy moved in a little closer so he wouldn't have to yell. "It's nice to meet you, Justine. My name's Hardy."

"It's nice to meet you, Hardy. I've never spoken with a duck before. I wasn't sure if you would be willing to speak with me or I would have said something sooner. I'm sorry if I startled you."

"That's okay. It's actually a good thing. It'll make me concentrate more in the future. I should have seen you sooner than I did. Well, I've never spoken with a crow before. I think it would be great to talk more with you and get to know you. You have a nice voice," responded Hardy, somewhat embarrassed by complimenting Justine. "So, what are you doing out here alone?"

"I'm not alone. My brother's nearby. I'm resting and waiting for him to return," said Justine. "His name is Nestor."

"Will he be upset if he returns and finds us talking?"

"Absolutely not; he's very curious about everything. He'll find it fascinating to talk with you. But I have to warn you; if you let him, he will wear you out with questions," giggled Justine. "So what have you been up to? You seemed out of breath when you landed, as if you'd been flying very fast."

"I played a great trick on my brother and I wanted to get a little distance between us. That'll give him time to cool off a little before he can find me," answered Hardy. "His name's Laslo. He should be showing up in the next ten minutes or so. And I have to warn you, he won't be very happy when he gets here. It was a great trick, really great. I loved it." Hardy laughed out loud again as he pictured Laslo tumbling head over feet.

"It sounds like you really enjoyed the trick you played on him, whatever it was."

"I did. It was fantastic. And he had it coming. Laslo always has it coming to him," said Hardy. "Do you live nearby?"

"I live in a pine grove near a woodlot on a hill about twenty minutes in that direction," answered Justine, pointing.

"That's amazing. I live in the woodlot not more than a minute or two from the pine grove. Maybe we can be friends. Uh, would that be a problem? How would your parents feel about that?" asked Hardy, remembering that his father may not approve.

"I think you and I can be friends. I think that would be just wonderful. But I think we should not let our parents know. In fact, I think we should be careful about letting too many others know we're friends, at least for right now." Justine spoke with a soft voice, attempting to convey to Hardy that there were issues with their being friends that she didn't agree with or fully understand.

"Yeah, I think that would be best, too," said Hardy, imagining what his father would say.

"Is that your brother?" asked Justine, looking up and out beyond where Hardy was standing.

Hardy turned, looked, and saw Laslo approaching. "That's him. Boy, he doesn't look too happy. Good."

Laslo must have seen Hardy at that moment. He banked sharply and immediately dropped into a glide path for a landing. He landed on the ground about ten yards from Hardy and immediately started waddling in Hardy's direction. He appeared to be seething with anger. "Hardy, I'm going to take you apart piece by piece. I'm sure you think that was real funny but you're not going to enjoy this. No, you're not going to enjoy this one bit," hollered Laslo.

"Hi, Laslo, where've you been? You look a little more ruffled than normal. Did you run into a problem?" Hardy had a big grin on his face.

"You know exactly where I've been. And now it's your turn to—" Just then Laslo noticed Justine, which startled him so much he gasped and stopped in his tracks. He took a long look at Justine and then looked at Hardy with a puzzled expression.

"I'd like you to meet someone, Laslo. This is Justine," said Hardy.

"Hello, Laslo. It's nice to meet you."

Laslo looked shocked. "Hardy, what are you doing talking to one of those carrion-eating crows? Have you lost your mind?"

"Excuse me?" said Justine. "What did you say?"

"Shut up, Laslo. Just because you're upset with me is no reason to be mean to Justine. She's nice. Now you're going to apologize to her right now." Hardy spoke sharply to Laslo in a tone that surprised him and Laslo.

"Who do you think you're talking to? I'm not apologizing to anyone, especially to a crow."

Hardy flew down to where Laslo was standing and walked off a short distance, taking Laslo with him. Justine could tell from their body language that they were having a spirited conversation, but she couldn't make out what they were saying.

"Laslo, just calm down for a minute and listen to me. We need to—"

"I'm not going to calm down. I owe you a butt whipping and that's what you're going to get."

"You're embarrassing me in front of my new friend. Let's straighten this out later."

"New friend? That crow is your new friend?" asked Laslo. "You just wait until I tell Dad about this. He'll set you straight real quick. Talking with a crow on our first day out without Mom or Dad. I don't think he'll be too happy when I tell him. And I'm going to tell him. Yes, I am."

"You'd better not tell him, Laslo. If you tell him I'll—"

"What? You'll do what?" asked Laslo, his voice filled with anger.

"I'll tell him and everyone I can find about the trick I played on you. I'll tell them what an idiot you are for falling for that. I'm sure everyone will get a big kick out of hearing that story. After I describe you falling on your face, and skidding, and flipping, you'll be the laughingstock of the woodlot," said Hardy. "I mean it. Only an idiot would do what you did. Everyone will know I outsmarted you." Laslo paused and appeared troubled at what Hardy had threatened. "I mean it, Laslo. I'll tell everyone. I'll tell every detail."

"Okay. Let's make a deal. I won't say a word about you and your crow friend. But you have to promise you won't tell anyone what happened. Not one single soul, do you hear?"

"I promise. But you also have to apologize to Justine. If you don't do that then there's no deal," said Hardy. "If you don't want to talk with her, then don't. Just try to be polite while I talk with her. And if you can't be polite then I'll settle for your not being rude."

"Oh, all right, but I don't see why you want to be friends with a crow. Good Lord." The two boys flew back over to the fence and landed opposite where Justine was perched in the tree.

Plato had been watching and was amazed to see these two young ducks with a crow. *Very interesting,* thought Plato, *very interesting, indeed.*

"Laslo has something to say to you, Justine," said Hardy.

"I'm sorry for what I said. I was angry with Hardy," said a reluctant Laslo.

"I can understand being angry with your brother but why would you say such a thing? Do you think I eat carrion?" asked Justine.

"Sure, I heard my father say crows eat carrion," said Laslo. "Isn't it true?"

"No. Well, not exactly. I certainly have never eaten carrion and neither has my brother, Nestor. I don't think I could ever do such a thing."

"So, you're saying crows don't eat carrion. You're saying my father doesn't know what he's talking about?" challenged Laslo.

"Let it go, Laslo. It's not important," pleaded Hardy.

"It's okay. I'll answer," said Justine. "Some crows have eaten carrion and some still do. Normally, crows will only eat carrion when there's not enough food. It's for survival purposes in hard times, like during a really bad winter. But some crows get used to it and will resort to it even when times are not tough. But that's the exception. Most crows don't eat carrion. You might be surprised what you might eat if you were starving."

"Well, I wouldn't eat dead things. I can assure you of that."

"Actually, that's not true. You eat dead bugs all the time. You ate some dead bugs that Mom gave us before we left this morning. And you and I both know you have some dead yellow beetles stashed somewhere in the nest." Hardy enjoyed correcting Laslo.

"That's different. Eating dead bugs is normal. If they weren't dead, they'd climb out of the nest. They have to be dead. But our food's not dead before we find it." Laslo made no effort to deny he had a stash of yellow beetles.

"It's not that different," said Hardy. "Anyway, it doesn't matter. Justine said she doesn't eat carrion so let it go, okay?"

"Okay. I'm sorry, Justine," said Laslo.

"Laslo has a tendency to just say and do things without thinking first. He doesn't mean to be rude," added Hardy.

"Well, I'm over it now. Can we talk about something else?" asked Justine.

"Sure. So, why are you out here?" asked Laslo.

"She's waiting for her brother, Nestor."

"I was speaking to Justine. Besides waiting for your brother what are you doing out here? I mean are you looking for food, exploring, what?"

"Well, Nestor and I were looking for a group of crows. Actually, one crow in particular." Justine was a little unsure if she should mention what she was doing but decided to take a chance. "You haven't seen any other crows, have you?"

"No," answered Hardy. "How about you, Laslo—seen any crows?"

"No. But I wasn't really looking for any. I'm sure I could find some if I wanted to. Why are you looking for these crows? Are they your friends? "

"Good heavens, no. One of them is absolutely the worst excuse for a crow I've ever encountered. All of them are misfits. We think, uh, Nestor and I think they may be up to no good and we were just trying to find out where they spend their day. That's all."

Hardy and Laslo exchanged glances and then Hardy spoke. "Up to no good; what do you think they might do?"

"Well, I'm not sure exactly. The leader's a troublemaker. He's always trying to start some kind of trouble and doesn't seem to care with whom. He started on Nestor and me not long ago. We think he may try to start trouble with the other birds in the woodlot." Justine was tentative, not sure she should be sharing so much information, but for some reason she trusted Hardy. She wasn't sure about Laslo, but he seemed okay.

"What? Like crap in a nest?" asked Laslo.

"Shut up, Laslo." yelled Hardy.

"Why would you ask such a thing?" Justine's voice was breaking up and she was near tears.

"Well, because a group of crows crapped in some duck nests just the other day. That's why," said Laslo.

"Oh no, really?" asked Justine. "I'm so sorry and embarrassed. Antus is behind this; I'm sure of it. Crows don't behave like that; not normal crows. Please believe me."

"We believe you," said Hardy. "Don't we, Laslo?" Laslo didn't say a word and just stared at Justine. Laslo wasn't sure what to believe but he thought Justine was good. "Laslo." Hardy's voice was loud and confident. "You believe Justine, don't you?"

"Thank goodness. Here comes Nestor. I have to tell him what's happened," cried Justine.

Nestor landed in the tree next to Justine. He looked at Justine and could tell she was upset. He then turned, lowered his head, and stared at Hardy and Laslo. His large eyes and stare made Hardy and Laslo feel uncomfortable— plus, his size was intimidating. Nestor appeared to be a powerful young crow.

"We didn't do anything," said Hardy. "We were just talking with Justine. You must be Nestor, right?"

"I'm Nestor. Justine, what's wrong? You seem upset." Nestor didn't look at Justine as he spoke but continued to stare right at Hardy and Laslo. Justine just sat there with her head bowed, unable to speak. Nestor stared into Hardy's eyes. "Did you hurt my sister?" He didn't raise his voice, but it was apparent he expected an answer.

"No," answered Hardy. "She and I are friends. I'm Hardy and this is my brother, Laslo. I think she's upset because of what Laslo told her about what some crows have done."

"Yeah," said Laslo. "They crapped in some duck nests in the woodlot where we live. So, what do you think about that?"

"Oh, I see. Justine, relax. It's going to be okay," said Nestor. His voice was soft and filled with understanding. He knew his sister was both embarrassed and also concerned that this could lead to conflict.

"So, what do you think about that, Nestor?" asked Laslo again. Nestor didn't respond but gave Laslo a look that strongly suggested he not ask again.

Plato recognized Nestor from the description Alexander had given. Crows and ducks talking together like friends. This was unusual. Then Plato remembered his father's words: "Forget the elders." This must be what he meant. Plato recalled the innocence and naivety of the two young ducks. *Of course, the solution is with the young. They haven't been prejudiced yet by others. They still have open minds. But how can I put that to use?* Plato was excited by this revelation. "I must tell Alexander about this."

"Nestor, what're we going to do?" asked Justine, finally composing herself. "You know Antus did this."

"You're right, Justine," said Laslo. "Our father said the crappers were a group of crows led by one called Antus."

"Let's not use the word *crap* anymore. Okay?" said Nestor.

"Well, what do you prefer, *poop*?" asked Laslo.

"No. How about *defecate*."

"What? Defa-what?"

"What's this all about?" asked Hardy. "Who is Antus and why would he do something like that?"

Nestor raised his wing and motioned for Justine not to answer. Nestor walked over to Justine and placed his head against her face. Hardy and Laslo watched in silence. Then Nestor turned and looked at them with a serious expression on his face. "This could be the beginning of real trouble. Antus is no good and he means to make trouble. That's all I can tell you right now. But we could use your help. Together we may be able to prevent Antus from upsetting the peaceful lives we all have in the woodlot."

"What do you want us to do?" asked Hardy.

"Why should we help you? It was crows that crapped in ducks' nests," said Laslo with a hint of anger in his voice. Laslo took a deep breath, puffed out his chest, and stared at Nestor.

"You should help us because together we may be the only ones that can put a stop to Antus and his plans. I'm not asking you to do anything difficult or dangerous. I would like you to meet Justine and me in this area each day and let us know if anything else happens; let us know if Antus is up to anything. I'll explain more about what may be going on as soon as we all have had some time to think about this. And whether we are all willing to fully trust and rely on one another."

The serious tone of Nestor's voice troubled Hardy. "We'll do it," said Hardy. "We'll be here tomorrow."

"No, we won't," said Laslo, looking at Hardy. "I don't trust them right now.

Why would I come back here tomorrow? Who knows how many crows will be here and what they might do? Heck, for all we know they may kick our butts and crap all over us."

Nestor spoke before Hardy could say a word. "It will only be Justine and me. You have my word there will be no others. Neither Justine nor I wish either of you any harm. And we certainly wouldn't do what you've suggested."

"I'll be here even if Laslo won't. I trust both of you. And you can trust me. I'm your friend." Hardy surprised himself. He knew this could be dangerous, but for some reason he liked Justine. And Nestor seemed like a good crow. There was something in Justine's expression that told Hardy this was really important. "And I can promise you, Laslo will tell no one about this. Isn't that right, Laslo?"

Laslo started to object and then remembered the deal he'd made with Hardy. "I'll tell no one."

"Good. Let's meet here about this time tomorrow, Hardy. I'm very pleased you have agreed to help us. And, Laslo, I wish you would reconsider."

"Not gonna happen," responded Laslo. "You've got Hardy, for whatever that's worth."

"Justine," said Hardy. "It's okay. I don't judge all crows because of what a few may do. Heck, I wouldn't want to be judged by what Laslo does," said Hardy with a grin.

"Shut up, Hardy."

"Or by what he *might* do. You've already had the chance to see him firsthand and you still want to be friends with me. That takes guts."

"Thank you, Hardy. I apologize for the behavior of Antus and his group. Their behavior is disgusting and humiliating. And, Laslo, I'm sorry you don't like us. I think you're nice and it was a pleasure meeting you."

Laslo looked a little surprised and then hung his head. "Thanks."

"Justine, it's okay. Really," said Hardy. "I'll see you both tomorrow."

"Tomorrow," echoed Nestor.

Chapter 15

Nestor and Justine returned home and said nothing to their parents about making friends with a duck. Nor did they say anything to them about what they had learned from Hardy and Laslo. That night the two quietly discussed what they had learned and whether they would help Alexander. They decided they would go to Alexander and tell him everything they had heard from Laslo and Hardy and let him know they were willing to help.

The next morning the two were up early, and within an hour they left the nest. They made their way toward the training grounds, taking great care to ensure they were not being followed. It wasn't long before they were intercepted and escorted to the camp where Alexander's headquarters was located. Paris met them after a brief wait, and they exchanged greetings.

"So, have you two made a decision yet? Alexander is hopeful. Your assistance could prove invaluable to our cause."

"We've made a decision. Both of us would like to help. We aren't committed to your cause, as you call it, especially in the manner you want to achieve it. But we do want to help avert trouble," said Nestor.

"We don't agree with the way you're planning on accomplishing your goals. We understand the desire to leave the pine grove and improve our living conditions, but we don't think it's right to accomplish that by forcing ourselves on others," added Justine. "It's important that what we do is right and just."

"We also have important information for Alexander." Nestor emphasized the word *important*.

"You have important information? What is it?" asked Paris.

"We'll tell Alexander; you can hear it then. This is not information we'll discuss out here among others. When you hear what we have to say, you'll understand why." Nestor's tone made it clear they were determined to speak with Alexander.

Paris nodded and turned. "Follow me." The three moved in among the branches of the trees. Soon they were in the opening among a number of crows busily going about their duties. "Wait here," commanded Paris. Paris walked across the opening and stood at the other side with his back to Nestor and Justine. A moment later he turned and Alexander emerged and walked over to greet his two guests. Paris accompanied him.

"Greetings, it's good to see both of you again. And, Justine, you're even lovelier than the last time we met." Alexander smiled and looked into Justine's eyes. Justine felt her face growing warm and her heart began to race. She didn't understand why, but she was excited to see Alexander again. His presence made her feel strange.

"Thank you," said Justine softly, lowering her eyes as she spoke.

"Yes, thank you," added Nestor. "It's good to see you again. We appreciate your taking the time to speak with us."

"I wouldn't have it any other way," answered Alexander, looking at Justine again as he spoke. Then turning to Nestor he continued. "Paris tells me you and Justine have agreed to help us. That's great. But I don't understand why you want to help if you don't support our cause."

"We'll help to prevent trouble. You were right about Antus. He and his group have already started acting up," said Nestor. "Tell them what you've learned, Justine."

Justine lifted her head and stood up straight and tall. "I made friends with a duck. His name is Hardy. He and I were speaking and—"

"Wait a second. Did you say you made friends with a duck? Why would you do that?" asked Paris. Alexander just looked at Justine with a slight smile on his face.

"Well, he and I met by accident actually. I was resting and suddenly he just landed nearby. When he saw me he was startled, thinking at first I may be a hawk."

Alexander laughed. "He thought you looked like a hawk? That duck apparently has bad eyesight."

Justine was a little embarrassed so she quickly answered to get past the uncomfortable feeling. "No, he didn't really think I was a hawk," answered Justine. "He didn't know I was there and when he saw me it took him a second or so to realize what I was. Anyway, we spoke briefly. He was very nice. I like him and we're going to be friends, I think."

"Wow. You are full of surprises." Alexander's smile had turned into a big grin. "Do you think being friends with a duck right now is a good idea, knowing what you know about our plans?"

"Yes, I do. And he's agreed to help us."

Alexander's expression changed immediately. "You didn't tell him about our plans, did you?"

"Of course not, why don't you quit interrupting and let me finish?" said Justine with a note of anger in her voice.

"Go right ahead, finish," answered Alexander. "Something tells me this is going to be interesting."

"Well, Hardy and I had been speaking for a few minutes when Hardy's brother, Laslo, showed up. Hardy had played some kind of trick on his brother. Laslo was so angry that he didn't notice me at first either and I startled him."

"Sounds like these ducks are rather skittish," said Paris. "Oops, I'm sorry. Go ahead."

Justine gave Paris a harsh look that lasted a full two or three seconds. "As I was saying, Laslo was startled. When Hardy introduced me, Laslo responded with a remark that I found insulting. He referred to me as one of those 'carrion-eating crows.' Well, we got that straightened out and—"

"I'll bet you did," said Alexander. Justine exhaled loudly and looked skyward in frustration. "I'm sorry, Justine. Go ahead and finish."

"I told the two boys I was waiting for Nestor and that we were looking for a group of crows. I asked if they had seen any other crows. They answered they had not. As the conversation continued I shared with them that these crows were not my friends, that Nestor and I were concerned they might start trouble. That's when Laslo said it." There was long pause. Everyone was waiting for Justine to continue.

Finally, Alexander broke the silence. "What did he say?"

Justine didn't answer. She just looked down at her feet.

Nestor spoke. "She doesn't want to use the language Laslo used. Laslo said that some crows had, quote, 'crapped in some ducks' nests.' He also confirmed that the leader of the group of crows was named Antus."

"That fool. Well, he's succeeded in muddling things now, hasn't he?" said Paris. "I think we need to remove him from the picture, Alexander, before he does any more harm."

Alexander raised his wing, indicating to Paris he had heard. "So, you said these ducks agreed to help. How will they help?"

"Only Hardy agreed. Laslo doesn't trust us. Hardy agreed to meet us later today." Nestor spoke with an air of excitement that was unusual for him. "He'll keep us informed in case Antus causes any more trouble. I think he can also give us some insight as to how the ducks and other birds are reacting to what's happened."

"Yes, that's good. That'll be a great help. Do you think you can trust this Hardy?"

"Hardy's nice. And he's gentle. He has an inner strength that I can't quite describe. I trust him," answered Justine.

"And I trust him. If that changes, I'll tell you," said Nestor.

"Okay. You two continue to meet with him. Share what you're comfortable sharing but keep in mind the risk. Learn all you can about Antus and what he's up to. We need to go on alert here; there could be trouble," said Alexander.

"I don't think you should overreact," cautioned Nestor. "There has to be a solution to this that's better than conflict. Promise Justine and me you won't start a war or do anything aggressive yet."

"The other birds have done nothing to us so far," added Justine. "It would be completely wrong for us to use force against them. Anyway, you said yourself that is what Antus wants and expects. So why give in to it?"

"What're we supposed to do, sit here and wait for the pine grove to be invaded?" asked Paris. "I don't think so."

"No," said Nestor. "There's no reason to believe that's going to happen. Right now Antus's actions will be seen as nothing more than an isolated incident of vandalism. As long as nothing else happens, it will probably be overlooked. Let Justine and me see what we can learn."

"We're not going to start anything. I'm considering sending out some patrols to find Antus. Paris may be right about removing him from the picture," stated Alexander.

Nestor responded instantly. "Right now, I think that would be a mistake.

That'll just make the ducks and other birds nervous. If they see increased activity in the area by crows, especially groups of crows, that kind of display of force could easily be interpreted as aggression. That could lead to confrontation and conflict. I beg you to be patient."

Alexander paced back and forth, deep in thought. Everything depended on his not making a mistake. "I think you may be right. Okay. But you need to keep me informed daily and immediately if Antus does anything else," said Alexander. "And one more thing, if there is any movement on the part of those birds to enter the pine grove, we will use all the force at our disposal to not only drive them out but to take control of a portion of the surrounding woodlot. Understood? That's not up for debate."

"Understood," answered Nestor. "Thank you."

"Understood," said Justine. "The only birds that have done anything wrong so far are crows. You've done the right thing, Alexander, the just thing. Thank you."

"I hope so. Be careful, Justine. You too, Nestor."

Nestor and Justine left and were escorted out of the area. They stopped briefly for a bite to eat and then headed out to the farm country to see if they could locate Antus and his gang and to meet with Hardy later.

Chapter 16

As promised, Laslo said nothing to his parents about Hardy and his new friends. When they got home, Mother asked them how their day went.

"Fine," said Hardy, giving a quick look in his brother's direction.

"Yeah, it was fine," echoed Laslo.

"Well, what did you do?" asked Mother.

"Nothing much, just hung out in the farmland. Explored a little," answered Hardy.

"Yeah, nothing much," said Laslo.

Mother and Father looked at each other for a moment and then they both smiled. "Kids," said Father, shaking his head.

The next morning the boys woke early. Hardy was anxious to get going but wanted to be sure Laslo was going to keep his promise. Hardy knew Laslo was nearly incapable of keeping his mouth shut about anything. Expecting him to keep a secret was like expecting a miracle.

"Remember what you promised," said Hardy.

"I remember. I'm not going to say a thing. You just make sure you remember what you promised."

"No problem. Why don't you come with me today, Laslo? This is going to be an exciting day. I think you would like Justine if you got to know her better. And I think Nestor will be a good friend, too."

Laslo just laughed and dismissed Hardy with a flick of his wing. "No way. I'm going to the pond. Do you remember the pond that's about ten minutes from the other side of the woodlot? Some of the older boys tell me that's where the girls hang out. I'm gonna go check them out," announced Laslo, speaking as if he was about to do something that Hardy would envy.

"What for?" asked Hardy. "Why do you want to go look at the girls? Oh, I think I know. Have you got your eye on anyone in particular?" asked Hardy with a big grin.

"Heck no, I've got my eye on all of them. No, I've got both my eyes on all of them," answered Laslo. "One of the older boys said if we get lucky we may be able to tickle a few tail feathers."

"What's that mean?" asked Hardy. Laslo laughed and just gave Hardy a look that indicated he knew something that Hardy didn't. Hardy was pretty sure Laslo had no idea what he was talking about. Anyway, he figured there was no use in trying to get him to change his mind. He could tell Laslo was determined to go to the pond and find out what that was all about. He was sure Laslo wasn't about to tag along with him just to go see crows.

Plato had secured himself in a nearby tree so he could keep an eye on the nest. He wanted to be sure he could see the two boys when they left the nest so he could follow. Plato was curious and excited about the possibility that the two ducks may seek out Nestor and Justine or other crows. He had briefed Alexander about the meeting and both concurred there was great promise in the youngsters. They just had to find a good way to get them involved.

After breakfast Hardy and Laslo left the nest together. They were supposed to stay together but as soon as they got out of sight of the nest, Laslo yelled to Hardy, "When you get back, come to the pond and meet me there." Laslo smiled, broke off, and flew in the direction of the pond.

Hardy continued on his way. He had plenty of time before he was to meet Justine and Nestor, so he thought he would do a little exploring. Hardy was surprised when he realized he was not only keeping an eye out for danger but also scanning the sky and ground for crows, although he didn't see any.

Plato climbed high and watched both Hardy and Laslo. He saw Laslo land in a pond and begin to interact with some other ducks. He was close to home and with other ducks, so Plato decided he would be safe. Plato followed Hardy.

An hour passed and Hardy was in need of some rest. He was also getting a little thirsty. He searched the area as he flew and located a small pond. He took a few minutes to survey the area around the pond and took a good look to see if there were any unidentified birds flying nearby. All looked good so Hardy circled, dropped down, and made a near perfect landing.

I'm getting pretty good at this, thought Hardy. He took a long drink and just floated, moving very little. He needed a rest and liked the way the water felt underneath him. It was nothing like flying but it was also not as tiring. Plus there was food and drink right there and very little energy was required to get his fill of both.

After he had rested sufficiently, Hardy took flight and started in the direction where he had met Justine and Nestor the day before. He was surprised at how excited he was—no fear or apprehension, just excitement. He liked the idea of getting to know crows. The only birds he knew were ducks. Sure he got along with other birds in the woodlot but he never had thought of becoming their friends. It was the challenge of getting to know a crow that excited him. He may be the first duck that had ever done such a thing. He had never heard of any other duck being friends with a crow. In fact, most of what he heard was that it was best to have nothing to do with them. Justine and Nestor seemed nice. He wondered why ducks and crows were not friends. Hardy also thought Laslo was a little afraid of the crows. He had put on a good show, but his reluctance to return made Hardy think he was a little scared. It made Hardy feel good to think that he may be doing something without any fear that maybe frightened Laslo.

There was the meeting place up ahead. Hardy was a little early but decided to land and wait for Justine and Nestor. He could check out the area and make sure it was safe before they arrived. That would be a polite thing to do and being there first, he thought, would demonstrate that he trusted them.

Hardy checked the area out and made himself comfortable. He kept an eye out for danger while watching for the arrival of Nestor and Justine. It was a beautiful day, warm, a little hot, but not too bad. The sky was clear with just a few scattered clouds. The bright sun made it difficult to see and was a strain on the eyes. Hardy just felt good to be alive. The air itself felt particularly good on his face. Everything seemed just right in the world.

Plato landed on a fence post a hundred yards or so from the tree where Hardy had landed. He pushed up against a fence post to avoid being detected not only by Hardy but by any hawks that might be in the area.

Lost in thought, Hardy's mind began to drift. He was not paying attention as he should have been. Suddenly, he saw a shadow move past. He was startled and immediately searched the sky, frantically trying to spot what had made the shadow. There was Nestor and Justine gliding in for a landing. They circled overhead. Hardy felt a little guilty that he had not been more vigilant. He didn't want the crows to think he was stupid or careless. He wanted to be trusted.

"Hi, Hardy," said Justine. Hardy still thought her soft voice was as pleasant as any voice he had ever heard.

"Hi, Justine, hi, Nestor. It's good to see you both again. Laslo's not coming; he went with some boys to a pond."

"I don't think Laslo likes us, does he?" asked Justine.

"Laslo doesn't know what he likes or doesn't like. He just does things and says things with little or no thought. But he's actually sort of nice, most of the time, for a brother. And I think he really likes you but he doesn't think ducks and crows should be friends."

"Why do you think he feels that way?" asked Nestor.

"I don't think he's thought about it. He doesn't think too much about anything. We've never known or heard of ducks being friends with crows so I guess he just thinks we shouldn't be. And you heard the crude things he said. I think he believed those things until he met you two. Now, I think he has doubts about what may or may not be true about crows. But, well, he's Laslo. If you ever get to know him better you'll understand what that means."

"So, what do you think, Hardy? Do you think crows are bad? Do you believe all crows are like Antus?" asked Justine.

"Of course not, I think there are good crows and bad crows. Just like I think there are good ducks and bad ducks. I also think there are smart crows and stupid crows and smart ducks and stupid ducks. As I said yesterday I don't judge all crows by what a few do. I don't judge all ducks by what some may do. I think if you and Nestor are as nice as I believe you are then we'll be good friends."

"Well, I think we'll be good friends, too. I sure hope so. Don't you agree, Nestor?"

"I do."

Hardy, Justine, and Nestor talked for a while about a variety of things. It was small talk, really. There were periods of silence interspersed within the conversation. All three were trying to find some common ground, a subject area they could talk about that would be familiar to each. Finally, Nestor decided to move beyond small talk and get right to the main subject: Antus and his gang.

"So, have you given any thought to what we talked about yesterday? Do you think you could help us out with the Antus problem?"

"I would sure like to but I don't really know what it's all about. And I sure don't know how I can help," replied Hardy.

"Then why don't we talk about those things? If we share some information with you, we need to know that you will keep it a secret; at least for right now. There may come a time when you'll have to share what you know but for the moment we need secrecy. Can you promise us that?" asked Nestor.

"Uh, sure I guess," said Hardy.

"No, Hardy," said Justine. "You can't guess. We need a promise. You can't even tell Laslo. Not your parents, no one."

"Well, that's a tough promise. I don't know what you're going to tell me."

Justine moved very close to Hardy, face-to-face, and looked into his eyes. "It's for everyone's good, Hardy. Do you trust me?" asked Justine.

"I do trust you. And I trust you too, Nestor." Hardy paused for a few moments and appeared to be lost in thought. "Okay, I promise."

"You'll tell no one?"

"No. I'll tell no one. And I'm pretty sure you can trust Laslo; I don't think he'd dare tell anyone anything he knows. I've got a little something hanging over his head. You and Justine have my word I won't tell. And when I make a promise, I keep it."

"Great," said Justine. "I knew you were special."

Hardy felt a little embarrassed. He liked the fact that Justine thought he was special. "What's this all about? What do you want me to do? Oh, wait, I've promised to keep the secret. I haven't promised to do anything else. Okay?"

Nestor and Justine laughed. Justine put her wing around Hardy and gave him a little hug. "We know. It's going to be okay. We're not going to ask you to do anything terrible."

"Good. I was getting a little nervous with all this talk about secrecy," said Hardy. "So, what's this all about?"

Plato saw Justine give Hardy a little hug and could tell by the body language that the three were getting along. "Interesting," said Plato. "Wonderful."

Justine looked at Nestor, indicating he should speak. Nestor began to pace back and forth, thinking about what he should say and how he should say it. Finally, he began to speak. "Hardy, many years ago, before any of us were born, crows and the other birds lived together in the woodlot. Then there was some trouble. That trouble was caused by a crow. Actually, the trouble was caused by a small group of crows."

"Nestor and I are ashamed of what those crows did," added Justine.

"What did they do?"

Nestor continued. "Well, the group had a leader that was, in many ways, like Antus—a troublemaker. He wasn't very smart and didn't have any reason for what he did. He just wanted to start trouble. He wanted to feel important." Nestor paused to study Hardy in an attempt to determine how he was reacting. Hardy didn't appear shocked or upset; just curious. Nestor continued. "It started out sort of like what Antus has done. But it continued and escalated. Eventually, all the birds in the woodlot had enough and confronted the crows. There was talk of open conflict; war. The elder crows knew nothing of what those renegade crows had been doing. They were ashamed. There was a lot of talk about the crows leaving but thanks to a wise young duck there was a compromise reached. The crows were expelled from the woodlot to the pine grove and banned from the woodlot lake."

"A young duck? Gee, I thought I might be the first duck to ever be friends with crows." Hardy was little disappointed. "So, Antus doesn't like the situation and now he's trying to start trouble? He wants things to change?"

"No, ducks and crows used to get along. As far as Antus is concerned, you're right, in a way, except it's more complicated than that." Nestor provided a brief explanation about the large army, Alexander, and the desire of most crows to move back into the woodlot peacefully. "I'm sure you have noticed the condition of the pine grove."

"Yes. It's mostly dead and dying trees. A lot of the trees have been blown down."

"Well, it's like this. If Antus causes trouble, any peaceful attempts would probably be impossible. Simply put, Antus wants to start a war. Many would get hurt and lives would be lost. If we can stop Antus, we may be able to avoid all of that."

"Wow," said Hardy. "That's serious. So, what can I do to help?"

"Well we, Nestor and I, are going to keep track of Antus and what he's up to. First we have to locate him. You could help us with that. You won't have to confront him. Just let us know where you see him," said Justine. "And if anything else happens in the woodlot, if Antus and his gang do anything else, you can let us know. We'll work to keep the crows from overreacting if something else happens. Maybe you can try to do the same with the ducks and other birds. The key, we think, is to do whatever we can to avoid conflict between crows and the birds in the woodlot."

"Then what?" asked Hardy. "Even if we stop Antus, how are we going to stop that army of crows from invading the woodlot? If that happens, you know there'll be trouble."

Justine looked at Nestor with a puzzled look. Nestor spoke with a soft tone, trying to sound reasonable and confident. "The army has no intention of attacking unless crows are attacked. Alexander doesn't want war. But first things first: let's work to avoid this crisis and then we can deal with the next problem. We need to keep things from escalating. We have to find a way to get everyone talking. Maybe we can be the spark, the inspiration. If the three of us can be friends and trust each other then there has to be hope that the others can find a way to get along."

"That sounds reasonable to me," said Hardy. "I'll do it. But I need a promise from the two of you." Hardy stared straight into Nestor's eyes and then turned his head and looked at Justine.

"What do you want us to promise?" asked Justine.

"You have to promise that if anything changes and the crows decide on war, you'll tell me as soon as you know. I need to protect my family and friends. I want the chance to warn them if it comes to that."

"I promise," said Justine without hesitation. "That would only be fair."

Nestor didn't answer right away. He looked off in the direction of the pine grove with a troubled look on his face.

"Nestor, it's only fair that we agree," said Justine.

Nestor finally turned to Hardy and spoke. "I promise, too. We'll warn you if we learn anything and you agree to do the same. We need to trust and stand by each other or we certainly won't succeed. Nor could we expect to inspire others to trust if we can't trust each other." Nestor paused briefly. "We'll meet here each day at midmorning and midafternoon to report on what we've learned. So, let's find Antus and see if we can keep track of his movements."

"Okay. I'll meet you both here tomorrow morning. Bye," said Hardy.

"Good-bye, Hardy," said Justine.

"Bye," said Nestor. "Be careful. And don't underestimate Antus. He's dangerous. We think he's capable of killing."

Chapter 17

Hardy left the meeting with his mind racing. He decided to do a little flying in an attempt to clear his thoughts and relax. He liked flying and needed to fly some distance each day just to stay in shape and hone his flying skills. Plato waited briefly and then took off and followed Hardy, staying well above and at a distance behind and slightly off to Hardy's right.

As he flew, Hardy began to reflect on the meeting and what he had promised. He began to have second thoughts. Maybe he should tell his father. After all, the safety of his family could be at stake. But he trusted Justine and Nestor. Nestor was right: if they couldn't trust one another there was no hope of success. And if they could be friends it would prove it was possible for all birds to get along. Hardy was struggling with mixed feelings of loyalty. On the one hand he felt he needed to be loyal to his family and tell them about the possible danger. On the other hand he trusted his new friends and believed their friendship may be the only chance of preventing a major problem and possibly a disaster.

I've given my word, thought Hardy. *If I'm going to change my mind, I need to tell Justine and Nestor before I tell anyone else. If I can't be trusted when I make a promise, I'll never be fit to be anyone's friend. No one will ever truly trust me.* Hardy decided that for now he would keep the secret and tell no one.

As he was flying, Hardy decided this might be a good time to look for Antus. But where should he look? Then he remembered the crows he saw the day he took his solo flight and how some of the crows had yelled at him.

Hardy spoke out loud to himself. "I bet that was Antus and his gang." Hardy turned and looked back. Justine and Nestor were already gone. *I should have remembered that and told them about it*, thought Hardy.

Hardy banked hard and headed out to where he had seen the group of crows. He estimated he was about fifteen minutes away. Hardy remembered Nestor's warning that Antus was dangerous. He decided he would approach the area and then circle at a good distance. He'd only get close enough to see if there were any crows there and would decide then if he could take a chance and get a closer look. Maybe he could see enough detail to describe the crows to Nestor and Justine. They would know if this was Antus and his group.

As Hardy neared the area, he located the spot where he had seen the crows. First he saw the fence line and then he spotted the tree. It was difficult to see if there were any crows there from that distance so Hardy circled around and swung in a little closer. He didn't see any crows so he circled in even closer. Still no crows, so he decided to land. Plato circled at a distance, keeping an eye on Hardy.

Hardy landed on a fence post about fifty feet from the tree. He slowly and cautiously moved closer. The area was a mess. Surely a group of birds had been spending a lot of time here. "They must be one really disgusting group of crows," mumbled Hardy.

Hardy took flight and decided to head home. Tomorrow he'd tell Justine and Nestor about this place. Hardy had been flying for nearly twenty minutes when off to his left he saw a group of crows flying in the opposite direction. There were at least a dozen. They were a noisy bunch. They seemed excited and were cawing and cackling almost nonstop. Trailing far behind was a lone fat crow. He looked like he was struggling to stay in the air and would glide a short distance about every twenty seconds. His gliding ability was poor and he lost altitude quickly. The fat crow wasn't making any noise.

Hardy kept an eye on the crows, but either they didn't see him or had no interest. In any case they made no effort to close the distance that separated them. Hardy was convinced the group of crows was Antus and his gang, as they looked like the group he had seen earlier.

Hardy continued to fly. Soon he could see the woodlot in the distance. He figured he would go straight to the pond and find Laslo so they could return to the nest together, thus avoiding any suspicion by their parents that they had not been together. He decided he should take a wide path around the woodlot so Mom and Dad wouldn't spot him. As Hardy banked and flew past the woodlot, it appeared there was a lot of activity near the lake. He could see a lot of birds flying into the area. Oh well. It was hot. *I guess everyone's trying to stay cool*, he thought.

It took Hardy about ten minutes to fly around the woodlot and reach the pond. He surveyed the area and almost immediately spotted Laslo. Laslo was gliding in for a landing on the pond. It appeared that a large group of ducks, boys and girls, was watching him as if he was putting on some kind of demonstration. Laslo landed in the water with way too much speed and immediately took one of the worst face dives Hardy had ever seen. As he fell on his face, Laslo overturned and began kicking his legs in the air. The group of ducks roared with laughter. Laslo righted himself, spit water out of his mouth straight up into the air like a fountain, and then coughed and gagged in a forced and exaggerated manner. He then swam over toward the group of ducks.

Hardy could hear Laslo's voice above all the laughter. "I swear. That's exactly how Hardy landed the first time we tried this." Laslo paused briefly. "And the second time was worse." The group of ducks laughed even louder as they welcomed Laslo back into their midst. "And the third time and the fourth time were even worse yet," said Laslo, laughing out loud at the top of his lungs. "I thought that fool would never learn how to land. I think my dad felt sorry for him because he made me stop laughing at him." Laslo had a big goofy grin on his face, and it was obvious he was enjoying being the center of attention. "Hey. Maybe I should tell ya all about the time I farted and it was so bad it almost killed Hardy."

The male ducks all laughed and Hardy heard a couple of the girls yell out in unison, "Oh, gross."

Laslo was swimming backward with his feet splashing water in front of him. "Yeah, Hardy claimed it killed bugs and made a buzzard vomit, but he was exaggerating. It was bad but not that bad."

"I'm gonna kill him." As angry as Hardy was he was also surprised when he realized Laslo's behavior didn't come as a shock. Not anymore. And then almost immediately, Hardy began to giggle and wasn't angry anymore. Laslo was … well, he was Laslo. He wasn't going to change and suddenly be different. Expecting him to behave any way other than he normally did was plain foolish. It wasn't going to happen. Hardy dropped into a glide path for a landing near Laslo and the group of ducks. He was determined to make a perfect landing just so Laslo would have nothing to make fun of.

"Here comes someone new. Does anybody know him?" yelled one of the ducks, pointing. All the ducks turned to look.

"That's Hardy," answered Laslo. "Keep your wingtips crossed; maybe he'll give us something else to laugh about."

Hardy came in at just the right speed and executed a perfect landing. He settled in the water, letting Laslo and the other ducks take a long look. Then he paddled over to the group.

Plato landed in the trees, well out of sight, and then made his way to a vantage point where he could observe.

"Hey, Laslo, what're you up to?" asked Hardy.

"Oh, nothing much; we're just telling stories and having a few laughs."

"Really, what about?" asked Hardy.

"Uh, just stuff. Um, ah, hey everybody, this is my brother, Hardy," said Laslo, changing the subject.

"Hi everyone, it's nice to meet all of you." Hardy looked around at the group and suddenly his eyes met the stare of a pretty, young female duck. They stared at each other, and then the girl duck lowered her eyes. She looked embarrassed and Hardy felt bad for staring and making her uncomfortable. The other girl ducks noticed what had happened and circled around their friend. Hardy could hear a lot of whispering. All the girl ducks looked in his direction and then looked away and giggled. Hardy was now feeling a little uncomfortable himself. Laslo gave Hardy a dirty look but said nothing.

"How long are you planning to hang out here before we head home?" asked Hardy.

"I don't know. I guess as long as everyone else hangs out. So, how did your day go?"

"It went great. I had an interesting day."

After a brief silence all the ducks began to engage in conversation, and before long the pond was alive with chatter. Hardy was getting to know some of the ducks. From time to time he would look in the direction of the young female that had caught his attention earlier and every once in a while he caught her looking in his direction. When their eyes met, they both would look away quickly, but on one occasion she hesitated and smiled at him. Hardy felt his heart race but wasn't sure why.

For the next half hour the little group of ducks talked, bantered, and laughed, enjoying the warmth of the late afternoon sun. Then a large bird appeared, circled the pond, and began to glide in for a landing. It was one of the elder male ducks, one of the parents. He landed and immediately swam over to where the group was assembled.

"Okay, kids, I've been sent here by your parents. All of you are to return home immediately. There's to be no hesitation and no delays. You're to go directly home. Is that clear?"

"Yes, sir," answered a number of ducks simultaneously.

"What's up? Has something happened?" asked Laslo.

"Your parents will tell you what you need to know when you get home. You're to go straight home and you're to do it now."

"Well, excuse the heck out of me," whispered Laslo to himself.

The young ducks began to depart, singly and in pairs, exchanging good-byes before they left. Hardy caught a glimpse of the female duck he had been interested in, and when she looked in his direction, he smiled. She smiled back and then left for home. Hardy and Laslo took off and were soon heading directly for home. Plato followed just to make sure they both got home safely.

"Laslo, remember not to make any mistakes. As far as Mom and Dad are concerned, we've been together all day. We'll say we were at the pond all day and you can tell all the stories of what we did if they ask. Okay?"

"Sure, not a problem. I've got it covered."

"What do you think's going on? Did you hear about anything unusual today?" asked Hardy.

"Heck, I don't know nothing," said Laslo. "It's a mystery to me. I was just fooling around all day. I didn't hear about anything. What happened with you? Did you meet Justine and Nestor?"

"Yeah, we met just like we planned. Everything went fine. After we met and separated, I flew around to see if I could find Antus but had no luck. But when I was coming back to find you I think I saw him and his gang flying in the other direction. I think it was him because there was this big, fat crow with them and I'm pretty sure he's part of Antus's group. I didn't want to get too close to them so I'm not sure it was really him. Anyway, I don't know what Antus looks like anyway so I wouldn't be certain even if I got close enough for a good look." Hardy and Laslo were soon at the other side of the woodlot and landed at their home. Mother and Father were engaged in conversation. They stopped talking and greeted the two boys.

"Welcome home, boys. Are you both okay?" asked Mother.

"Sure," said Laslo. "What's going on? We were told by one of the fathers to come straight home. Did something happen?"

"Yes," answered Father. "It was those damn crows again. They came in here in broad daylight and started crapping in every nest they could find. They're some evil sons of bitches, they are."

"Father, please. Watch your language," said Mother sharply.

"I'm sorry, Mother, but I have had enough of these crow-crapping raids. Boys, they spoiled a whole lot of homes. I personally visited some of the nests and what I saw was enough to make you sick. There was one nest in particular that was beyond belief." Father paused briefly and then continued. "From what I was told, a big fat crow crapped in that nest. He was by himself. And you can't imagine the mess. The whole nest was covered. In one area there was crap and blood mixed together." Father paused to collect himself as the thought of what he had seen nearly made him gag. "That damn crow must have strained so hard to crap in that nest that he blew an O-ring."

Hardy and Laslo looked at each other. Hardy had a puzzled look on his face but Laslo shook his head and grinned as though he knew exactly what Father was talking about. Hardy knew Laslo didn't have a clue.

"I'll tell you this; that sphincter won't be sphinctering anytime soon, that's for sure. It'll make identifying that no-good SOB easy though. All we'll have to do is find a big fat crow with a blown O-ring and we'll have our man. That shouldn't be too hard."

"Father, I think you need to calm down a little," said Mother.

"I can't calm down. Boys, those crows not only ruined a bunch of nice homes but one of the young ducks, a little boy, was attacked and injured."

"Really?" exclaimed Hardy. "Was he hurt bad?"

"Bad enough; we weren't sure at first how badly he was hurt. He was a mess; covered with blood. He's going to be all right in a few days. He was returning home and saw a crow in his nest. He landed, confronted the crow, and was attacked without warning. He was pecked right above one of his eyes; could've lost his sight. His parents found nearly ten wounds from being pecked. Fortunately, the crow just quit and flew off before he killed him."

"I think you boys should stay home for now," said Mother. "I don't think it's safe."

"Mom, do we have to stay home in the nest?" asked Laslo.

"That's not fair. The attack happened here, in the nests. We'll be careful. Don't make us stay in the nest," begged Hardy.

"Mother, I think the boys are right. It's probably less safe here in the nest than if they're out on their own. A duck can outfly a crow any day and these boys can really fly. I think we should let them go out. But you boys have to promise your mother that you'll be extra careful."

"We promise," Hardy and Laslo yelled at the same time.

"Please, Mom, we'll be careful. We can outfly any crow that ever lived," said Laslo. "Even Hardy can do that."

"Oh, I guess you're right. I was so worried about you boys. If anything were to happen to you, I don't know what I'd do."

"Well, I know what I'm going to do. I'm going to kick some serious crow ass. This has got to stop *now*," said Father.

"Dad, I think this is just a small group of bad crows," said Hardy. "I don't think all crows are like that. If they were, we would have had trouble long before this. There are lots of crows around, and you said the other day this was just a small group."

"I don't care. An example has to be set. If not, we'll be up to our eyeballs in crow crap. And who knows? The next time they might just kill someone."

"So, what are we gonna do?" asked Laslo.

"We're not going to do anything," said Father, emphasizing the word *we're*. "The other fathers and I will be meeting at the lake with Plato tomorrow evening to decide what to do. Until then the other fathers and I are all going to take turns patrolling the perimeter of the woodlot. If we see any crows heading this way, a warning will be sounded. Then we're going out and deal with those crap-filled bags of wind. There's going to be some serious crow ass whipping if they try to come back here. You can bet your sweet ass on that. But you, Laslo, aren't going to do anything."

"Father, I've asked you to watch your language. Please?" Mother was so upset she was near tears.

"I'm sorry, Mother. I need to calm down, that's all. I didn't raise this family to have a bunch of renegade crows threatening their safety. Anyone threatens my family and it gets my blood going. I'll calm down. Again, I'm sorry."

"Dad, I'm pretty grown up now. I think I can whip some crow ass, uh, sorry, some crow butt. Just give me the chance. Please?" Laslo looked at his father straight in the eyes and puffed himself up to look as big as he could.

"Not a chance. Crows are tougher than you think. You aren't ready for that yet."

"Have you boys had anything to eat?" asked Mother.

"Yeah, we ate at the pond with the other kids. We're good," said Laslo.

"Okay. You boys go sit down and get some rest. Your mother and I need to talk in private." Mother and Father went out to the end of a large limb to talk.

Hardy and Laslo sat down next to each other, thinking about what Father had just told them. Finally Laslo broke the silence. "Well, are you gonna tell Dad and Mom about Nestor and Justine? I think you should."

"No, I gave my word I would keep it a secret. If I decide I need to tell Mom and Dad, I need to let Justine and Nestor know first. Laslo, I trust them. They told me some things today that are really serious."

"What all did they tell you?" asked Laslo.

"I think you need to come with me tomorrow. I'm gonna tell Nestor and Justine what happened here today and then we'll see what's next. Will you come with me?"

"I guess I'd better," answered Laslo. "You said you thought you saw Antus and his group. Where do you think were they heading?"

"Probably back to the place they hang out. I went there today. There's a fence line about fifteen minutes past where we met Justine and Nestor. I think they hang out in a lone tree that's there near the fence line. You won't believe the mess; they must be some really disgusting crows."

"Pretty much all crows are disgusting, Hardy," said Laslo with a somewhat condescending tone. "Justine and Nestor may seem nice but I bet in the end you're gonna find out they're nothing but two more disgusting crows. I hope for your sake I'm wrong but I think not; I can feel it in my bones."

"You and your bones; you can't feel anything with your bones. Why don't you try using your brain once in a while? 'I can feel it in my bones.' Good Lord."

As the boys talked, Hardy saw Father leave the nest. Father flew a short distance where he met with Plato. Plato briefed Father on the boys' activities. Father was not surprised when he learned that Laslo and Hardy had not stayed together. He was pleased to hear that the boys were very capable and, in spite of his concern about Laslo's fearlessness, decided Plato didn't need to follow the boys any longer. Plato did not tell Father about the meetings with crows. Father told Plato about the events of the day and closed the conversation by telling Plato he had not made much progress in convincing anyone to support letting crows into the woodlot. And in light of the raid today, nothing he said now would. Father advised Plato he would no longer help him with his mission to reunite with the crows.

The boys sat quietly contemplating the day's events and thinking about what tomorrow might hold in store. Hardy was anxious to tell Justine and Nestor what had happened and to see what their reaction was going to be. Laslo sat there lost in thought: *Hardy thinks he is going to save the day. He won't, he can't, but maybe I can.*

Chapter 18

Hardy and Laslo woke later than usual. Both were a little worn out from the previous day's activities and had had trouble falling asleep as the events described by their father swirled in their brains.

"It's about time you two sleepyheads woke up," said Mother. "I know you'll want to head off right away but you need to have a little something to eat first." Father was already gone.

"Okay, Mom, sure," said Hardy. "Mom, what's an O-ring?"

"Your father's going to have to explain that to you, Hardy. I don't want to hear any more about that. Do you hear me? Not another word."

"Okay."

The boys quickly ate a small breakfast, bid their mother good-bye after assuring her they would be careful, and flew off. They flew side by side, not saying anything to each other for about ten minutes.

Finally Hardy spoke. "Laslo, I want you to promise me you'll behave when we meet with Justine and Nestor. I know how you feel about crows but for once, please, keep your feelings to yourself. Keep the conversation strictly about the Antus problem so we can come up with some answers. Okay?"

"All right, I won't mention anything about crow crap or ass whipping," replied Laslo.

"For God's sake would you please—"

"I'm just fooling with you. I don't think I'm going with you. You know me when I get ticked off, and I'm plenty ticked off at crows right now. You'd be better off talking to them yourself. I'll just scout around until you're done and then we'll join up and look for Antus and his crap happy gang."

"I think you should go with me. We have a chance to stop this and we could use your help. Get a grip on your feelings and help us out."

"I am helping out. That's why I shouldn't go. They trust you and the three of you will do better without me there with an attitude. Even if I keep my mouth shut, they'll be able to tell I don't like crows. And I don't like crows; not even a little bit."

"Okay. I'll be with them for about an hour, maybe less, I guess. I'll circle out around the meeting place looking for you. Try to come back about then so we can find each other. I really want your help."

Hardy was sincere and Laslo could sense it. He briefly thought about changing his mind but didn't. "I'll be there on time."

The boys flew a while longer, searching the sky for danger and for crows. Soon they arrived at the meeting place. Laslo said good-bye and then banked left and flew off. Justine and Nestor were already there so Hardy landed without circling.

"You're a little late, Hardy. We were getting concerned that maybe you'd changed your mind about meeting us," said Justine.

"No way; I just woke up late. I had trouble sleeping last night. Something bad happened yesterday. Antus and his friends raided the woodlot again."

"Oh no," cried Justine. "Did they do the same disgusting things again?"

"Hi, Hardy," said Nestor. "Do you want to catch your breath before talking about it?"

"I'm sorry, Hardy," said Justine. "Good morning."

"Good morning to both of you. No, I'm fine; we need to talk. It was the same thing, except this time they also attacked a young boy and hurt him pretty bad. If my dad is an indicator of how the other birds are feeling, then there's trouble brewing. I've never seen him this upset before."

"Is the boy going to be okay?" asked Nestor.

"Dad said he'll recover but it was a pretty brutal attack. And he has an idea of who one of the crows is, or at least how he can be identified."

"Great," said Nestor. "What did your father tell you?"

"He said there was one fat crow in particular that really messed up one of the nests. He said if we find a big fat crow with a blown O-ring then we'll have our man."

"What?" exclaimed Justine.

"What?" asked Hardy.

"What are you talking about?" asked Nestor. "What's a blown O-ring? That doesn't make any sense to me."

"Me neither," added Justine.

"I don't know what it means. I was hoping you did. My dad was in no mood for questions yesterday. I asked my mom but she said I would have to hear that from Dad. Laslo was acting like he knew but I could tell he didn't really know."

"Well, that's just great. Did he say anything else that may help?" asked Justine.

"Yeah. He said, uh, let me think. I want to get this right. Okay. He said, 'That spinker won't be spinkering anytime soon.' Yeah, that's it. 'That spinker won't be spinkering anytime soon.' That's what he said."

"Good Lord. Now what does that mean? What's a spinker?" asked Nestor.

"I don't know. You're the smart one. I figured you'd know."

"Well, that doesn't help us at all. O-rings and spinkers? It doesn't even make sense."

"So, what do you think we should do?" asked Hardy.

"Let's approach this logically," replied Nestor. "First, do you have any idea how the birds in the woodlot are going to respond to what happened? Did you learn anything about what they may have planned?"

"Dad said they're going to take turns patrolling the perimeter. If any crows approach, they'll send a warning back to the woodlot. That will summon more birds and then I think they will use force to run the crows off. I think they're all probably in a fighting mood. But my dad said there'll be a meeting later this evening to decide what they're going to do. I don't think it's gonna be good unless they cool down some."

"Well, they have every right to be upset. And they have every right to defend their homes and families, especially if one of the children has been harmed." Justine was nearly shouting she was so angry. "Antus has got to be stopped. We can't let him raid the woodlot again. If he does, there will certainly be more bloodshed."

"Absolutely, you're right," said Nestor. "But first we have to locate him."

"I think I know where they hang out," said Hardy. "I remembered yesterday after we met that I saw a group of crows one day and they yelled at me; I should have remembered it sooner. I went by the place after we split up yesterday. They weren't there but the place was a real mess. I mean, it was disgusting. I think they must spend a lot of time there. Oh yeah, and I think I saw Antus and his gang yesterday. I was returning home and they were flying in the opposite direction. I bet they were returning from their raid; they seemed pretty excited about something."

"Did they see you?" asked Nestor.

"I don't think so. I can show you the place where I think they hang out. If they're there, you could confirm if it's Antus or not."

"I think it best if I go alone. They'd be spooked if they saw a duck and two crows flying around there together. You stay here with Justine and I'll go take a look. Tell me where." Hardy gave Nestor directions and Nestor immediately left. Hardy and Justine stayed put and talked. Nestor returned about a half hour later and reported that no crows were there but crows had definitely been there recently. And the mess looked like something Antus and his gang would leave behind.

"Okay. This is what I think we should do. Hardy, you go back to the woodlot. Try to find out what's discussed at the meeting this evening. Maybe you can talk with your dad before he goes and try to calm him down. There needs to be at least one bird at that meeting who keeps his wits about him. If we can avoid the start of a war today, we have a chance of preventing it completely."

"What'll you do?" asked Hardy.

"We're going to speak with Alexander, the leader of the crow army. We'll do all we can to keep him from overreacting to any action the other birds may take. But, just so you know, they will defend the pine grove against an attack."

"Should I tell my dad about you two and what you've told me?"

"How will he react to that?" asked Justine.

"He'll be angry at first, I think. But maybe it'll give me a chance to calm him down. If I tell him that it's just a handful of renegades that's causing all the trouble and, if he understands just how serious the risk of war is, he may try to convince the birds in the woodlot from doing anything right now. At least he may be able to keep them out of the pine grove."

"Okay. I think you should only tell your father whatever will keep him calm. Don't tell him any more than necessary." Nestor gave Hardy a long look and then continued. "If we fail on our end and you see or hear of large numbers of crows heading for the woodlot, warn your family and get out of there. Alexander's army is large and powerful."

"Okay. Do you think they'll attack?"

"Alexander's very reasonable and he's a good leader. I think we can keep him from attacking. We don't want you hurt. You're our friend."

"Both of you are my friends, too. Good luck. And we'll always be friends no matter what happens."

"Without question we will. Good-bye. Let's not rely on luck. Let's make sure we do what we need to do. Failure is not acceptable," replied Nestor.

"Bye, Hardy. We'll meet you here tomorrow morning," said Justine.

Justine and Nestor flew off. Hardy decided to find Laslo and then return home. Maybe he would get a chance to talk with Father before the meeting this evening.

Chapter 19

After Laslo left Hardy, he flew for about ten minutes. He wanted to be sure he was out of sight so Hardy wouldn't see him change directions. Then he banked and began flying in the direction of the tree where Hardy indicated Antus and his gang might be hanging out. As Laslo flew, he was deep in thought. *Hardy thinks he's gonna be some big shot and solve all these problems. But there's no way he can do that. He's too afraid to do what's necessary. He's too trusting; he trusts crows. You can't trust crows.*

Ahead in the distance Laslo could see what he thought was the tree Hardy had told him about. Yes, there was the fence line. As he continued to fly, Laslo thought about what he was going to do. *I'll confront the crows and explain to them what will happen if they return to the woodlot. Whatever their reasons for doing what they did they'll have to stop. I'll make them understand that the fun is over. I'll tell them there will be real trouble if they return. I'm not afraid of crows and if they start any trouble I can always outfly them. When I tell everyone what I've done and that the crows won't be coming back everyone will be happy and I'll get all the credit. And Hardy won't get in any trouble for being friends with crows. It's a good plan.*

Laslo had neared the tree and could see a number of crows roosting among the limbs. He saw a big fat crow and figured this must be the group Hardy had seen yesterday, probably Antus's group. Laslo circled around and glided in for a landing. He landed on the fence rail about thirty feet from the tree. All the crows stood up and looked directly at him, obviously puzzled that he had landed there. Laslo looked at each of the crows, trying to locate one that appeared to be the leader. They were all disheveled and dirty looking, nothing like Nestor and Justine. The one fat crow was, in Laslo's estimation, absolutely enormous. The whole area under and around the tree was a mess, and the stench nearly made him sick.

"Excuse me, but is one of you named Antus?" Laslo spoke loudly and with a slightly deeper voice than normal.

"Who wints to know?" asked one of the crows.

"My name's Laslo and I want to know."

The crow closest to Laslo took two steps forward and spoke. "I'm Intus. Whit do you wint?" The crow's voice was hoarse sounding, almost growling. Laslo immediately felt a strong dislike for this crow.

"I wint, uh, excuse me, I want to speak with you about you and your friends coming into the woodlot and crapping in our nests. You may think that's funny and harmless. But yesterday one of you hurt a young bird."

"Who siys we did it?" asked Antus.

"Some of the birds heard your name mentioned during the raid."

"I see. So, whitever you hiv to siy, siy it."

"Well, I want to warn you, uh, rather tell you that the birds in the woodlot are all pretty upset. I don't think you should return. If you do there'll be trouble. You'll be outnumbered by a large group of very angry birds. I'd like to be able to go back and tell them I spoke with you and that you've promised to stop."

Antus raised his head and laughed out loud. His laughter prompted the other crows to laugh also. Suddenly, Antus stopped laughing and stared at Laslo. There was a look in Antus's eyes that made Laslo feel afraid, really afraid, for the first time in his life. "We're not going to stop. We do whitever we wint to do en we're not afrid of eh bunch of little birds en some clumsy old ducks. Whit mekes you think you're going to be eble to go beck? You mid eh big mistik coming here, duck."

Laslo wasn't sure what to say. Antus said something to the crow next to him and in an instant two crows flew from the tree and landed next to Laslo, one on each side. "I guess there's no point in talking. I should be going. I'll leave now. I'm sorry if I disturbed you." Laslo was surprised by the sound of his own voice. It sounded weak and was breaking up. The fear in his voice was obvious.

Without any hesitation or warning Antus flew from the tree and glided right toward Laslo. Laslo tried to move but it was too late. Antus bumped him and Laslo fell backward off the fence and landed hard on the ground. He quickly got to his feet and tried to take off. Laslo felt something grab the feathers on his back. He looked back and saw that one of the crows had grabbed his feathers in his beak. Laslo began to struggle to get free when he felt a sharp pain in his neck. And then another sharp pain on his shoulder. Suddenly Laslo realized that the other crows in the trees were landing around him. The sound of crows cackling and wings rustling was both confusing and scary. The crows were all pecking at him and he felt the pain of each blow. It felt like hundreds of sharp objects grabbing his flesh and pulling off pieces. Then he was pecked directly on the head just above his eyes. Laslo saw a bright flash of light and felt dazed. Laslo went down and was off his feet, lying on his side. The crows swarmed on him, pecking and pulling at him. It was then that Laslo realized that if he didn't escape right now the crows were going to kill him.

Laslo used all of his strength, flapping his wings wildly, and was able to get to his feet. He screamed at the top of his lungs. It was a sound he had never heard before and it came from deep inside. It wasn't a scream of pain but a thunderous battle cry. Laslo's scream startled the crows and they all stumbled back a few feet. That was just the opening Laslo needed. He ran right at a small lone female crow, and as she turned to escape his charge, Laslo bowled her over. He began to get airborne and could hear the gang of crows yelling. He also heard the sound of rustling wings; they were coming after him.

Fly hard, Laslo thought. *Any duck can outfly a crow.* Laslo called on all of his strength and flew as hard as he could. He gained altitude and soon began to outdistance the crows. Within a minute or two the crows gave up and turned back.

Laslo hurt all over. He was having trouble seeing out of one eye and thought maybe he had been pecked in the eye. He blinked several times and realized it was just blood running into his eyes from a wound on his head. Laslo slowed down and tried to catch his breath. He was exhausted from the effort to escape. It didn't take him long to catch his breath and soon he started to relax a little.

Laslo headed for home. As he flew he began to feel tired. His wings hurt; his whole body hurt. He felt his muscles beginning to cramp. Laslo slowed down and began to glide whenever he could. He realized he couldn't continue that for long because he was losing altitude and he didn't have the strength to climb. He slowed down even more, maintaining a slow but steady wing beat, flying only fast enough to maintain altitude.

I have to get home. Keep flying; no matter how tired you feel, keep flying. You can't land. If you land you'll never be able to take off. You won't last anytime on the ground; it's dangerous there. Thoughts raced through Laslo's mind as he struggled to fly. It was as if another being was speaking to him and encouraging him not to give up. Tears began to mix with the blood in his eye. Laslo realized his situation was desperate. He wasn't sure he could make it all the way home. *I should have stayed with Hardy. Where's Hardy?*

Laslo looked around and realized he didn't know exactly where he was. He was headed for home but in his haste, his panic to escape, he had paid no attention to his surroundings. *Dad taught me to always, no matter what, pay attention so I'd always know where I was. I'll just keep flying; I think this way is toward home. If I get lucky, maybe I'll find Hardy. He can go get Dad. Dad will know what to do.*

Laslo continued to fly but his strength was fading and he was losing his will to go on. Laslo thought of home, Mom and Dad, and Hardy. He longed for the comfort and safety of the nest. He thought about the time he spent growing up in the nest, the fun he had teasing Hardy, and the lessons Mom and Dad taught him. Mom and Dad loved him and they showed it in everything they did. He loved his mom and dad and he loved Hardy. Laslo wished he had told all of them how much he loved them. He wished he could tell Hardy that his teasing didn't mean anything. Hardy was the best brother in the world. Laslo began to cry, to sob, as he struggled to fly. He looked ahead but was unable to see the woodlot. He was still a long way from home.

Chapter 20

Hardy left the meeting with Justine and Nestor and decided to look for Laslo. He flew out some distance to gain speed and then began to climb. He wanted enough altitude so he could spot Laslo at a distance but not go so high that he could miss seeing him if he passed.

Hardy reached the proper altitude and, as planned, began to circle the area. Each time he circled he flew farther out so he could cover more ground. He scanned the sky above to be sure there was no danger and scanned ahead and below looking for Laslo. After fifteen minutes, Hardy had expanded his search area as far as he thought reasonable and found no sign of his brother. *Laslo; you can never depend on him to do what he's supposed to do. I can't spend any more time looking for him. I need to get home and find Dad. There are far more important things I need to do than spend the afternoon looking for Laslo.*

Hardy turned and headed for home. As he flew, his mind was filled with all the things going on. He had become friends with Justine and Nestor. If that wasn't odd enough in and of itself, a crisis had started in the woodlot and he, Justine, and Nestor were all thrust into a position of trying to prevent an all-out war. And to complicate matters more, he had kept all of this a secret from his parents. Now he had to go talk to his father and, if necessary, tell him about Justine and Nestor, about Antus's plan, and about the large and powerful crow army. Dad was not going to be happy with him. Maybe things had settled down and Dad had cooled down enough so he could accomplish his mission without having to tell him too much.

Hardy had been flying toward home for a little over five minutes when he

118

noticed a duck up ahead and off to his right flying at a much lower altitude. The duck appeared to be struggling in his flight. Hardy decided to go see if anything was wrong; maybe he could help. Hardy increased his speed and started a slow descent on a path to intercept the struggling duck.

As Hardy got closer, he was struck with the impression that something about the duck looked familiar. A few seconds passed and Hardy realized the duck looked like Laslo. It didn't fly like Laslo; Laslo was graceful in flight and powerful even though he was young.

"That is Laslo!" Hardy recognized his brother. There was no doubt. As the distance closed between them, he could tell that Laslo had been injured and was straining hard just to remain airborne. What could have happened to him?

Out of habit, Hardy checked the sky around him. As he scanned above him, his eyes passed right by an object and then immediately returned. Hardy strained to focus on the object. Hardy felt his heart skip as he recognized what it was: a hawk. There was no doubt about it. Father had described hawks to him and Laslo. Even though Hardy had never gotten a good look at one, he knew beyond a shadow of a doubt that what he was looking at was a hawk.

Hardy looked quickly to see how Laslo was doing. He started to call out a warning but realized he was too far away to be heard. Ahead in the distance was the woodlot, barely visible. The way he was flying Laslo would never cover that distance before the hawk could get to him. Hardy began to fly to Laslo as fast as he could fly. Laslo was flying very slowly and Hardy was closing the distance between them rapidly.

"Where's the hawk?" Hardy looked up, scanning the sky again. "There." The hawk began to descend in Laslo's direction, beat his wings with several powerful strokes, and then pulled his wings in against his body. The speed of the hawk shocked Hardy. Hardy began yelling to Laslo. After several screams, Laslo looked in his direction.

"Hawk!" yelled Hardy. "Fly faster; head for the woodlot as fast as you can." Laslo looked up but didn't locate the hawk. He looked back at Hardy. "Hawk!" Hardy was screaming at the top of his lungs. "Don't look; just fly. Fast."

Hardy looked at the hawk and then at Laslo. Gauging the distances and speeds, he thought he could get to Laslo just before the hawk could get there. Hardy chose an angle that he calculated would allow him to pass in front of the hawk about a hundred yards above Laslo. He had to time this just right. If he was too early, the hawk would not be distracted or could turn and attack him. If he was too late, the hawk would certainly get Laslo, injured as he was.

Hardy flew as hard and as fast as he had ever flown. His wings ached and he was out of breath. The hawk was diving with blinding speed. Hardy was having trouble following the hawk; it was moving so fast. The distance between the three closed, and the closer they got to each other, the faster the hawk appeared to be moving. Hardy adjusted his angle down slightly and in a blinding flash of speed passed between the hawk and Laslo, passing so closely the hawk was startled. The hawk flared his wings and banked hard left, reacting on instinct in an effort to avoid a collision. The hawk passed on Laslo's left and was now below Laslo but pulling up as he continued to bank. The hawk was circling back and climbing, trying to get above Laslo so he could attack again. Hardy had bought Laslo some time but not enough. Laslo was struggling and trying his best but he was not flying fast enough to get to the woodlot before the hawk would be in a position to strike.

Hardy yelled to Laslo, "Keep going! I'll try to distract the hawk. You're the best flyer I know so get going."

"I can't. I'm hurt. I'm hurt bad."

"I don't care how bad you're hurt. Fly. Fly or you're dead," yelled Hardy.

Hardy banked and climbed. He needed to get enough altitude to stay above Laslo and, if possible, the hawk. He would need the altitude to get enough speed to distract the hawk and yet not get caught himself. Now that the hawk was aware of his presence, Hardy had lost the element of surprise. He would have to find a way to distract the hawk away from Laslo. Hardy's mind raced as he tried to figure out what he could do. *If I can get the hawk to chase me instead of Laslo, I think I can get to the woodlot before the hawk can get me. But if I make even the smallest mistake, it'll be all over.* Hardy was scared. The fear made him stronger. Hardy realized he was also angry. *That hawk is not going to get my brother. I'll do whatever I have to do but he's not going to get Laslo.*

Hardy climbed as the hawk climbed. He tried to keep just the right distance between himself and the hawk so that when the time came, he could act. The hawk stopped climbing and glided briefly, probably to catch his breath. Then with a series of strong strokes of his wings he was diving again to attack Laslo.

Hardy didn't hesitate and began flying as hard and as fast as he could. He was off to the right side of the hawk and slightly behind and just a little higher. But he was closer to the line of interception to Laslo than the hawk was. He had planned well and was in the right position. Hardy needed to get this just right. His plan was to come slightly from behind and at an angle so the hawk would not see him until the last moment. He would pass in front of the hawk a little farther away this time, hoping the hawk would see him as an easier, closer target than Laslo. Hardy wanted the hawk to chase him instead of Laslo.

The hawk was moving with astonishing speed and was focused intently on Laslo. Hardy was flying as fast as he could on the intercept course he had calculated and was constantly adjusting. Hardy saw the hawk's head turn in his direction just as he was entering the intercept path. Hardy passed in front of the hawk about forty yards away. It worked. The hawk veered from his course and went after Hardy. Hardy banked hard left and stayed in that banking maneuver, hoping to make a tighter turn than the hawk. All the training Father had provided was paying off. Hardy used every technique he had learned to make his turn as tight as possible. He was able to turn more sharply than the hawk. Hardy completed the circle and was heading for the woodlot. The hawk finally completed his turn and was flying hard, trying to gain altitude on Hardy. Hardy just kept flying as hard as he could toward the woodlot. Ahead, Laslo neared the woodlot and disappeared among the trees. He was safe.

The hawk was fast—faster than Hardy imagined. He was not going to make it to the woodlot in time. The hawk was closing the distance much too quickly. Hardy looked back and realized the hawk was only about fifty yards away. Hardy prepared for the impact and certain death, convinced the end was only seconds away. Suddenly a large duck passed Hardy to his left, flying on a direct path toward the pursuing hawk. It was Father! Hardy turned his head just in time to see his father collide with the hawk. There was a sickening thud and an explosion of feathers. Both Father and the hawk spun out of control falling toward the ground. Both appeared to be unconscious or possibly even dead. As Hardy watched in horror, Father began to struggle, trying to fly. He was able to slow his descent but hit the ground hard. Father lay still for a moment or two and then began to struggle to his feet.

"The hawk, where's the hawk?" Hardy looked in the direction he had seen the hawk fall. There was no sign of him, but then movement caught his eye. It was the hawk. The hawk had regained control of his flight and was circling, heading for Father. Hardy banked and turned sharply trying to get in a position to distract the hawk, but it was too late. The hawk descended rapidly. Father saw the hawk and struggled to find cover. Then when it was obvious escape was impossible, Father just stopped and looked up at Hardy.

Father raised one wing. "Take care of the family, Hardy. I love you all. I'm proud of you, son."

Then the hawk was on him. There was a brief struggle and then Father was still. Hardy could watch no longer so he turned toward home, sobbing as he flew. Father was gone, killed by a hawk while protecting his son. Laslo was seriously injured by the same hawk. War was imminent and, if there was war, there would be more tragic losses. Hardy felt overwhelmed with sorrow and the responsibilities he knew were now his. And he was angry—angry and determined to prevent a war. But first he needed to go home and make sure Laslo had made it to the nest and was okay. And he had to tell Mother about the loss of Father.

Chapter 21

Nestor and Justine left the meeting with Hardy and started on their flight directly to Alexander's headquarters. They felt the situation was serious enough that they needed to report it immediately. Justine was unusually quiet during the flight, not saying a word. Nestor glanced over at his sister and could tell she was worried, lost in thought.

"What are you thinking about? What do you think we should tell Alexander?" asked Nestor for no other reason than to get Justine to speak and take her mind off the thoughts troubling her.

"You're the smart one, Nestor. I'm just afraid this is the start of big trouble. And it's so unnecessary. Antus is evil, I tell you, pure evil. What do you think we should tell Alexander?"

"We have to tell him everything. We have no choice. But somehow we need to convince him not to attack the woodlot. Hardy's a very unique duck. We need to give him a chance and see if he can prevent the birds in the woodlot from seeking revenge."

"Hardy is unique. I like him, Nestor. It takes courage for him to trust us the way he does. We need to tell Alexander that Hardy is brave and resourceful. We can rely on Hardy to help us prevent war. Alexander and the others need to understand that we can prevent war if we trust Hardy and we all work together. It just wouldn't be fair for a war to start over this. Antus needs to be stopped."

"If we all work together? You just gave me an idea. Let me think on it as we fly."

Nestor and Justine flew for about twenty minutes. The navigation training they had received from their parents was paying off. They circled around the woodlot and pine grove and took a direct route toward the training area. They were soon intercepted by members of Alexander's army. After exchanging greetings and advising their escorts that they had information to personally give Alexander, they were all off, heading toward headquarters.

Soon they landed and were immediately taken to meet with Alexander. Alexander was surrounded by five crows, including Paris, and they seemed to be engaged in an intense discussion while looking over something that lay at their feet. Alexander looked up and saw the pair. He smiled wide and greeted them.

"Nestor and Justine, how good to see you again." Alexander noticed they wore expressions of concern. "Is there something wrong?"

Paris and the other crows stopped what they were doing and looked on as Alexander approached Nestor and Justine.

"It's good to see you again too, Alexander," said Nestor.

"Hello," said Justine.

"Is there something wrong?" asked Alexander again. "You look troubled."

"Well yes, there is something wrong. Antus and his gang have attacked more nests in the woodlot, defecating in them again. But this time a young duck was attacked and seriously injured."

"I knew it. We should have removed Antus," yelled Paris. Alexander gave him a stern look that indicated he should remain silent.

"How badly was the duck injured?" asked Alexander.

"It sounded bad," said Justine. "But fortunately he'll recover."

"How did you learn of this?"

"We met with Hardy," answered Nestor. "He told us. He also said the adult ducks are pretty angry, maybe fighting mad."

"Well, they have every right to be angry. And they're perfectly within their rights to defend their homes and family," said Justine. "Maybe Paris is right. Maybe you need to deal with Antus right now."

"Wait a minute. Let's not jump into something without thinking it through fully," said Nestor.

"I don't see where we have a choice. We need to eliminate Antus and his gang for everyone's good. There's no other option," replied Alexander.

"Damn right," added Paris.

"There are always other choices," said Nestor.

"We'll need to prepare to defend against an attack on the pine grove." Alexander was getting excited and had raised his voice. It was easy to see why he was in charge. He was large, strong, powerful, and smart, and he spoke with a confident, commanding voice.

Agreed," said Nestor. "But listen to what I have to say before you act."

"Speak," commanded Alexander. "Time is wasting."

Nestor stared at Alexander for a full ten seconds and then glanced at Paris and the others. He turned and walked a few steps away and then quickly turned back and faced Alexander. "The ducks are not going to attack today. They've set up a defensive perimeter around the woodlot. The only way there will be trouble today is if a crow or group of crows approaches the woodlot. If that happens, they'll fly out and confront the crows. Only then will there be any trouble today."

"And how do you know this?" asked Alexander.

"Hardy told us that's what his father said. The ducks and other birds in the woodlot are having a meeting this evening to decide what to do. Hardy's going to try and reason with his father. Hopefully, his father will be able to convince the other birds not to do anything aggressive; they really only need to defend the woodlot. There's no reason why they need to attack the pine grove."

"Great. Hardy said this. A duck, and a child duck at that," replied Alexander. "We can't put our home at risk based on what Hardy says."

"Hardy's good. Not only can we trust him but we can put our faith in him. He'll do all he can to calm his father down," said Justine. "And don't underestimate him because he's young. Nestor and I aren't much older than he is and you've trusted us with a lot."

"It's not that I don't trust him because he's young. I'm not sure the other birds in the woodlot will pay much attention to him, because he's young. There's just too much at stake. He may do all he can but if he's not successful we have to be ready."

"Understood and agreed," added Nestor. "But how you go about preparing the defense of the pine grove can influence what happens. Just add the forces in the pine grove that you need to defend it—no more. And send them there in small groups. As long as it is done in a way that doesn't appear aggressive the birds in the woodlot won't be alarmed and they'll have time to talk among themselves. But if they feel threatened, they'll have to act to defend themselves. You can keep sufficient forces out of the pine grove and dispersed in a way that they can be sent into the pine grove quickly if there's an attack. That'll buy some time for Hardy. And it'll give you a tactical advantage if there is an attack."

"Which there won't be," added Justine. "The birds in the woodlot have never been aggressive toward us. They don't want trouble. Do the right thing, Alexander."

Alexander thought briefly and then looked at Paris and the other commanders. They nodded that they could live with that approach. "Okay," said Alexander. "Make it happen, Paris. And do it carefully. Send only the most disciplined; we don't want some fool doing something stupid and getting us into a war." Alexander smiled at Justine and then spoke again. "You two are a pair to reckon with. Nestor, you're smart and deliberate in your thinking. You may be the smartest crow I've ever met. And you, Justine: always concerned about being fair and just."

Justine stepped forward and spoke. "Well, I think you're the perfect crow to lead our defense. Your cool head and willingness to listen may prevent a war. I really appreciate your handling things this way. It takes great restraint to do what you're doing. You're a true leader."

"Was that a compliment? Why, thank you. I never thought the day would come when you would compliment me. I assumed you disliked me because I'm a warrior."

"No, I dislike those who think war is a good solution. War is only a solution of last resort and only in defense. You know, if it becomes necessary, we can still leave the area rather than go to war."

"That's not an option. This is our home and this is where we will stay. But I promise I'll do everything I can to avoid war."

"Thank you," answered Justine. "I now know you will."

"Thank you," added Nestor. "I have something else I want to talk with you about. I think there may be a way we can avoid war, get rid of Antus, and who knows, maybe we can even get a place in the woodlot."

"Wow! Is that the idea you said you had earlier?" asked Justine.

"Yes."

"I'm all ears. If you have an idea that'll accomplish all that, I definitely have the time to listen. Let's go over there and sit where we can talk alone." Alexander put his wing on Justine's back. "Come. I want to hear what your reaction is to Nestor's idea." Justine felt her face get warm and her heart race at the touch of Alexander's wing.

Chapter 22

Hardy flew toward the woodlot and home. Ahead he saw two large ducks heading his way. It was two of the fathers who had been patrolling the woodlot perimeter. As they neared, one of them spoke.

"Are you okay? We saw what happened; at least some of it."

"I'm okay. Did Laslo make it home?"

"He's with your mother."

"Is he going to be okay?"

"He's hurt bad, Hardy."

The ducks saw that Hardy was still crying. They looked at him and then out toward the area where the hawk had tried to attack Laslo and Hardy. "And your father, Hardy, is he okay?"

"No!" sobbed Hardy. "The hawk got him. He just flew right into the hawk to save me."

"I'm sorry. Your dad loved you and was very proud of you. When he saw that hawk go after Laslo and what you were doing to try to save your brother, I could see the pride in his eyes. He just yelled to us to get help and off he went to try to save you and Laslo."

The other father spoke softly. "We saw what you did. We saw you put yourself in great danger trying to save your brother. You're one of the bravest ducks I've ever known. I know you made your father very proud."

"I have to get home. I need to check on Laslo and tell my mother what happened," said Hardy.

"We can go with you, Hardy, and tell your mom, if you would like us to."

"No, thank you. I need to do that. I'm the oldest male in the family now. My mom will need me to be strong," answered Hardy. "But I appreciate the offer."

The two ducks escorted Hardy back to the woodlot. All three flew in silence. Finally, Hardy spoke. "I'll go on alone from here. Thanks again."

"No problem, Hardy. Be strong. I hope your brother makes it," said one the ducks.

"Let us know if you need any help. Take care. We're both really sorry about your father."

Hardy flew to the nest. As he approached, he saw Laslo lying on his side in the bottom of the nest. Mother was leaning over him tending to his wounds. Another mother duck had come to help treat Laslo's injuries.

Hardy landed in the nest. Mother looked up at him and burst into tears. She ran over and hugged him as tightly as she could. "I was so worried about you. Are you okay?" asked Mother as she tried to control her crying.

"I'm fine, Mom. Is Laslo going to be okay?"

"I don't know. He's been seriously injured. What happened to him?"

"I don't know for sure. It was a hawk. Laslo was already injured when I saw a hawk trying to get him. Father and I were able to save him from the hawk."

Mother turned and went back to Laslo. Hardy walked over and looked at his brother. Laslo's feathers were soaked with blood and he wasn't moving or making a sound. He appeared to be unconscious and his breathing was deep and gasping. Hardy began to cry again. He was sure Laslo was not going to survive.

"Hardy, get me some moss from the side of the nest over there. I need it to stop this bleeding."

Hardy turned and began to pull some moss from the side of the nest. As he tugged, a large piece came out rather easily. There, hidden behind the moss, were four yellow beetles. It was Laslo's stash. "I knew it," mumbled Hardy. "That little ..." Hardy gave the moss to his mother and she began taking small pieces and placing it on Laslo's wounds.

"Go and find your father. Tell him I need him here." Hardy didn't move; he hung his head and was silent. "Did you hear me? Go and get your father right now."

"I can't, Mother," answered Hardy.

"Hardy, I don't have time to argue with you." She turned and looked at Hardy. "You get going right now, young—" Mother saw the sad look on Hardy's face and knew something was wrong. She feared the worse. "Oh no," cried Mother. "Tell me what happened."

"It was the hawk, Momma. Father gave his life saving Laslo and me," Hardy cried. "I'm sorry, Mommy."

Mother was sobbing now. After a moment or two she composed herself and spoke softly to Hardy. "It's going to be okay. Just stay right here while we take care of your brother. I may need you to help." Mother turned and went back to work trying to save Laslo.

Hardy sat down and leaned against the side of the nest as far as possible from where his mother and the other momma duck were working on Laslo so as not to get in the way. Hardy soon realized that he was exhausted from the ordeal. He felt sad and empty inside. He just sat there and cried softly while watching the efforts to save Laslo.

"Hardy, wake up, sweetie." Mother was sitting next to Hardy. Hardy had fallen asleep while watching his mother tend to Laslo. He was feeling a little guilty for having fallen asleep.

"How's Laslo, Momma? Is he okay?" asked Hardy.

"He's resting now. It'll take some time before we know if he'll recover. He's young and strong so I think he has a good chance."

"I'm sorry I fell asleep when you needed me."

"Hush. You have nothing to feel sorry for. When Laslo came back to the nest, the only thing he said before he passed out was, 'Hardy saved me, Momma.' One of the father ducks saw what you did and told me all about it. You were very brave and you saved Laslo's life. I'm so proud of you."

"Momma, I watched Daddy get attacked by the hawk. It was terrible." Hardy paused as his eyes filled with tears. Mother wrapped her wing around him. "But just before the hawk got him he looked up at me and said that he loved us all. He said for me to take care of the family. I'll do that, Momma. You can count on me."

"You're a wonderful son. We're going to be just fine. Your father loved you and Laslo more than you can imagine. He was the proudest father in the woodlot." Hardy and his mother just sat there in silence, holding each other, for several minutes.

Suddenly Hardy got to his feet. "What time is it?" He looked around at the sun and shadows, trying to determine how late in the day it was. "Have the fathers had the meeting yet?" Hardy asked excitedly.

"The meeting should be starting in a few minutes but you don't need to worry about that."

"I need to go, Momma. I'm going to the meeting in Daddy's place."

Mother looked surprised. "That meeting's for the adult birds. I don't think you'll be welcomed there. Stay here with me and we'll hear about the meeting from the other ducks later."

"No, Momma. I need to go. It's important, real important. You trust me, don't you, Momma?" Hardy looked into his mother's eyes.

"Of course I trust you. But, Hardy—"

"I need to go. I'll come back as soon as I can. If Laslo wakes up, tell him I love him. I love you, Momma. Bye." Hardy flew from the nest before Mother could say another word.

Chapter 23

Nestor paced back and forth in front of Alexander and Justine, who sat together waiting to hear the idea Nestor had mentioned. Justine felt slightly nervous sitting so close to Alexander and her heart raced, just a little. Alexander sat closer to her than she expected, but secretly she was pleased he did.

"Well?" asked Alexander. "I thought you were going to share your idea with us."

"Shhh," said Justine. "Sometimes you have to be patient with Nestor. His mind gets going and he needs to settle it down before he can speak. Or at least before he can speak in a way the rest of us can understand."

Alexander looked at Justine and smiled. Justine returned it with a slight smile of her own and then lowered her eyes, feeling a little uncomfortable.

"This is what I have been thinking about. The birds in the woodlot are concerned about their safety and welfare because of what Antus has done. And they have every reason to be concerned. However, right now they don't know anything about who did it or why. They just know that crows did it." Nestor paused for at least thirty seconds.

Alexander started to speak and Justine motioned with her wing for him to stay silent.

"In response, they've decided to patrol the perimeter of the woodlot in a defensive manner. They have not reacted aggressively in any way; at least up to now. Hardy's going to try to convince his father to urge restraint when the birds in the woodlot meet this evening. I think there's a good chance he can be successful. But there's one problem they will not be able to overcome." Nestor paused again, this time resuming his pacing back and forth.

A least a minute passed. Alexander looked at Justine, and when she looked at him, they both just smiled, almost laughing.

"The problem for them is this: how can they patrol the woodlot perimeter in the long term? They must all seek food and take care of their young. In short, they must go on living their lives. They can't spend all their time patrolling. Even if they divide the workload, it will be too burdensome for them to continue for very long. There is the opportunity for us to resolve this crisis peacefully." Nestor stopped pacing and looked directly at Alexander. "I think we should offer to help patrol the perimeter. Let them monitor our activities while we patrol so they can confirm that our intentions are sincere. We'll also promise to hunt down Antus and his group and put an end to the raids. There."

Alexander seemed surprised that Nestor had stopped there. "Well, that is an interesting idea. But how do you propose we get the birds to agree? I don't think they trust us enough to meet with us."

"Hardy will arrange the meeting," yelled Justine. "We can discuss it with him tomorrow. I just know he'll do it."

"Exactly," replied Nestor. "And, Alexander, I think you should meet Hardy. Judge him for yourself. If you agree, we'll bring him to a neutral place where you can meet with him in safety. You need to have as few escorts with you as possible so he'll be comfortable. I think a good place would be the tree where Justine and I met with Hector, Frederick, and Marshall—the same day we met with you the first time."

"So how will this get us back into the woodlot?"

"I was thinking that if we help patrol the woodlot and secure the safety of the birds, deal with Antus and resolve that situation permanently, we would be in a stronger position to ask for a place in the woodlot. If we explain how the pine grove has deteriorated and that we only need a small portion on the edge of the woodlot, they may see that as reasonable and agree."

"Interesting," said Alexander. "That's certainly better than war. It would be great if we could continue to live together in peace and maybe even eliminate some of the distrust that exists. But what about access to the lake, how does that fit into your plan?"

"I think we need to solve the bigger and more immediate problems first.

If we succeed in avoiding war and dealing with Antus, we can also propose a solution to the water issue. I'll think on it."

"Dealing with Antus isn't going to be a problem. We just need to track him down before he makes things any worse. And we certainly have sufficient forces to patrol the woodlot. I like your idea. If you and Justine can get Hardy to agree, I'll meet with him tomorrow."

"Oh great!" yelled Justine. She was so excited she threw her wings around Alexander and gave him a big hug. Realizing what she had done, she immediately pulled back, turned, and hugged Nestor.

"Wow," exclaimed Alexander. Now his face was warm and his heart was racing. Smiling, Alexander said, "Thank you."

Justine smiled and said, "No, thank you."

"And thank you, Nestor, for a great idea. Let's get started and let's make this work."

Chapter 24

Hardy flew the short distance to the woodlot lake where the meeting was to be held. It appeared everyone who had been invited was present and the meeting was about to begin. Hardy decided it would be best if he stayed on the outskirts of the assembly so as not to draw the attention of anyone. He landed on a tree limb where he was secluded but able to see and hear everything.

The ducks were all gathered at the lake and were floating in the water. The other birds were perched in the trees. There was the downed tree in the lake about twenty five feet from the shoreline. It was ideally located as a platform for the elder duck, Plato, who was going to preside over the meeting. From that location, everyone would be able to hear what was said and Plato could recognize anyone who wanted to speak when the time came.

Plato walked out to the middle of tree trunk, about three feet above the surface of the lake. He faced the shoreline. The assembly of ducks was immediately in front of him and the other birds were in the trees directly behind the ducks in the water.

"Greetings, everyone; I appreciate all of you coming together this evening to discuss the crisis we all face."

"What are we going to do about the crows?" yelled a bird from the trees.

"Yeah, what are we gonna do?" hollered one the ducks. "I think it's time we go right into that pine grove and drive those no good crows away from here."

A chorus of voices rose, yelling and shouting, each having a different opinion and something they wanted to say. Plato raised his wings, motioning all to be silent but to no avail. He screamed a high-pitched sound that was halfway between a squeal and a honk. The volume was sufficient to be heard over all the chatter and the sound was so unusual that everyone fell silent.

"This won't do. We have to maintain order; only one shall speak at a time or we'll get nothing accomplished." Plato paused, allowing his words to sink in. "Here's what I propose. Let me get the meeting started and then I'll recognize those that want to speak. I'll start with one of you in the trees and then one from the lake and continue to alternate until all have spoken who wish to speak. Those who speak shall come down here on this tree next to me so everyone can hear. I ask each to be brief in your comments, and there is no need for too much repetition. If a point has been made once, that should be sufficient. If all are agreed, I'll begin."

Plato paused and no one spoke or objected. "Okay then. What we seek is a course of action on how we're going to deal with the raids by the crows. As you should all know by now, some crows have entered the woodlot on at least two occasions and damaged many of the nests. And during the most recent raid one of the young boy ducks, a child, was attacked and injured. Our woodlot is not safe. So let's get started."

Plato pointed at one of the birds in a tree who indicated he wished to speak. "Please, you go first. Come down here so everyone can hear what you have to say."

A blue jay flew down and landed on the tree next to Plato. He looked briefly around at the assembly of birds. "I guess I have a question rather than a statement. Have the crows only raided duck nests or have the nests of other birds been damaged also? Simply put, I'm wondering if this is a problem for all of us or just the ducks."

"What difference does it make?" yelled one of the ducks. "None of us is safe." A cacophony of chatter followed with all the birds discussing the question among themselves.

"Please." Plato spoke in a loud, powerful voice. "All have a right to speak their minds. It's a valid question and must be answered." Plato paused and then said, "Let's see how many have been affected by the crow attacks. Ducks, flap your wings if your nest has been raided." About two-thirds of the ducks indicated they had been raided. "Okay, how about you in the trees. Raise your wings up and down if your nest has been impacted." Plato looked around the trees, assessing the response. "It appears that about 15–20 percent of you have indicated your nests have been raided. I don't think this is just a duck problem but a threat we all face together. Agreed?" A chorus of voices indicated agreement.

"Is there a duck who would like to speak?" Plato looked around and pointed at a healthy, strong-looking young duck. "You come up and speak."

The duck flew up onto the tree trunk and paced back and forth nervously. "I'm a new father. This is my first year raising a family. There's no way I intend to sit by and allow a bunch of crows to threaten the safety of my children or the safety of their mother. My parents told me this happened years ago and that there was a confrontation. The crows were allowed to stay." The duck paused briefly. "We can't patrol the woodlot day after day forever. There's only one solution. I say the crows had a chance and now they've forfeited it. I say we confront them in the pine grove and give them a choice: leave peacefully or we'll drive them away with whatever amount of force it takes. We outnumber them at least two to one, maybe three to one. There's no reason to stand by and continue to do nothing. If it's war they want, then I say let's give them war."

"Well said," yelled a duck from the lake. "Let's give them what they asked for and what they deserve."

"I agree," yelled another.

"Me too," hollered several more. The birds in the trees were nodding in agreement.

Plato raised his wings, and after a few moments the crowd grew quiet. "It appears we have a consensus among most of us assembled here. This will be a serious, dangerous course of action. We may outnumber the crows but they're formidable. They may leave peacefully but maybe they won't. Maybe they'll fight. They've lived here for years. This is their home." Plato turned his back to the crowd and lowered his head in thought. All the birds remained quiet, waiting to see what he would do. After a minute or so he turned back around and faced the crowd and spoke again. "If there's anyone here who disagrees, this is your chance to speak. Does anyone want to speak against this course of action?" No one moved or said a word. "Well then, I guess that's it. It looks like—"

"I have something to say," yelled Hardy, who then flew down and landed next to Plato.

Plato looked surprised to see Hardy standing beside him. He started to advise Hardy he couldn't speak as the meeting was for the adults only but lost the opportunity when Hardy began to speak.

"My name's Hardy. Many of you probably know my—"

Hardy was interrupted by a large duck sitting in the lake in front of him. "I know who you are. This meeting is for the adults. You're just a boy."

"You can't speak here," said a bird from the trees.

"You need to leave right now. You're just a boy," yelled another duck.

Plato raised both his wings high and held them there until everyone was quiet. He then spoke in a quiet voice to Hardy. "They're right; this meeting is for the adults. You can't speak here."

"I must speak," answered Hardy. "I have information that's important. I will be heard." Plato saw the determination on Hardy's face and could hear it in his voice. He nodded and indicated to the group he would let Hardy speak.

Hardy turned and faced the assembly of birds. "My name's Hardy. I know you think I'm just a child and have nothing of value to offer but you're wrong, completely wrong." Hardy emphasized the word *wrong* and then paused for a moment, allowing the assembly to ponder what he had said. " This morning when I left the nest with my brother, it's true: I was just a boy. But today my brother was almost killed by a hawk. He's fighting for his life right now. And I watched as that same hawk killed my father. I left the nest this morning a boy, but I'm no longer a boy. I'm an adult."

"I saw Hardy risk his life today to save his brother. It was one of the bravest things I've ever seen," yelled one of the ducks who had escorted Hardy home earlier in the day. "He's earned the right to speak. Let's listen to what he has to say."

"Thank you," said Hardy. "I have information that's very important. I'm sure it will come as surprise to you; maybe you will find it shocking. But please hear me out. What I have to say could save a lot of lives." The lake was quiet. All were looking at Hardy, waiting to hear what he had to say. Hardy was surprised. He did not feel at all uncomfortable speaking to this large group. *I really have grown up today*, he thought.

"Not long ago I met two crows and we've become friends." The group of birds let out a collective gasp of surprise. "Let me finish before you make any judgments," said Hardy. "The two crows are brother and sister. Their names are Nestor and Justine. And I give you my word on my father's memory that they are good. They can be trusted. And they're doing what they can right now to avoid any conflict between the crows and those of us living here."

"If they're so good, how do you explain the attacks on our nests? How do you explain the unprovoked and violent attack on the young boy yesterday?" yelled a blue jay from the treetops.

Hardy looked up into the trees and stared long and hard at the blue jay. He then let his eyes roam and meet with the eyes of each bird assembled there. "It wasn't Nestor or Justine who raided our nests or attacked the young boy. Let me say that again so it's clear to everyone: it wasn't Nestor or Justine who raided our nests or attacked the young boy."

Hardy paused, adding more emphasis to what he had just said. "They and many other crows have been working in a concerted effort to try and prevent the attacks. But so far they've failed. The attacks are the work of a rogue band of crows led by a sick, mean-spirited troublemaker named Antus. It's his intention to start a war between those of us living here in the woodlot and the crows in the pine grove. None of the crows in the pine grove have participated in these attacks. Most don't even know it's happened." Hardy paused to catch his breath. The other birds were silently waiting for him to speak again. "Antus wants all birds out of the woodlot. No exceptions. Only crows can live here as far as he's concerned. He'll do whatever it takes to start a war so the other crows will drive us from the woodlot. It's his plan to take all the credit for that, and then grab power and become the leader—no, the dictator—of all crows."

"I have a question," said one of the ducks near the rear of the group of assembled ducks. "If none of the crows other than those in Antus's band are involved in these raids, and they are really trying to prevent this, then how could Antus take credit for running us out of the woodlot? Why would the other crows be impressed with that?"

"Good question," said Hardy. "The pine grove's a mess. Many of you probably have seen all the dead and dying trees and all the trees that have been blown down in storms. Most of the crows are concerned with the safety and welfare of their families. The pine grove doesn't provide good shelter or protection anymore."

"So what? Let them go somewhere else," yelled one of the birds in the trees.

"That's what a large group wants to do. They want to move into the edge of the woodlot. This is their home and—"

Hardy was interrupted by a chorus of voices expressing strong opinions. No crows were welcome in the woodlot was the collective response. Hardy raised his wings, indicating he needed silence so he could respond. Plato also motioned for the group to quiet down. "The crows will not leave this area; this is their home. They wish for a peaceful solution to the issue."

"We'll give 'em what's coming to 'em if they try to move into the woodlot, and it won't be peaceful," hollered the blue jay who had spoken earlier.

"Please let me finish," said Hardy. "The immediate threat is Antus and his group. If we don't deal with that threat and find a way to prevent war, there'll be a terrible price to pay. There'll be bloodshed and deaths on both sides. Here's what I suggest: I think you should continue the perimeter patrol for another day. Let me meet with Nestor and Justine and see if they've developed a plan. There are more crows than most of you think; I've learned that in the last day or two. And they have a powerful army. Nestor and Justine are speaking with the leader of the army to see if they can come up with a solution to what Antus is trying to do. They've been reluctant to go after Antus with force as they think we may see that action as a threat against us. Then if we were to respond with force, the whole thing could just get out of control."

"I think Hardy's made a good point here," said Plato. "We can stay in a defensive mode for another day. We have enough force to deal with Antus and his group if they return." Plato looked at Hardy for several seconds and then turned back to the group. "We'll let him speak again with the two crows, Nestor and Justine. But someone else needs to accompany him. I'll go along and make my own assessment of the two crows and the situation. It makes sense to try to find a solution that avoids conflict and bloodshed."

"You could fall into a trap, Plato," said one of the ducks.

"I'll take the chance. I'm old and probably won't be around much longer anyway. But I have the experience to make sound judgments about this. I say we continue the patrols tomorrow. Hardy and I'll go and meet with the two crows." Plato paused. No one said anything. "It's settled then."

"I don't like it," yelled the blue jay. "But since everyone else is agreeable, I'll wait. But if we don't have a plan for putting an end to this by tomorrow evening, I'm going to call for an attack on the crows. We can't sit here and wait to be attacked in our homes."

Plato stared at the blue jay with an expression that showed clearly that he would not tolerate rabblerousing. "We have a plan. Everyone needs to stay calm. We must all work together in everything we do. Unity in this effort is not only essential for success but lives depend on it." Plato then looked at the blue jay again and spoke in a loud and booming voice. "Anyone, and I mean anyone, who starts trouble will be run from this group and from the woodlot by me personally. Meeting adjourned."

"Hardy, I'll meet you about an hour after the sun rises at the woodlot perimeter," said Plato. "Good night."

"Good night, sir. Thanks for trusting me."

Chapter 25

It was dark as Plato floated alone in the lake, the moonlight shimmering on the surface and illuminating the surrounding forest. He had been alternately sleeping and listening to the songs of the night that he loved so much. Drifting in among the reeds and cattails, he now paddled slowly out into the open water to greet the morning and be warmed by the first rays of sunlight. It had been a peaceful, restful night even though Plato had much on his mind.

As Plato paddled into open water, the lake grew quiet. It grew darker and when Plato looked up he could no longer see the moon or stars. The water grew warm and the air thick. Plato recognized the signs. As he glanced back toward the reeds, there was his father. Or the image of his father, whatever this vision really was. Plato turned and paddled softly toward the image of his father. He stopped and stared but said nothing. Finally the silence was broken.

"Plato, what have you done? Things are a mess. How will you keep your promise now?"

"Things are as they are, Father. But it's not my doing. I am doing all I can to keep my promise to you. I'm hopeful that there is an answer in this crisis."

"The woodland is on the verge of war. How can there be an answer in that? You'll never keep your promise now."

"I believe that longstanding wrong sometimes requires a crisis to resolve it. Sometimes even violence is necessary before the wrong is recognized and appreciated for what it really is. I don't know how this will turn out. I can't control everything. I can only do my best. I'm not responsible for the crisis that exists just like you are not responsible for the injustice that exists. We do what we can. And that is what I am doing: my best. All that I can."

"I'm disappointed, Plato." His father stared hard into Plato's eyes. Plato held his father's stare until his father spoke again. "I appreciate what you have tried to do."

"I'm doing all I can, Father. And I think there is opportunity here."

"Time is short, Plato. Good-bye." The image rapidly faded from view. Plato turned and swam into the open water of the pond to greet the new day and all it held in store.

Chapter 26

Hardy woke at daybreak and checked on his brother. Laslo was asleep or unconscious, Hardy wasn't sure. But Laslo's breathing was regular and not labored as it had been the day before. As Hardy looked at Laslo, he was suddenly aware of how many wounds Laslo had received. He was covered with dried blood and moss bandages. Hardy was worried about Laslo, and as the memory of yesterday's events entered his mind, he thought of his father, his brave father who had defended his sons fearlessly. Hardy was determined to be a brave duck and do whatever it took to prevent a war with the crows. He would honor his father's sacrifice by the way he conducted himself from this day forward.

Hardy ate a quick breakfast Mother had left for him. As he prepared to leave the nest, he waddled over to where his mother was sleeping. He pressed his cheek against hers.

"Good morning. You're a good son, Hardy," said Mother.

"I'm sorry I woke you, Mother. I was leaving and wanted to … well, just be close to you before I left. Is Laslo sleeping or is he unconscious?"

"You didn't wake me. Your brother hasn't awakened since he passed out after returning to the nest. But he seems to be resting peacefully."

"Is he going to be okay?" asked Hardy.

"Only time will answer that question. Where are you off to?"

"I'm meeting Plato. I need to, uh, show him something I think is important." Hardy didn't want to worry his mother by telling her he was meeting with crows.

"Plato? You're meeting with Plato? My goodness but you never cease to amaze me." Mother looked at Hardy with an expression of love and pride. "Be careful. I'll watch after Laslo, and if he wakes up, I'll tell him you love him."

"Thanks, Mom. I love you. Good-bye."

"Good-bye, Hardy."

Hardy left the nest and quickly flew to the meeting place. He was a little early so he took the opportunity to grab a quick snack. He figured he would have a busy day and wasn't sure when he would get a chance to eat again. Hardy looked up and spotted Plato flying to the meeting place. Hardy took off and landed next to him in a large hickory tree.

"Good morning, sir," said Hardy nervously. Plato was the leader and everyone admired him. Being alone in his presence was a little intimidating for Hardy.

"Good morning. Right on time; that's good. Punctuality infers reliability. Both are good traits."

"Thank you, sir. Are you ready to get going? The flight's not long but I think it would be wise to try and get there first. That way you can see how many crows approach and won't have to worry about a trap, uh, if you are worried."

"I quit worrying a long time ago. Things will be what they will be. You're a good boy and I trust you. My instincts tell me we'll be fine." Plato looked at Hardy with a slight smile. "And no more of that 'sir' stuff. My name's Plato."

"Yes, sir, uh, I mean Plato, sir," Hardy laughed. "I'm sorry it's just that you're … well … I don't know but I'll try to call you Plato."

Plato laughed loudly. "I like you." Plato paused briefly and then spoke softly to Hardy. "You had a terrible experience yesterday, witnessing the death of your father. How are you handling it? Are you doing okay?"

"I try not to think about it. When I do, it makes me feel like crying. I feel guilty that he died saving me. It isn't fair and I wish it didn't happen."

"You're not to feel guilty. You did a brave thing and were willing to put your life at risk to save your brother. Your father did the same thing for you." Plato put his wing on Hardy's back. "I've been around a long time. During that time I've lost a lot of good friends. I've seen a number of ducks and other birds killed. It's the way of nature; nature's way of renewing the world. Your father understood this."

"I know you're right, but I still wish it didn't happen."

"Of course you do. But wishing for something different than what nature ordains is foolishness. You need to look at life, not just your father's but all life and put it in perspective with all that has existed, all that exists now, and all that ever will exist. Listen to me. Do you think your father was a great duck?"

"Of course I do."

"You're right to think so. He had a great soul. He understood that our lives are just a blink in time. Do you think someone with a great soul and who understands nature and the great expanse of time in the past and the great expanse of time that lies ahead would think their own life to really be of great importance?"

"Well, I guess not," answered Hardy.

"Of course not, do you think the thought of death would frighten such a soul?"

"No. Not really."

"Your father wasn't afraid yesterday. He did what he did because it was the right thing for him to do because he had a good soul. He could not have lived with himself if he had let that hawk get you. He was going to do whatever he had to do to save you, just like you were doing for Laslo. Cherish the memory of your father but move on and enjoy the life your father gave you and all it offers. The only thing we can be sure of is this moment. Nothing else is guaranteed."

"You speak of my father as if you knew him," said Hardy.

"I did know him, Hardy. He was my brother."

"Really? You're my uncle?"

"Yes, I'm your uncle."

Hardy and Plato stood quietly for several minutes, each lost in thought. Finally Hardy spoke. "Thank you, Plato. I think I understand what you said and I feel better now. We need to be going. Are you ready?"

"Yes. Let's go."

Chapter 27

Hardy and Plato took off and flew directly to the place where they would meet with Nestor and Justine. No other birds were allowed to follow. The two had settled in and were talking when they saw two crows approaching.

"There they are," said Hardy, pointing. "That's Nestor and Justine."

Nestor and Justine circled and seemed to be hesitant about landing. Hardy waved and immediately Nestor and Justine banked and landed about ten feet away.

"Good morning, Nestor. Good morning, Justine," said Hardy.

"Good morning," responded Nestor and Justine in unison. They then looked at Plato. Plato said nothing but stared back at them.

"This is Plato," said Hardy. "He's the wisest bird in the woodlot and he's our leader."

"Hello," said Justine. "It's a pleasure to meet you."

Nestor nodded at Plato. "Hello."

"Good morning. Hardy's told me a lot about you two. He tells me you're working to prevent war. He's also certain you can be trusted." Plato paused and considered their reaction. They didn't react at all except for a brief look Justine gave in Nestor's direction. "And disregard what Hardy said about my being the wisest bird in the woodlot. I'm just very old and have seen a lot. Others trust my judgment, but that doesn't necessarily mean I'm wise."

"I hope you don't mind Plato coming here with me. It's the only way I could, er-uh, I mean, we could prevent the birds from taking some kind of action in revenge for the attacks on the nests."

"It's fine. We've arranged for you, Hardy, to meet with Alexander later. Things are critical right now, and if we don't cooperate, the whole thing could easily erupt in widespread violence." Nestor paused and then continued. "Alexander's a good leader. He wants to prevent war. But he has a lot of pressure on him. Many are convinced the birds will attack the pine grove because of what Antus has done. This may be our last chance."

"Plato? Why, you're the duck who prevented the crows from being chased from the pine grove years ago." Justine was surprised it took her so long to realize Plato was the same duck Alexander had spoken about. "You're the one, aren't you?"

Hardy looked puzzled and awaited Plato's answer expectantly. "I'm not that duck. That duck was my father. That was a long time ago and not important now."

"It may not be important to you but it is to me. Your father did a very just thing," said Justine, "a wonderful and courageous thing."

"It appears you were able to convince your father to speak with the other birds then. Is that how you ended up here with Plato?" asked Nestor.

Hardy looked down and then raised his eyes. "My father's dead. He was killed by a hawk yesterday. He died saving Laslo and me."

"Oh, that's terrible. I'm so sorry," said Justine. She walked over a put her wing on Hardy and gave him a hug.

"I'm sorry too, Hardy," said Nestor.

"Actually, Hardy saved Laslo's life. Hardy's incredibly brave. He put himself in an almost certain death situation to save his brother from that hawk," said Plato. "It was his bravery that impressed the other birds so much that they gave us another day to find a way to achieve peace. Hardy spoke to the group last night, taking his father's place, and did an amazing job."

Justine gave Hardy another hug. "I told you he was special," said Justine.

"He certainly is," said Nestor. "Is Laslo okay?"

"No. He was hurt bad. He's unconscious. We're not sure he'll recover."

"Oh heavens," exclaimed Justine.

"Well, I hope Laslo recovers. I know he doesn't like us much but he's a good brother to you and we like him," added Nestor.

"Thanks, everyone," said Hardy. "We should get down to business now. What're we gonna do? Do you have a plan?"

"Well, we do have a plan, I think. It's up to Alexander. He won't commit until he meets you, Hardy. He thinks too much is at risk to commit to any plan unless he meets you personally. We're supposed to bring you to him in about an hour from now."

"Hardy won't be going without me," said Plato. "I'm on a mission on behalf of the residents of the woodlot to determine if we can trust you. If Hardy goes somewhere today, then I go with him."

"Actually, I think that'll work to our benefit," answered Nestor. "It'll be good if the two leaders can meet and talk. If we can adopt a plan, we can act much more quickly if both leaders are in agreement from the start."

The four spent the next half hour discussing the situation at length. Justine and Nestor got to know Plato better and indicated, privately to Hardy, they were impressed with Plato's intelligence and wisdom. Finally, Nestor said it was time for them to depart and meet with Alexander. "When we arrive it'll be best if you two circle the area. Let Justine and I go in and advise Alexander about Plato joining the conversation. I don't want any surprises that could cause things to fall apart. Plato, there'll be a few crows in the area for the protection of Alexander; there's some concern he could fall into a trap of some sort."

"I understand. There was similar concern on our end when I decided to come with Hardy. We'll stay clear until you indicate we can join you. Are we ready?"

"Yes. Follow us." Nestor and Justine took off. Hardy and Plato left right behind them. They flew together in groups of two; Nestor and Justine flew side by side with Hardy and Plato about a hundred yards behind.

"Are you comfortable with this?" Hardy asked Plato.

"Of course, I told you I don't worry much anymore. And you, are you okay meeting Alexander?"

"I'm a little nervous. But I trust Nestor and Justine. I don't think they would take me anywhere unsafe."

"I agree. I think your assessment of these two was right on target. They seem to be truly interested in keeping the peace."

Nestor hollered back, "We're approaching the meeting place. It'll be in that group of trees up ahead. Watch where Justine and I land and then give us a few minutes and someone will indicate to you when it's okay to land."

"I prefer that you be the one that indicates to us that we can land, Nestor," said Plato.

"Okay. I'll do it." Nestor and Justine then dropped into a glide path for a landing while Hardy and Plato circled the area at a safe distance. They watched as three crows intercepted Justine and Nestor. There appeared to be a brief conversation, then Nestor and Justine continued in and landed among the tree limbs. The three crows then circled the area and spaced themselves in a way that allowed them to both observe Hardy and Plato while keeping a wary watch on the entire flight area around the landing site.

Several minutes passed and then Nestor flew out and intercepted Hardy and Plato. "It's okay. We can all go in. Alexander's actually excited that you're here, Plato. He said he's heard a great deal about you. He said he heard you're wise and just."

"Obviously he's been listening to someone who doesn't know me well," joked Plato. Hardy and Nestor laughed and then the three dropped into their glide path and landed.

Nestor introduced Hardy and Plato immediately upon their arrival.

"Greetings, Hardy. It's nice to finally meet you. Nestor and Justine have told me a lot of good things about you."

"It's nice to meet you, Alexander sir. I hope I can live up to your expectations."

"And this is Plato. Plato, Alexander." The two stared at each other briefly. There appeared to be a look of recognition as if the two had met before. Then Plato spoke.

"It's an honor and a pleasure to meet you, Alexander."

"The honor and pleasure is all mine. I've heard stories from time to time about you since I was a child. I think it'll be very helpful to have your experience, wisdom, and judgment available as we try to resolve the crisis that's developed."

"I hope I can be of valuable service," replied Plato. "Shall we get started? Maybe he or she with the most comprehensive information regarding what has happened and how we got to where we are at this time should begin, if that's acceptable to all present of course."

"I think we should let Nestor speak, and when or where it's needed, others can add pertinent information to avoid confusion or to fill in any missing information that they consider important," offered Alexander.

Everyone agreed and Nestor provided a thorough overview that touched on the needs and concerns of the crows, Alexander's role as leader of the army, how Antus became a renegade, how Nestor and Justine met Alexander, how they both met Hardy, and what they knew of the recent attacks on the nests by Antus and his gang. Nestor's overview was accurate, complete, and concise. Occasionally one or another added something they thought was a key component to the discussion or to help clarify something. The overview conversation lasted nearly an hour.

Plato, who had remained quiet up to this point and just listened, then spoke. "So, that gets us to where we are now. The big issues that remain are to determine what we can do to set things right between us all and also try to meet everyone's needs and wishes regarding living arrangements, if all that's possible. But first we need a plan for dealing with Antus and stopping the raids. Is that an accurate assessment of what we should try to address from this point? And do we all agree that priority one has to be to deal with Antus and his group?"

"I certainly agree with all you said," said Alexander. "Nestor, how about you, are you in agreement?"

"I agree."

"Justine?"

"I agree."

"And, Hardy, how do you feel about what Plato said?"

"I agree. Heck, it seems pretty obvious that Antus has to be stopped before we can do anything else." Everyone laughed at Hardy's comment. Justine giggled longer than the rest.

"So, does anyone have any thoughts on how best to deal with Antus?" asked Plato.

Alexander answered immediately. "Nestor presented me with an interesting idea. I've thought about it since and I think we have a plan that not only will work but may be acceptable to everyone. I shared this plan late yesterday with the elders in the pine grove and they'll support it. For the record, no one in the pine grove other than some of my troops knew of what Antus has been up to. Shall I brief you on the plan?"

"Go ahead," said Plato.

"Well, we have two competing concerns. We know we have to deal with

Antus and put a stop to what he's doing. I'm reasonably certain the birds in the woodlot are concerned with what all crows are up to since Antus's raids."

"That's true," answered Plato.

"I'm concerned and so are many other crows that the pine grove could be attacked as a means of defense of the woodlot. Therefore, I can't utilize all my forces to go after Antus. You're facing a similar challenge. If you send sufficient forces after Antus, you won't be able to defend the woodlot."

"All true," said Plato.

"So, this is what I propose. I think—"

"We should join our forces? By doing so we can defend both the woodlot and the pine grove and still search for Antus," offered Plato.

"Wow. That didn't take long," said Alexander. "So, what do you think? I have some thoughts on how to deploy the forces. It's important everyone is comfortable with the plan."

"I think this approach might work," said Plato. "Let's hear your thoughts."

"All right," yelled Justine, unable to contain her excitement.

"All right," yelled Hardy. Justine and Hardy both laughed and gave each other a hug.

"Can we get back to the issues? If you're done playing, that is?" asked Nestor.

"Lighten up, Nessy," said Justine playfully.

"Yeah, lighten up, Nessy," said Hardy. Everyone laughed, including Nestor.

"Okay. I've lightened up," said Nestor, making a funny face with his eyes squinting and his wings spread out in front of him at a forty-five degree angle.

"These are my thoughts, Plato," said Alexander. Everyone quieted down and focused their attention on Alexander. "I'll place enough crows at your disposal so they can be deployed in the woodlot. To be sure you and the others are okay with that, you can choose the number so that you have a three to one or greater advantage in numbers in the woodlot. I'll keep enough forces in the pine grove sufficient for an initial defense, no more. That'll provide a balance in forces that should give everyone peace of mind." Alexander paused and looked intently at Plato awaiting his response.

Plato thought for a few moments and then answered. "It has promise, as long as we can agree on the numbers. So how do you propose we deal with Antus?"

"I'll send out a force great enough to overpower and either kill or capture Antus and his gang. You can send some of your forces along if you want, to monitor and observe. But any attack on Antus must be by crows only. That's important. If Antus is attacked by a force other than crows, it could incite further trouble."

"I agree; only crows should attack Antus. I'm not sure we need to send any forces with yours on that mission. I'll think on that a bit." Plato paused briefly; he seemed a little tired. "So, what if your forces can't find Antus? What if Antus eludes them and tries to attack the woodlot again? How will we handle that?"

"If Antus approaches the woodlot, the forces I've deployed there will fly out and intercept him. They'll kill or capture him and his gang. Your forces will stay near the woodlot perimeter. If by some chance any of Antus's gang get past my forces, you can defend your homes without any objection from me or any other crows. This plan will work if you allow me to deploy sufficient forces in or near the woodlot to effectively deal with Antus if he attacks. Hopefully, we'll find and capture him elsewhere, but if not, I'll need enough force—probably no more than twenty-five to thirty crows. Antus and his gang are not very good fighters and they're not in fighting shape; they're just mean-spirited. My forces, in the numbers I just mentioned, can deal with them quickly."

"Where will you be?" asked Plato.

"I think I should be with you in whatever location gives you comfort."

"I agree. You and I should be together. But I also think Hardy, Nestor, and Justine should be with us. I think if the others in the woodlot see us together interacting as friends and trusting one another, that'll give them all a feeling of safety. It'll foster greater cooperation from everyone. I also think that if you're successful in taking down Antus and putting an end to the attacks there will be a much greater chance of your other objectives being met. Everyone would see you and your crows as friends and not as threats."

"Do you mean you think the crows can move into the woodlot?" asked Hardy.

"If we can pull this off together and things go like we've planned, then I'll use all my influence to make it happen. I think we'd all be better off getting along and living together peacefully than to go on being suspicious of each other. The present living situation is what has led to this crisis and, if unresolved, will lead to more in the future."

"You are the wisest, most-just duck in the whole world," yelled Justine. "And you're the sweetest."

"Goodness. Thank you but I deserve no credit for this. I think most of the credit goes to you, Nestor, and Hardy. If you three hadn't had the courage to trust one another, we wouldn't be here right now. And, Alexander, thank you for exercising such restraint. That took courage. I know you were under a great deal of stress the past few days."

"Thank you. But I agree with you that Hardy, Justine, and Nestor have made this happen. Justine was right, Hardy—you are very special. And, Plato, you are as wise and fair-minded as I've heard. I look forward to our continued friendship. So, let's nail down some details and then we can go prepare everyone. I think we should try to implement this tomorrow, if possible. One more attack by Antus and we may miss our opportunity."

Chapter 28

Plato and Hardy said good-bye and left to return to the woodlot. They flew side by side for a few minutes in silence and then Plato spoke.

"Hardy, when we meet at the lake this evening, I want you right next to me. Understood?"

"Sure, if you want me there, I'll be there. But don't you think it would be better if—"

"No, I don't," said Plato abruptly. "But let me do the speaking. If I think you need to speak, I'll prompt you. I want you right next to me the whole time."

"Yes, sir," said Hardy.

"My name is Plato. It's not sir. I want you to call me by my name, especially at the lake tonight."

"I'll remember, Plato." Hardy smiled at Plato and shook his head in disbelief that he had developed such a close relationship with the most important bird in the woodlot.

As they neared the woodlot, Plato spoke again. "You need to go home and check on Laslo and determine if your mother needs your help. I'll see you tonight at the lake, same time as last night. Be prompt. Better yet, be a little early." Plato then banked and disappeared into the woodlot. Hardy continued home and landed in the nest. Mother was standing next to Laslo, who was sitting up. When Hardy landed, Mother turned and smiled.

"Welcome home, Hardy. Look who is back among us and wide awake."

"Laslo," yelled Hardy as he quickly waddled over to where Laslo was seated. Hardy reached out and threw his wings around Laslo, and they both began crying. "I thought you were going to die."

"Not a chance. I still need to get even with you for that trick you played on me." Laslo smiled briefly. "Thanks for saving me. You have to be the bravest duck in the whole world, or the dumbest. I can't believe what you did to save me."

"I'll leave you boys alone to talk while I clean up the nest," said Mother, moving to the other side of the nest.

"You're my younger brother. I've always had to look after you and probably always will. It's the burden that's been assigned to me."

"You are so full of it. If I've told you once I've told you a hundred times: there is nothing I can't do better than you. But anyway, thanks again for what you did for me."

"Well, it's apparent you're still the same old Laslo. I was hoping that hawk knocked some sense into you."

"Thanks to you that hawk didn't touch me or maybe he would have knocked some sense into me."

"The hawk didn't touch you?" asked Hardy.

"No. You were there and saw it all. You kept him off me."

"I thought the hawk hurt you. How did you get injured if the hawk didn't do it?"

"It wasn't the hawk. It was Antus and his gang. They tried to kill me. I think they would have but I was able to get away, barely."

"Antus and his gang did this to you? How? There is no way they could catch you. You can outfly any crow and you and I both know it."

"It was my fault. I did something really stupid. I went to talk to Antus. I thought if I told them just how upset everyone here was I could convince him to stop the raids."

"Good Lord, Laslo. You are crazy. It's a miracle you're still alive. You heard what Nestor said about Antus. You knew he was dangerous. Why would you do something so stupid? We were putting a plan together to deal with Antus. I don't understand."

"Well, first, I don't trust Nestor, at least I didn't. I figured he was exaggerating about Antus being dangerous just to keep any of us from trying to stop him. And I didn't want to wait for some plan to be put together, especially by crows. I figured if I could convince Antus to stop the raids everyone would think I was a hero. I told you I did something stupid."

"That's an understatement. It was more than stupid. It was, uh, I don't know a word that can describe it. I can't believe you. Don't you remember what Dad told you? He said, 'Being brave doesn't mean being foolish.' Good Lord."

"Yeah, I remember. Promise me you won't tell Dad when he gets home. He warned me and I ignored him."

"When Dad gets home?" asked Hardy hesitantly.

"Yeah, promise me you won't tell him. He'll never let me leave the nest on my own again."

"I think you need to focus your energy on getting better and not on worrying about how much trouble you might be in. How are you feeling?"

"I'm sore, real sore. And stiff. But surprisingly, I don't feel that bad. I think I'll be able to fly tomorrow or the next day. I just need to move around a little and get loosened up."

"Don't try and rush things. You had a real close call," said Hardy in a rather authoritative manner.

"Look, you're my older brother but I'm not required to take orders from you. I'll know when I'm ready to fly."

"Well, I sure am glad you're okay. Why don't you try and get some rest. I need to talk with Mom."

"I don't need any more rest. Resting is all I've done lately. I think I'll try and stretch out a little and see if I can't get rid of some of this stiffness."

"That sounds like a good idea. I'll talk with you again later and fill you in on what's been going on." Hardy waddled across the nest to speak with Mother. As he did, he could hear Laslo making grunting sounds as he started to stretch. "Momma, Laslo thinks Dad's coming home. Didn't you tell him what happened?" asked Hardy.

"No, I didn't tell him. I thought I should wait until you were home and we could tell him together. Laslo pretends to be tough and strong but I'm not sure he'll handle this well." Mother's eyes were filled with tears.

"I'll tell him, Momma. I think it would be better if I told him alone."

"You're a good son. You're the strong one, always have been. Thank you. I need some time alone. I'm going to go collect some food and I'll return shortly. That'll give you some time alone with your brother."

"Okay, Momma. Be careful. I'm sorry you're sad."

"It'll be okay, Hardy. We're going to be fine. It'll just take a while to adjust," said Mother while looking at Hardy with an expression of pride. Hardy had never realized just how strong his mother was.

"I have to go to a meeting with Plato this evening, Momma. It'll be the same time as the meeting yesterday. Will you be back before I leave?"

"Yes. I'll be back in time." Mother turned and took flight from the nest.

Hardy looked across the nest at Laslo, who was still stretching. Laslo looked stronger than Hardy thought he looked earlier. Maybe Laslo would be able to fly in a day or two. Hardy took a deep breath and waddled over to where Laslo was stretching. "So, how do you feel? Are you getting the stiffness out?"

"I'm pretty sore but everything seems to be working okay. The stiffness is gone as long as I keep moving. I think I'll be able to fly in a day or so."

"Well, don't rush it. Take some short flights and stay near the woodlot until you're sure you have your strength and speed back. That hawk's probably still around."

"Yeah, I'll be careful. You were right about keeping an eye out for hawks. But I could have outflown that hawk if I hadn't been injured," said Laslo.

"No, you couldn't. Hawks are fast, really fast. They can fly much faster than us when they are dropping from above. Don't underestimate them. I thought I could outfly that hawk and get back to the woodlot. I was wrong. It wasn't even close."

Laslo looked at Hardy with a puzzled expression. "But you found a way to get away. How did you do it? Did you outsmart him somehow?"

"No. Father saved me from the hawk." Hardy paused and looked at Laslo. "If it wasn't for him, the hawk would have killed me."

"Wow," exclaimed Laslo. "I thought you got away from that hawk on your own. I didn't even see Dad in the area. How did he save you from the hawk?"

"Take a break from your stretching and sit down for a minute."

Laslo noticed Hardy spoke in a voice that sounded serious and noticed the sad, troubled expression on Hardy's face. Laslo sat down. "What happened? How did Dad save you?"

"Well, remember this: Dad couldn't outfly that hawk, so don't ever think you can. I'll tell you what happened but don't interrupt me. And listen closely because I'm only going to tell you this once." Hardy paused and remained silent for a full minute or more. Laslo just looked at him and waited quietly. "Do you remember what happened with the hawk? Do you remember how I flew in front of him and how he changed direction to avoid flying into me because I surprised him?"

"I remember. You were amazing; if it hadn't been for your doing that, the hawk would have had me for sure."

"Well, that bought you some time but not enough. The hawk circled up and was well above you in no time. I watched him and tried to keep myself in a good position, but I really didn't know what I was doing. The hawk started to dive on you again and I knew I couldn't surprise him again. So this time I thought if I flew in his path at just the right distance I could get him to stop going after you and get him to chase me. And it worked."

"I don't know what to say, Hardy. You—"

"Don't interrupt me, Laslo. Let me finish. The hawk turned and came after me, so I banked as hard as I could. I thought I would be able to make a sharper turn than he could because he was flying so fast. I've never seen anything move that fast. Never. Dad's fastest is slow compared to that hawk."

Hardy took a deep breath and continued. "I made a much sharper turn than the hawk, but he used his speed to gain altitude and get above me. Then he dove on me. I was flying as fast and as hard as I have ever flown and I couldn't get away from him. He was right on top of me when I saw Dad pass by; it was like a blur. I turned and looked. Dad flew right into the hawk. It was the only way he could save me." Hardy began to cry.

"What's the matter?" asked Laslo. "Why are you crying? What happened?" Laslo suspected the worst but didn't want his thoughts to go there. Hardy needed to tell him what happened.

"Well, I thought they were both killed. But then I saw Dad struggling to fly. I think he had been unconscious for a moment. He couldn't stop his fall and he hit the ground hard. But then he got up. I looked for the hawk and couldn't find him at first. But then I saw him. He had recovered and was going for Dad. I tried to turn and get back to help but it was too late. Dad looked for a place to hide but there was no place for him to go. Then Dad looked up at me and told me he was proud of us. And that he loved us. And then the hawk was on him. I watched the hawk kill him." Hardy had recovered and was no longer crying.

Laslo looked stunned. He just sat there staring at Hardy in disbelief. "Dad's dead? It's all my fault."

"It's not your fault. Anyway, it's not about you or me. Mom needs us to be strong and help out by taking care of ourselves."

"But it is my fault, Hardy. If I hadn't gotten hurt by those crows, that hawk would never have come after me. And you wouldn't have had to help and Dad wouldn't have had to do what he did to save you. It's my fault."

"No, it's not your fault. You shouldn't have gone to talk with Antus. That was stupid. And that's what got you hurt. But the hawk was just there. You had nothing to do with that. And even if you weren't hurt, the hawk would probably have attacked you. And, Laslo, you can't outfly a hawk. Dad knew what he was doing and he did what he felt he had to do. He gave us a chance to live and now we have to live our lives and be grateful. There's no one to blame. What happened, happened. It just is. Do you hear me? We owe it to Father. He was proud of you and told me so just before the hawk got him. So don't go blaming yourself for what happened. There's no blame, period. So promise me, no more blaming. We just keep our good memories of Dad. And we'll help Mom as best we can."

"You're right. I promise. I just can't believe Dad's gone." Laslo turned and sat down with his back to Hardy and started to cry softly.

Hardy checked the sky and realized it was nearly time to leave for the meeting. He glanced around and saw Mother returning to the nest. She landed and immediately noticed Laslo crying. She looked at Hardy with a questioning expression.

"I told him what happened to Dad. He's upset but he'll be okay."

"Thank you." Mother wrapped her wings around her son and gave him a long hug.

"I need to leave and go to the meeting. I'll be back later."

"Be careful, Hardy." Mother then turned and went to sit with Laslo.

Chapter 29

Hardy took off and headed for the lake. Along the way, his mind retraced the conversation that had taken place earlier with Alexander. He wanted to have all the facts straight in his head in case Plato asked him to say anything during the meeting.

As Hardy neared the lake, he could see that everyone had arrived. There was a great deal of chatter and activity. Hardy looked at the log in the lake but Plato was not there yet so he decided not to land until Plato arrived. Only a minute or two passed before Plato glided in and landed on the log. The chatter ceased and the lake got quiet. All eyes were on Plato. Hardy flew in and landed on the log next to Plato.

"Good evening. Right on time," said Plato with a slight smile.

"Good evening, Plato," answered Hardy.

Plato nodded, indicating his approval that Hardy had called him by name. Plato then turned to face the assembly of birds. He scanned the crowd, looking briefly at each bird.

A full minute or two passed before he finally spoke. "Greetings to all; it pleases me that so many are here. It demonstrates that all of you fully appreciate that we face a serious crisis." Plato paused for another ten seconds. "Hardy and I met with the two crows, Nestor and Justine. I've determined that Hardy's judgment was sound. They are good crows and can be trusted. We also met with the leader of the crow army. His name's Alexander and he's a remarkable crow, an intelligent and brilliant leader. He also has earned my trust."

"So ... what are we gonna do about the raids?" asked a blue jay hesitantly.

Plato looked up into the trees and spotted the speaker. It was the same blue jay who had received a warning from Plato the night before.

"I'm glad you asked. Sometimes I take too much time getting to the point. There's much to do and not much time to do it. We've developed and agreed to a plan of action. This is how—"

"We haven't agreed to anything yet," yelled the blue jay.

"Oh yes, you have. And don't interrupt me again," said Plato sternly. "Just in case there's a misunderstanding about what we're facing, let me clarify things. We are at war. Our woodlot and our homes have been invaded, but not by our neighbors the crows but a group of renegade crows who serve only their own selfish purposes." Plato paused briefly and then continued. "Now, you've selected me as your supreme commander in time of war. Unless you've lost confidence in me and want to remove me from that position, I intend to command decisively and without hesitation. I will not tolerate anyone who does not act in concert with the plan that's been developed. So, have you lost confidence in me?"

A chorus of voices rose in unison. "You're our leader, Plato. We'll follow you."

"Does anyone object to my serving as your leader in this crisis?"

No one said a word.

"Good. Let me remind everyone that in a time of war the penalty for failing to support the joint effort is severe, very severe. We've agreed to a plan and everyone, and I mean everyone, will support it. Anyone who disrupts this in any way will pay a heavy price. There's too much at stake for us to permit any individuals going off in some other direction. We must and we will be united in this effort. Is that clear? If there's anyone who objects, let him leave right now and find another place to live. That'll be much more preferable, I assure you, than the penalty you'll pay if you try to disrupt this plan."

Plato paused and again scanned every face in the crowd. "I'll continue. This is how we're going to deal with the crow raids." Plato then proceeded to lay out the details of the plan over the next fifteen minutes. There were some initial expressions of shock when Plato told them they would be cooperating with crows, but as he spoke and explained the plan, most concluded the plan made sense—if the crows could be trusted.

"So, there you have it. Now, I know some of you are still wondering if we can trust the crows. I do trust them. I wouldn't have agreed to this if I didn't trust them completely. They don't want conflict with us any more than we want conflict with them. It's in their interest to work with us and avoid a confrontation which would only lead to injury and death on both sides." Most of the assembly nodded in agreement.

"I have to tell you, Hardy has made quite an impression on me. He's a very special young duck. He's young but he has more courage coupled with sound judgment than anyone I've ever known. Hardy, do you trust the crows we met with today?"

Hardy had been listening to Plato and was surprised when he was suddenly complimented by Plato and asked to speak. Hardy turned and faced the assembly of birds. "I trust Nestor and Justine completely. I would trust them with my life. I would trust them not only with my life but with the lives of my brother and my mother. In the name of my father I tell you they are good. They can be trusted. And I trust Alexander."

"We have a lot to do," said Plato. "So let's get started with assigning roles and putting things in order. I want this done right. I want sound discipline and I want us prepared to implement this tomorrow. And I expect total and complete cooperation with Alexander's troops."

Plato kept Hardy by his side the whole evening while he assigned duties, gave direction, answered questions, and solved problems. Hardy was amazed by the quickness of Plato's mind and how he could attend to so many details. Hardy learned more about leadership in one evening working alongside Plato than he could have learned in a lifetime on his own. By dark, most of the details had been worked out and everyone knew their assigned roles.

"It's time to go home and get some rest. We don't know how long it'll take to find Antus and put an end to this. And if things don't go as planned, we could all be very busy." The birds began to depart and soon Hardy and Plato were alone.

"Thank you for everything you've done, Plato. I believe things are going to work out fine."

"Things will work out for the best regardless of how it comes about. And thank you for what you've done. You've given us an opportunity to prevent the loss of lives and maybe improve our lives in the process by working closer with the crows. It's very important to everyone's future well-being that they're permitted to move into the woodlot and live among us. Meet me at the edge of the woodlot just after sunrise. We'll have to go and meet Alexander and his troops so we can escort them back here and get them deployed properly with our forces."

"I'll be there. Oh, I haven't had the chance to tell you; Laslo's awake and doing well. He was weak from the loss of blood, I think, but it doesn't look like his injuries will be permanent or crippling or anything like that."

"That's good news. Give him and your mother my best wishes. Good night."

"Good night, Plato."

Chapter 30

The next morning Nestor and Justine met with Alexander and Paris. They took a brief flight and landed in an area where a large number of crows were assembled. These were the forces Alexander intended to use to implement the plan. The crows were dispersed in groups of five, and each group had a leader. Each group of five was matched with four other groups. There were five of these matched groups and there was a leader of each of these five larger groups. Each of these leaders reported directly to Paris. There were more than a hundred crows perfectly organized—an impressive sight for Justine and Nestor to see for the first time.

"Wow," said Justine as she stared in awe.

"You can say that again," whispered Nestor.

Paris approached Alexander, and the two exchanged greetings. Paris then briefed Alexander. "Our forces are assembled as ordered. The recognizance force has already left in their search for Antus and his gang. They left as a single group but will search in five groups of five. They were ordered to keep as much distance between their groups as possible in order to search large areas but to remain close enough together that they can regroup quickly and attack in force as a single unit."

"Excellent," said Alexander. "Who's leading the recognizance team?"

"I assigned Hector that task," replied Paris.

"Good choice. He'll do a great job," said Alexander. "Have your troops been fully briefed? I don't want any trouble in the woodlot with the other birds there. I don't want trouble from any of our troops even if they're provoked."

"I briefed them all personally. They know exactly what's expected and what the price will be if they misbehave. These are well-trained troops, Alexander; you know that. You oversaw their training yourself. There'll be no problems from us."

"Okay. We're ready to move out. You know the plan. I'll go with Nestor and Justine. We'll meet with Plato and Hardy. You'll stay off at a distance. If everything's in order, I'll advise you and you'll disperse our forces as planned."

"Yes, sir," answered Paris.

"And if anything goes wrong, if I am attacked or taken prisoner by the birds in the woodlot, you're not to do anything. Understood? You return to camp and put together a plan based on whatever situation exists at the time. I have complete faith and trust in you to do the right thing."

"I understand and I appreciate the faith and trust you've placed in me. I won't disappoint you. Don't you trust Plato?"

"I know you won't disappoint me. I trust Plato but you never know what a large group filled with anger may do. I'm reasonably sure everything will be fine. Thank you for all your work last night. You've done a great job. Let's move out."

Alexander, Justine, and Nestor took off and flew toward the agreed-upon meeting area. As they flew, Paris got the army airborne. Nestor looked back, and what he saw was impressive. More than one hundred crows were perfectly assembled and flying in formation. The groups were tightly structured, each separated from the others with what appeared to be the exact same spacing. It was a sight to behold.

"Look, Justine," said Nestor, motioning for her to look behind them.

"Wow," said Justine breathlessly. Justine stared for a full ten seconds and then glanced over at Alexander. Alexander was completely focused ahead and appeared to be deep in thought. *What an amazing leader. He's the most impressive crow I've ever met*, she thought. Then she felt her heart race and she immediately turned and focused her attention ahead of her. But every so often she would sneak a brief look at Alexander, and each time her heart raced.

The three soon neared the meeting location. Up ahead, they saw Plato and Hardy approaching. Plato and Hardy circled and then dropped into formation with Alexander, Nestor, and Justine.

After they all exchanged greetings, Plato said, "Is everything ready to go as we agreed?"

"Yes. Our recognizance force is already out searching for Antus and his group. We're ready to deploy our forces in the woodlot when you give the approval. Is everything a go on your end?"

"We're ready. I do have a concern about one blue jay and a couple of his friends. He may try to act independently. He's been warned but I don't know if we can depend on him. I suggest you brief one of your best teams and assign them to him. If he or his friends get out of line, they have my approval to help stop him. I have some of my trusted troops keeping an eye on him also. They'll take him down if he gets out of line, but your troops can assist if needed."

"Understood; I'll go get that taken care of. When you're ready just give the signal and we'll deploy as your designated leader directs."

"Hardy will let you know when it's time. You and the four of us will deploy together in the top of that large tree there," said Plato, indicating the tree he had selected. "That's the perfect place, I think, for us to observe and direct the action if the need arises."

"That's an excellent location. I'll go brief Paris and the team about your concerns. Send Hardy when you're ready for us." Alexander flew off to brief Paris and the others.

Plato, Hardy, Nestor, and Justine flew to the tree that would serve as the command post. All the birds deployed along the perimeter of the woodlot had watched the interaction with Alexander and most could easily see the command post location.

Plato then spoke. "Hardy, I think you should pair up with and support Alexander. Nestor and Justine, I think you should work closely with me and support me. I'm old so it'll take both of you to support me. That kind of interaction between all of us will provide an example to the troops on both sides that we're all in this together as one team."

"Sure," said Hardy.

"No problem," answered Nestor.

"You can depend on me, Plato," said Justine. "I want this to go well. Antus needs to get what's coming to him."

"Justine, this is about stopping a war. It is not about giving Antus what you think he deserves. If we're successful and capture him rather than kill him, we can then concern ourselves with how to deal with him. I'm going to recommend you make that decision so you may want to think about what a fair and just sentence you'll pass if the opportunity arises." Plato looked at Justine. "I have every confidence that you'll find a perfect answer to that."

Justine looked stunned. "I don't think I'm qualified to do that."

"Sure you are. I just heard you say Antus needs to get what's coming to him. Obviously, you have that answer already in your mind. Right? Why else would you say such a thing?" Plato smiled at Justine. "You're well qualified for the job, Justine. All you have to do is make sure whatever you decide is fair and helps prevent any future problems with Antus or anyone else that may have similar ideas in the future. See? It's easy."

Plato looked around the perimeter of the woodlot. Then he looked toward the direction Alexander had gone. He could see all the crows flying in formation, circling the area. "Hardy, go to Alexander and tell him to deploy his troops. Nestor, you fly along the perimeter in that direction and pass the word that the operation has started and the crows will be deploying in the woodlot. Justine, you fly the perimeter in that direction and do the same. Then all of you return here."

"What then?" asked Hardy.

"Then we wait," answered Plato. "The commanders will make sure everyone gets a chance to forage for food, not only for themselves but for their families as needed." Hardy left to get Alexander. Nestor and Justine left, flying the perimeter of the woodlot and giving notice that the operation was starting and that the crows would begin deploying.

Plato watched Hardy fly out and join Alexander. They flew together briefly, and then Alexander began shouting orders. Immediately others began to shout instructions, and then the crow units began to separate and most headed for the woodlot. Hardy led one group to an area of the woodlot where the blue jay was stationed and then flew back and joined Alexander. They flew to one end of the woodlot and then along the entire perimeter while Alexander checked the deployment.

Occasionally, Alexander shouted instructions to some crows or birds not properly secured and who could be easily spotted by Antus if they approached. After they flew the entire perimeter, Alexander and Hardy returned to the command post and joined Plato. Nestor and Justine had also returned.

"Everything seems to have gone well, Alexander," said Plato.

"Yes. Your forces were deployed just as we'd discussed, and they seemed to welcome ours without reservations. That's good. We have one of our most trusted group leaders with the blue jay you were concerned about. And we have two groups back by the lake area with some of your troops in case Antus tries to come through the back door."

"Great. I'm pleased. We have a schedule established for our troops to collect food, so the activity will appear normal," said Plato.

"My troops are also on a schedule to leave for food. One member from each group will go through the woodlot and use the lake and the area in the rear for food and drink. We can expect a messenger by early afternoon and another just before dark advising us how the recognizance team is doing."

"I suggest we get comfortable. We could be here for some time." Plato sat down, lowered his head, and fell asleep. Alexander sat down and seemed to be resting but did not sleep. Hardy, Nestor, and Justine moved away some distance, sat, and talked quietly.

Chapter 31

everal days passed with no sign of Antus. The recognizance force reported that a few times they were close to catching up with Antus, having found evidence of a roosting area that obviously belonged to Antus's gang. However, the areas appeared to have been abandoned just prior to the arrival of the troops.

Everything was going well at the woodlot. The cooperation was good and the feeding schedules were working effectively. It was apparent, though, that the confinement was starting to wear on everyone. Alexander and Plato were concerned about the possibility of tempers growing short and problems developing as a result. They had even discussed suspending operations for a day to give everyone a break. However, after conferring with the various commanders and group leaders, they decided the operation could be maintained for another three days before a break was needed. If the commanders and group leaders saw any evidence of problems, they would report them and the situation would be reassessed.

Laslo had made great progress. He had gone out on several flights, and his most recent trip lasted the better part of a full day. Mother had gone with him on most of his flights, until she was sure he was capable of taking care of himself. After Hardy got home each night, he and Laslo would talk about what was going on with the defense operation. Laslo wanted to be part of the operation and pressured Hardy to ask Alexander and Plato to assign him a role.

On day five of the operation, Hardy approached Plato and Alexander.

"Excuse me, could I speak to both of you briefly about something that's kind of important to me?"

"Sure, Hardy. What is it?" answered Alexander. Plato nodded his approval.

"It's about Laslo. He's recovered and is nearly back to full strength. He's been flying and is ready to resume a normal routine."

"That's great," said Plato. "What will that normal routine be under these circumstances?" Plato glanced at Alexander, and they exchanged brief smiles.

"Well, he and I were wondering if you would let him join the operation. We were wondering if you had a role for him." Hardy seemed a little uncomfortable bothering Plato and Alexander with a concern about one duck. But this one duck was his brother, and he thought having Laslo involved in some way might help Laslo get over any lingering guilt he was feeling about Father.

"What did you have in mind?" asked Plato.

"Well, I didn't have anything specifically in mind. I was hoping you would know where to place him."

"Where's Laslo right now?" asked Alexander.

"He's at home."

"Why don't you go get him and bring him here? Plato and I can then judge for ourselves what we think he's capable of doing," said Alexander.

"Great, I'll be right back. It will only take a minute or two. We live right over there," said Hardy, pointing.

"I know where you live," said Plato. "Get going."

Hardy left and returned a couple of minutes later with Laslo. "This is my brother, Laslo," announced Hardy.

"We assumed it was Laslo and that you had not left and brought back some other duck," said Plato with a big grin. "It's nice to meet you, Laslo."

"Thank you, sir. It's an honor to meet you." Laslo spoke timidly and appeared to be nervous.

"I'm Alexander. Hardy's told us about your being injured. It seems you've recovered well. I'm glad you're feeling better."

"It's an honor to meet you, Alexander. Hardy's told me about the two of you. He says you two are the most amazing birds he's ever met."

"Well, that was nice of him. But your brother's pretty amazing himself," said Plato. Laslo just nodded in agreement.

"I understand you don't like crows. Is that correct?" asked Alexander.

Laslo looked shocked and a little embarrassed. "Well, sort of. I mean, I used to not like crows. I met Nestor and Justine and they seemed nice, but I didn't trust them. I don't know why. There are still some crows I don't like very much, like Antus and his gang."

"Antus and his gang are not easy to like," said Alexander. "But try to understand, most of that group was led astray by Antus. I know all of them. A few are mean-spirited just like Antus, but not all of them."

Justine was listening closely and appeared surprised to hear Alexander say that.

"Well, all of them seemed pretty mean to me," answered Laslo. Everyone laughed.

"Well, I guess we understand why you feel that way," said Alexander.

"Hardy tells us you want to help with the operation. Is that correct?" asked Plato.

"Yes, sir. I'll do whatever you tell me to."

"You'd better, if we decide to give you an assignment," said Plato.

Laslo lowered his head, embarrassed.

"Okay. I suggest you fly with the recognizance team. They're all crows and they're out on a search and destroy mission, looking for Antus and his gang. How's that sound?"

"They're all crows?" Laslo looked at Alexander. "Will I be safe with them?"

"Safety is never guaranteed in this world, especially at a time of war. But the team won't hurt you. In fact, they'll defend you as they will any member of the team."

"Sure, I can do that."

"There's one condition. You're not to engage in any fight with Antus and his gang. You stay back and watch. You'll learn a great deal from what you see. Only crows are to attack other crows unless Antus and his gang somehow make it to the woodlot."

"Sure. I'm not real excited about fighting them anyway. Dad told me crows were tougher than I thought. He was right."

Alexander smiled. "Ducks are tough, too. But you haven't learned how to fight yet. And apparently you haven't learned when to fight and when to run."

"Oh, I've learned when to run. You can believe that," said Laslo. Everyone got a good chuckle from that remark.

"Yes, you probably have learned that lesson," said Plato. "One more thing. You're recovering from serious injuries. The recognizance team works very hard. If you get tired, you're to return home. Everyone will understand."

"Yes, sir. But I'm stronger than I look."

"I'll bet you are," said Alexander. "Okay, you'll join with the recognizance team tomorrow morning. You can stay here today if you like."

"I'm part of the recognizance team? Wow. Thanks everyone. Thanks, Hardy."

Chapter 32

The day passed uneventfully. The messenger arrived just before dark and advised that no contact had been made with Antus or any of his gang. The operation was shut down for the evening, and everyone returned to their homes with instructions to report back the next morning. Nestor complained about his head and bones feeling out of sorts. He said he thought a storm was coming and advised everyone to spread the word to be prepared.

That night a severe thunderstorm invaded the woodlot and the surrounding area. Lightning flashed, thunder crashed, and the winds thrashed the trees. The birds in the woodlot and the pine grove had a rough night, but all weathered the storm. They all woke to scattered clouds and intermittent rainfall with occasional glimpses of the morning sun.

Hardy and Laslo woke early. They decided not to tell their mother Laslo was going out with a team of crows searching for Antus. They reasoned there was no sense in worrying her needlessly. They sat and ate breakfast together without speaking. Mother was still asleep on the other side of the nest.

"Mom, we're heading out for the day. Laslo's going with me again."

"Good-bye, boys, be careful and make sure you get enough to eat. Watch the weather closely. I love you."

"Good-bye, Mom. I love you," said Hardy.

"Love you, Mom," said Laslo and he went over and pressed his face against hers. "Don't worry about us. We'll be fine." The boys took off from the nest and headed directly to the command post. As they flew, Laslo spoke. "Hardy, I want to thank you for asking Plato and Alexander to give me a

174

chance to participate. I really appreciate it. I won't do anything stupid. I'm pretty sure I've learned my lesson about not thinking before I act."

"No problem. That's what brothers do. But you be careful and no showing off. If you get tired just admit it, tell the team leader, and come back here. Okay? Promise me you'll do that." Hardy gave Laslo a look that communicated that he was still concerned about his physical condition.

"I'm in better shape than you think. I'm pretty sure I can keep up." Hardy gave Laslo another long look. "Okay. I promise if I get tired I'll come back." Hardy gave him another look. "And I promise I won't do anything stupid."

"Thank you. I trust you," said Hardy and then he rolled his eyes.

"I mean it. I promise."

"I'm kidding you. I think you know how important this is and the last thing you would want to do is let Plato and Alexander down."

"That's for sure. I don't think either of them will tolerate any nonsense."

"You can bet on it," said Hardy. "The command post is right up ahead. Let's land together, side by side."

"Sure, but my landing will be better than yours, as usual." The boys landed.

Plato was already there. He greeted them and then spoke in a commanding tone to Laslo. "You need to get going. Now you behave yourself and do as you've been instructed. If not, I'll personally deal with you. I may be old but don't underestimate what I am capable of."

"I'd never underestimate you, sir. I'll behave. And thank you for the chance you've given me. I'll do exactly what you've told me to do."

"Good. Now get going."

"Bye, Hardy." Laslo left, and Plato turned his back on Hardy and appeared lost in thought.

Hardy stood quietly by, reluctant to interrupt. Finally, he spoke. "Is there anything you want me to do? Is everything okay?"

"You don't need to do anything right now. And yes, things are okay. I'm just a little puzzled that no contact has been made with Antus. The recognizance team has been finding plenty of evidence that crows are around, but they haven't found Antus. That seems strange to me. Here come Alexander, Nestor, and Justine. And there's Paris leading his troops back." Alexander, Nestor, and Justine landed and everyone exchanged greetings. Plato and Alexander moved off to speak in private while Hardy, Justine, and Nestor engaged in idle conversation.

Laslo had flown out and met Paris, who immediately assigned him to the recognizance team. The team leader, Hector, greeted Laslo and gave him instructions. He told Laslo how they would search, where Laslo was supposed to fly within the group, and what to do if they encountered Antus. Laslo was instructed to remain at a distance, remote from any fighting. He was only to approach when the fighting was over and only after he had been summoned. Laslo assured Hector he would do exactly as instructed.

"You'd better," said Hector, giving Laslo a stern look. "I won't tolerate lack of discipline from my troops, and I sure won't tolerate it from you. I have every intention of finding Antus and dealing with him. I don't want you causing me any distractions."

"I'll do exactly what you have told me to do," responded Laslo. "I don't know what you've heard about me. I've learned a lot of lessons in the past week. I won't do anything stupid. I'll do exactly what you've told me to do. I promise."

"I heard you confronted Antus and his gang by yourself. That wasn't smart or brave, it was plain stupid. I don't want anything stupid happening on this mission." Hector paused and looked at Laslo "Okay. Let's go."

Hector shouted instructions to the team, and they spread out in their search formation. Laslo fell in with a group just behind Hector, who was out in front leading the formation. Several hours passed with no sign of Antus. The group reformed at Hector's command, and they landed near a small lake, drank some water, and foraged for food. Laslo was particularly hungry. He was still recovering his strength and Hector had maintained a vigorous pace. Laslo saw a yellow beetle, hesitated briefly, and then ate it. He saw two more, succumbed to his hunger, and ate them both. Laslo was a little concerned but hoped the exertion would keep him from developing any gas. Anyway, he needed the nourishment. After a brief period of rest they were off again, flying in search formation. About thirty minutes passed when Hector turned and flew back to the group where Laslo was assigned.

"Spread the word among the units. I've sighted a group of crows ahead. There's about fifteen of them; I think we've finally located Antus. Everyone's to stay in formation and remain quiet. All groups are to unite into attack formation on my command. I want the two outside groups to stay well to the outside of us. They're to flank Antus's group and come in from the rear. Now go." Hector then flew out to lead the way.

Laslo was excited; his heart was racing. Finally, Antus would get what was coming to him and Laslo would get to watch the entire thing. Laslo noticed the strength of these crows and the discipline among them. He was certain Antus and his rabble would be no match. Five minutes passed, and Laslo saw a wooded area in the distance. Just then Hector rocked repeatedly from side to side. This was the signal. The groups of crows moved in and joined forces. Laslo could see the outermost groups fly off to the left and right in their flanking movement. Laslo saw a group of crows landing in a field ahead.

Just as the last one landed, Hector screamed a command. "Attack!" The entire unit immediately began to descend on the group of crows. Laslo fell back and began to fly in a circle, staying at a safe distance.

The crows on the ground must have heard Hector's scream. They turned, looked at the attacking force, and began to try to fly off. But it was too late. Hector and his troops were on them and the fighting started. Laslo watched in awe. The combat was intense and violent. Laslo was relieved he wasn't in the fight.

Laslo looked up and beyond where the fighting was taking place. What he saw surprised him. The two flanking groups had both encountered groups of crows that outnumbered them at least three to one, and they were engaged in aerial combat. The crows were flying, diving, circling, and crashing into one another. It was entrancing to watch. Then Laslo saw something that shocked him to his core. A large group of crows, at least fifty in number, were flying directly in the direction of the fight. They had come from the wooded area ahead. Laslo immediately flew toward the area where Hector and his troops were engaged with the crows on the ground. Laslo yelled a warning.

"Hector!" screamed Laslo. "Hector, it's a trap. A large group of crows are coming." Laslo motioned in the direction of the oncoming crows. Hector looked, saw the approaching crows, and yelled orders to his troops, who immediately broke off their fight and took wing.

"Go warn Alexander. Tell him we'll engage these crows and try to slow them down. Now go," yelled Hector. Laslo immediately turned and began flying as fast as he could toward the woodlot. He briefly looked back. Hector and his troops had engaged the crows in aerial combat. But they were overwhelmed; the number of crows they had to deal with was just too great.

A large group of at least forty crows had passed through the battle lines while the remainder kept Hector and his troops engaged. The crows on the ground that Hector had originally chased and attacked had taken wing and were joining the group of forty. Laslo had seen enough. He turned and flew as hard and as fast as he could. He had to put as much distance as he could between himself and these crows so he could give Alexander as much advanced warning as possible.

In spite of his injuries, Laslo was still fast. He was quickly leaving the crows behind. He briefly felt some abdominal cramps from gas. He was concerned this might slow him down but it quickly passed. He had been flying hard for about twenty minutes when he finally saw the woodlot ahead. He looked back and could no longer see the pursuing crows. He had put a good deal of distance between himself and the crows. Laslo approached the woodlot and could see Paris and two other crows flying out to meet him. As they came together, Paris dropped in next to Laslo. He could tell Laslo had been flying hard and that he seemed troubled.

"What's wrong, Laslo?"

"Hector found Antus's group and attacked about fifteen crows on the ground," said Laslo breathlessly.

"Great," Paris exclaimed. "Hector will quickly deal with that group."

"No, it's not great. It was a trap. Maybe twenty-five more crows attacked Hector's two flanking units. Then at least fifty more crows came out of the trees. I was able to warn Hector, and he was able to get his troops in the air before the large group of crows arrived," said Laslo. "Hector sent me here to tell Alexander what happened. Hector engaged the crows in an attempt to slow them down but I saw at least forty, maybe more, get through his battle line. They were joined by ten or more crows that Hector had attacked on the ground. There must be at least fifty crows heading this way. I was able to outdistance them but I'm sure they're coming."

"Take him to Alexander," yelled Paris to one of the crows with him. "You follow me," he said to the other. Paris and the other crow flew off in the direction of his advance force. Laslo and the other crow flew toward the command post. As they did, Laslo saw that Paris had organized his advance forces, about fifteen in number, and they were heading out to intercept the enemy. Laslo looked back and saw the approaching crows. They'd be here in minutes.

Laslo landed at the command post and explained what had happened. Alexander immediately went into action. He gave Hardy instructions to fly down the tree line and tell the crows to advance and form on Alexander. Nestor was sent in the other direction with the same orders. Alexander flew out in front of the tree line so everyone could see him.

Plato instructed Justine to fly along the tree line after the crows had moved out. She was to tell the birds to remain in place and to not engage in any fighting unless Plato left the command post and moved out. Then they were to form on his right and left. Justine waited until the crows had left and began her flight along the lines. Hardy and Nestor returned to the command post and joined Plato.

"What are we going to do now?" asked Hardy.

"We'll just watch and see how Alexander does. He should be able to stop those crows. If any get through, we'll have to deal with them but only on my command."

Ahead, Paris had tried to engage the crows, but his force was too small. At least forty crows were heading toward the woodlot. Hardy looked at Plato to see if he was going to attack the oncoming crows. As Hardy watched, he saw movement off to his left along the tree line. It was the blue jay and about ten other birds. They were flying directly toward the oncoming crows in an attempt to engage them before Alexander's forces could.

"Look," yelled Hardy, pointing. "It's that blue jay."

Alexander saw the blue jay and the other birds. He deployed a team of twenty crows to prevent their advance. An aerial combat took place. The blue jay and smaller birds were more maneuverable than the crows, but there were at least two crows for each bird.

Alexander led a now depleted force of about thirty out against the oncoming crows. The attacking crows didn't hesitate at the sight of Alexander's forces but came on in a single tightly bunched group. The fight was on. Alexander was unable to use all of his troops to attack the tightly formed group. He held a number back, approximately fifteen, to use as reinforcements if any of his units that were engaged looked like they needed help.

Alexander's force was well trained and strong. They soon began to get the upper hand. A number of the invading crows had fallen to the ground. As they fell, Alexander sent the necessary number of troops from his reinforcements down to kill or capture them. In most cases, the injured crows refused to

James G. Tauber

surrender and were killed. As the battle waged, more and more of the invading
crows fell from the sky. The fight was nearly over and Alexander's troops had
captured about fifteen crows. There were three crows still engaged in aerial
combat. Alexander sent in about fifteen fresh troops and almost immediately
the remaining invading crows were taken to ground and killed.

In the interim, the blue jay and the remaining birds, seeing they had no
chance to engage the enemy, returned to their place in the woodlot. Two birds
had been injured and were held in protective captivity by a group of crows.
Plato sent Hardy down the tree line in one direction and Nestor in the other.
They were to tell all the birds to stand down. Plato was going to leave the
command post and they were to stay put. Plato looked at Laslo and Justine.

"You two stay right here. When Hardy and Nestor return, you tell them
to stay here. Understood?"

"Yes, sir," they answered.

Plato then took wing and began to fly out toward Alexander. Laslo
looked for Hardy and Nestor. They had completed their mission and were
returning.

"Oh no," yelled Justine, pointing almost straight up.

Laslo looked and he saw four, no five, crows heading for Plato. It was
Antus and some of his gang. They had stayed out of the fight and were
now sneaking in for one purpose—to kill Plato. Laslo looked again in both
directions. Hardy and Nestor were too far away to help.

"Stay here," yelled Laslo to Justine. Laslo took off and flew toward Plato
and yelled a warning.

Plato turned and saw Laslo flying in his direction. "I told you to stay
put."

Laslo flew right past Plato and up toward the attacking crows. Laslo
figured his best chance to save Plato was to attack Antus. Maybe if Antus
was taken out of action the others would break off the attack. Laslo climbed,
and as soon as he was near the same altitude as the crows, he banked hard
and went right at Antus.

Two crows broke off and turned toward Laslo to intercept him. Laslo flew
right at them at top speed and they banked away to avoid a collision. Antus
had turned his attention toward Plato, who was climbing to engage him.

Laslo focused on Antus and flew directly into him. The impact was violent
and Laslo grabbed the back of Antus's neck in his bill. The two spun wildly

and fell toward the ground with Antus struggling and screaming at the top of his lungs. About thirty feet from the ground, Laslo let go of Antus, spun off to his left, and regained flight. Antus could not recover and hit the ground hard. The two crows that had been with Antus had both banked hard in an effort to assist Antus but were too late.

Plato had zeroed in on one crow, and with great skill grabbed the crow by the neck, turned and flew toward the ground. As he neared the ground he released the crow. The crow then fell the final fifty feet and struck the ground with a thud. That crow remained motionless. Plato banked, climbed, and began searching for another crow to attack.

Nestor and Hardy approached the area. Nestor immediately attacked one of the crows. Hardy attacked another. They were engaged briefly when the three remaining crows broke off. Nestor immediately banked and dove straight down. He landed directly opposite Antus, who had recovered and was watching the action from below.

"Well, if it isn't the scriggly clown. I've been witing for this chince for eh long time. Now I'm going to show you whit—"

"Shut up, Antus. There's only you and me here now. The time for talk is over. You can give up and go with me peacefully or I have every intention of killing you here where you stand. Too many lives have been lost because of you and it's all going to end right now."

"You kin't kill me. I em a wirrior en you er just ... you're nothing. Nothing," yelled Antus.

Without any hesitation, Nestor went right at Antus. He moved so quickly he caught Antus completely off guard. There was only a brief struggle and Nestor had Antus pinned to the ground. Nestor had a tight grip on Antus and was using all his strength to drive his beak into Antus's neck.

"Nestor, let him up. There'll be no more killing. Antus will be our prisoner and will face our justice." It was Plato, and he spoke with a commanding tone. Nestor continued his attack on Antus. "Nestor, let him go."

Nestor looked up and saw Plato with Alexander. Just then Hardy and Laslo landed and almost immediately Paris and several other crows joined them. Nestor let go of Antus, who was immediately surrounded by several crows.

"Take him away," said Alexander. "But keep him safe. We'll deal with him later."

"You're nothing, ill of you. You're eh disgriss. You shouldn't be kelled crows," yelled Antus. "I should've killed you long ago, you scriggly clown."

"Should have, could have … you're done, Antus," replied Nestor.

Antus looked at Laslo with unveiled hatred. Then he turned his attention to Plato. "You, duck. I'll deal with you some diy. En when I do, be certain of this: there will be no mercy. I will kill you."

"I really doubt you could do thit no mitter how bid you mi wint it," replied Laslo with a smile. "Not where you're going."

Plato didn't respond to Antus but motioned to Paris. Paris directed several crows to take Antus into custody.

Suddenly, eight crows dropped from above and landed behind Antus, who smiled and then spoke. "I'm not going inywhere. We er going to kill you, ill of you."

Laslo groaned, bent over, and turned his back on the crows. This surprised Antus and the other crows, causing them to hesitate and not immediately attack. Just as Hardy started to go to Laslo and check on him, Laslo began passing gas. He had never eaten more than two beetles before, and one of those was small. This was a three-beetle performance. It started with a symphony of sound, ranging from low pitch to high pitch. The notes blended together and created a noise unlike anything anyone present had ever heard. After two seconds or so, the gas kicked into full gear, creating a high-pitched scream that could only be described as something between a squeal and a whistle. This lasted a good five seconds and then tapered off into a series of rumbles that sounded like distant thunder, ending with a slight fluttering noise.

Fortunately, Plato and his group were off to the side of Laslo and not directly behind him. Antus and his group were not so fortunate and neither were the crows Alexander had directed to take Antus into custody. They were all directly behind Laslo, downwind, and immediately rendered helpless by the gas. All started to gag. Several crows collapsed vomiting. Antus started trotting around in a circle. His wings were outstretched and he was heaving nonstop.

The stiff breeze quickly carried the worst of the gas away. Paris sent in some fresh crows to take Antus and his companions into custody, which was easily accomplished as all were incapacitated.

Antus stopped retching and, with eyes filled with tears, looked at Laslo. "You er the most disgusting duck in the world. I mik you a promise, here en now. I will kill you. Nothing that can do whit you just did should be illowed to live. You er good es dead. You ilready smell dead."

Laslo looked at Antus with a big grin on his face. "Careful what you say, Antus. There's a lot more where that came from." Laslo then looked at Plato and giggled like a fool.

Antus was then escorted away, screaming threats and insults at the top of his lungs. Plato looked at Laslo and shook his head.

"What am I going to do with you? I told you to stay put. But thank you for what you did, I think."

"I'm sorry I disobeyed you, sir. And I'm sorry about farting. I guess I shouldn't have eaten those beetles. But we can't afford to lose you. You are too important to all of us."

"Well said." Alexander was all smiles.

"You more than all should know the need for discipline, Alexander," said Plato.

"True, but I also know the need for bold initiative when it's necessary. Laslo did us all a great service in saving you. Although I admit his methods are unusual. And, Hardy and Nestor, you're both to be commended."

"Nestor, I am surprised at your fighting spirit," said Plato, "and your ability. You're big and strong but I didn't think you were the fighting kind."

"Thank you, both of you. I'm not a fighter. I don't aspire to that sort of thing. But I'm capable if the need arises."

"Laslo, you know better than to eat those beetles. What were you thinking?" asked Hardy.

"You know me. I wasn't thinking. I was hungry. But it appears everything worked out okay," said Laslo with a big grin. Everyone started laughing and shaking their heads.

"Laslo is now our secret weapon. Let our enemies beware," said Alexander.

Justine flew in and landed next to Nestor. "Are you okay, Nessy? Is everyone okay?"

"Everyone's fine," said Plato. "Alexander, perhaps you should go and assess your losses and secure your prisoners. We'll get together later for a situational briefing. Hardy, Justine, and Nestor, I want you there also. You'll be notified of the time and place." Plato paused and looked at those surrounding him. Tears began to well up in his eyes, tears of pride and gratitude. A beautiful rainbow had formed and was visible out over the field of battle. The sight filled them all with a sense of relief and peace after the violent night and day they had experienced.

"Thank you, all of you, for what you've done. Now, I have a blue jay and some other misfits to deal with. And you, Justine, need to start thinking about what's to be done with Antus and the other prisoners. You'll decide their fate tomorrow morning."

Justine looked surprised. She had hoped Plato had not been serious earlier when he told her that would be her decision. She looked around at everyone surrounding her and saw nods of approval. "Yes, sir," responded Justine. "I'll do my best to ensure justice is done."

Chapter 33

The next morning Hardy and Laslo flew to the woodlot lake. Many birds of all kinds were already assembled, some from the woodlot, as well as a number of crows from the pine forest. An air of excitement and anticipation was apparent, and the chatter among those present was lively, creating a thunderous din. Plato arrived just as Hardy and Laslo approached. Plato landed on the log in the lake, and as he did, the area became so quiet a field mouse could be heard rustling in the forest leaves. Hardy and Laslo joined Plato on the log. Soon Alexander, Nestor, and Justine arrived and joined Plato and the two boys. Paris and Hector arrived and landed in the trees opposite the log. Plato spoke briefly to Laslo, who immediately joined Paris and Hector in the trees. Plato took a long look at his companions and then turned to address those assembled.

"Yesterday, through a cooperative effort with our neighbors and friends, the crows, we put an end to the threat posed by Antus and his gang. The attacks we had been subjected to nearly sent us to war. That war would not only have been tragic, it would have been disastrous for all. And it was just what Antus was trying to cause with his attacks. Antus had a plan and it failed. It failed due to the cooperation of all and the sacrifices of some."

Plato paused and looked at Alexander, who then spoke. "It's been a great honor and privilege to work side by side with Plato this past week or so. The cooperation of all has made our efforts successful, and I thank each of you from the bottom of my heart. But this cooperative effort and our success would not have been possible if it weren't for the wisdom and courage of these three extraordinary young heroes. In fact, if it weren't for them, I'm convinced we would have been drawn into a terrible and deadly war."

Plato then spoke again. "The efforts of Nestor, Justine, and Hardy made this all possible. We owe them a debt of gratitude. Let's hear it for our three champions of peace and justice." A loud chorus of cheers went up and Nestor, Justine, and Hardy each stood there in awe, embarrassed by the attention.

As the cheers subsided, Plato spoke again. "Alexander, you've proven yourself to be not only a great warrior and commander of troops in battle but also a wise leader. Without your wisdom, restraint, and incredible leadership during some very difficult times, this day would not have been possible. Thank you." Another loud round of cheers went up and lasted for several minutes.

Finally, Alexander raised his wings, asking for quiet. "Thank you. But that restraint was not mine. It was the result of the influence Justine exerted in the name of justice and fairness. The basis of the battle plan and, hopefully a new era of cooperation among us all, was Nestor's idea. Nestor is not just smart. His wisdom is incredible and grows each day. And finally, the courage of Hardy must be noted. We all have heard of his physical courage, which he displayed on the day his father was killed. But the courage he displayed in trusting Justine and Nestor at a time when trusting crows had to be nearly impossible for any woodlot bird speaks to what Hardy's made of. Hardy may be the bravest of us all."

"Well said, Alexander. Paris and Hector, your service has been invaluable and led to the success of our operations. Your skill and perseverance made the victory possible. And I must also personally say thank you to Laslo. He is an impetuous young duck, and that nearly got him killed not long ago. But if it weren't for him I wouldn't be here to celebrate with you. Thank you, Laslo."

Hardy yelled, "Way to go, Laslo."

Everyone laughed and then Alexander yelled, "You're damn right. Way to go, Laslo."

A loud cheer rang out among all present, and Laslo just stood there and beamed.

Plato raised his wings and everyone quieted down. He lowered his head and was silent for at least thirty seconds. Slowly he raised his head and looked around, staring into as many faces as he could. Then he began to speak. "Let's not forget those who gave their lives protecting us. In their honor and memory we all need to commit to a new time of cooperation. We have a lot of work ahead of us. First we'll deal with our prisoners. We have a few among us who violated wartime orders and they must face justice. They nearly brought about the failure of our combined efforts. Then we'll deal with Antus and his gang. In a moment I'll decide the fate of our woodlot soldiers who disobeyed orders. Tomorrow, Justine will demonstrate if she can determine the true nature of justice by deciding the fate of Antus and the surviving members of his gang. Bring out the prisoners."

Several birds flew off and after a minute or so the group returned. The blue jay and his accomplices were led to the shoreline, where they landed and faced Plato.

"Blue jay, step forward and state your name," said Plato in a stern, powerful voice.

The blue jay stepped forward and said, "My name's Blake. But you already know that."

"That I do, but all those assembled here do not. You're charged with disobeying orders in battle and endangering your fellow soldiers. How do you plead?"

"I admit I disobeyed your orders, but I was defending our woodlot. I don't consider those crows my fellow soldiers. It's our job to defend our own homes. We don't need to rely on crows for that. As for you, you endangered yourself. That was not my doing."

"You've admitted your guilt. Is there anyone here who can present any evidence that would contradict his admission?" No one said a word. "Guilty as charged. How about the rest of you, do you admit your guilt also?"

One of the birds stepped forward. "My name is Colby. I've been asked by the others here to speak for all of us. We admit our guilt. And we're all sorry for putting the operation and especially you, Plato, at risk. We know now that the crows are our friends and we admit what we did was wrong. But we thought at the time Blake was right and we followed him. He was wrong. We were wrong. We accept whatever punishment you decide to impose."

"Cowards," mumbled Blake.

"Blake, normally the punishment for your crime is death. But you've never caused any problems before. Even though I warned you earlier I feel merciful. You're hereby ordered to serve as a recruit in the crow army. You'll serve for one year in the rank and file. You'll complete all training required of all soldiers under Alexander's command. And you will demonstrate total commitment and pledge your loyalty to your new commander. Understood?"

"And if I refuse?" asked Blake.

"You can't refuse. You've been sentenced. If you fail in any way, you'll be escorted from this area, banished permanently. And your family will not go with you. You'll go alone. Take him away. As for you others, you're forgiven. However, any actions on your part that in even the slightest way disrupts our new friendly relationship with the crows will result in you and your families being dispelled from this community. That will not be negotiable. Now you're free to go home."

"Thank you, Plato," said Colby.

"Thank you," said the other birds in unison.

Plato looked at Justine and then turned back to the assembly of birds. "Tomorrow morning we'll assemble in the clearing at the edge of the woodlot near the big tree where our command post was located. Justine will then decide the fate of Antus and his associates. I bid you good day."

The birds, speaking freely with one another, raised a hubbub that made conversation difficult unless one raised their voice. That in turn made the racket even louder. Soon the birds began to leave in small groups. Plato, Hardy, Nestor, Justine, and Laslo stood quietly and watched the others leaving. Alexander motioned to Paris. Paris nodded, turned, and spoke to Hector, and the two flew off in the direction of the pine grove.

When the sounds quieted sufficiently, Justine spoke. "Plato, I'd like to meet with you later, if that would be convenient."

"Certainly," said Plato. "We can meet at the command post location about two hours before dark." Plato paused and looked at Justine and smiled. "In the meantime you need to give a lot of thought to what you're going to do tomorrow."

Justine nodded. "I have been."

Alexander said good-bye to Hardy, Laslo, and Nestor and then spoke to Justine. "Is there any chance I could spend some time with you after tomorrow morning? Maybe when things settle down a bit?" Justine felt her face get warm and she stood there speechless, looking at Alexander. She started to speak but hesitated, not knowing what to say.

Plato, seeing Justine's lack of composure, spoke up. "You'll being seeing a lot of her Alexander, I think. In fact, I'm sure we'll all be seeing a lot of each other in the coming weeks. We have a lot to do. We have a lot of problems to solve if we're going to all live together in peace."

"Wonderful," yelled Justine. "This is unbelievable. Just a few days ago I didn't think this would happen." Tears filled her eyes and she spoke quietly. "Thank you, all of you." She hugged Nestor and Hardy. She then turned and looked at Alexander. "You're a great leader. If anyone else had been in charge of the army, we would surely have gone to war. Thank you, Alexander."

"Don't I get a hug?" asked Alexander. Justine laughed and threw her wings around Alexander. Alexander wrapped his wings around her and they hugged each other for at least ten seconds, their cheeks pressed against one another. Justine stepped back and realized her face felt as if it were on fire. Alexander was confused and just stood there staring at Justine.

"Good-bye, Justine. Good-bye, Hardy. Good-bye, Nestor. Good-bye, Laslo. Alexander, my friend, I look forward to seeing you again in the morning," said Plato. Everyone bade each other farewell and then went their separate ways.

Chapter 34

Justine flew to the tree where she and Hardy had first met. Nestor and Hardy had asked her to join them for a little celebration and conversation, but she declined, preferring some time alone to think. Hours passed with Justine lost in thought. She sat motionless for long spells and then would get up and pace back and forth along the large tree limb. Finally, she looked around at her surroundings, realizing it was nearly time to meet Plato, so she took wing and flew off toward the command post, and as she grew nearer she observed that Plato had already arrived.

She landed and spoke. "I'm sorry I'm late. I lost track of the time."

"Greetings, Justine," replied Plato. "You're not late."

"I apologize for not greeting you properly. Hello, Plato. Have you been waiting long?"

"No. I've been here most of the day reflecting on all that's happened. I'm ecstatic we were able to avoid war. We now have a good chance of creating a community where all of us can live together. That's as it should be."

Justine seemed a little puzzled. "A good chance? I thought we were going to do that."

"We are, but there's a lot that needs to be done. There's much that can still go wrong. Nobody's really saying anything out loud but there are many crows and other birds who likely don't think living together is a good idea. There are a lot of false beliefs held based on what's been taught or just accepted. This separation goes back many years and … well, we just have a lot of work to do. We need to get it right and be vigilant in our efforts. So, what did you want to talk with me about?"

"I think you know," said Justine with a smile. "I'm worried about tomorrow. I know justice needs to be done. I know Antus and his gang need to be dealt with. That part is easy. But figuring out exactly what would be fair, well, that's not so easy. I don't know if I can do this."

"Of course you can do it," replied Plato without hesitation. "Let's just analyze this a little. And remember, there's no absolute right answer. If there was, we wouldn't have to think about it, we could just impose justice from a list and be done with it."

"So, what should I do?"

"Oh, you're going to have to figure that out for yourself." Plato paused briefly and then spoke again. "But maybe I can help a little. Let's start with a basic question. Why does Antus need to be dealt with? To put it another way, what did he do that requires us to impose justice?"

"Well, that's obvious. He raided the woodlots and nearly started a war. Many were injured or killed because of what he did."

"That's not what I meant by my question. What did he do that was wrong? I'm not asking for a response based on morality. It's more of a legal question. What did he do that gives us the right to impose justice?" Plato asked while staring into Justine's eyes and holding her gaze while waiting for a response.

"Well, he broke our rules. He violated the laws we all live by and accept," answered Justine hesitantly. "Is that what you're asking?"

"Yes." Plato didn't say anything further but kept staring at Justine. Seconds ticked by while the two just stared at each other.

"What?" Justine asked. Frustration was apparent in her question.

Plato continued to stare for several seconds and then spoke. "So, why is that a problem? Why can't we just overlook his violating the laws or rules? That would make things easy for you, wouldn't it?"

"We can't do that. If we did that, then others would think they could break the rules and we would have ... chaos."

"Laws and rules have purpose then. Is that what you're saying?" asked Plato.

"Of course they do."

"What purpose do they serve?"

"Well, for starters they control individual behavior to prevent trouble and to keep others from being harmed." Justine appeared a little unsure sensing her answer wasn't complete.

"That's good. So does that mean that laws can keep us from doing what we want or saying what we want if others don't like it? Or are there limits to the control laws can exercise?"

"Oh, there are limits, obviously. We're all born with certain rights. We have a right to do or say whatever we want provided it doesn't harm others. Others don't have to like what we do or say but we can't harm others. That's where the limits are set."

Plato considered Justine's response for about thirty seconds before responding. "You said we are born with certain rights, including the right to say or do what we want, but that laws or rules place appropriate limits. Is that correct?"

"Yes," replied Justine. "That's correct."

Plato turned and looked away from Justine and spoke in a soft voice. "So, what about the crows being confined to the pine grove, shouldn't they be permitted to live in the woodlot like everyone else?"

Justine was taken by surprise by the question. She paused, and thought, and then responded with conviction. "The crows were confined to the pine grove to protect the other birds from harm and to prevent war. It was crows who started the trouble years ago and ..." Justine hesitated. "Oh, I see where this is going. All crows, even the innocent, have been punished for the actions of a few."

"Is that justice?" asked Plato.

"No."

"So what else should the law do?"

"It must protect the rights of everyone."

Plato looked at Justine and smiled. He walked over and stood by her side and then stared out across the field where the battle had raged. "Justine, you know more about justice by instinct than most who have studied it and thought about it their entire lives. You already know what you need to know. You'll make sound decisions tomorrow, decisions that will be fair and just."

"But I don't know what to do," protested Justine. "The penalty for what Antus and his gang did can be death. I don't know that I can impose that. It would guarantee that they don't do any more harm but I don't know that killing them is fair."

"You don't have to impose death if you don't think that's just. What do you have to accomplish with your decisions tomorrow? What did we just conclude the law should do?"

"It should protect everyone from harm and protect the rights of everyone. But don't Antus and his cohorts have a right to live?"

"He does unless you decide he's forfeited that right by his actions because of the harm he has done, and because of the threat he still poses. Justine, go back to the basics. What does your decision need to accomplish?"

"It needs to ensure that Antus and his gang are no longer a threat to everyone in this community."

"And?" asked Plato.

"And it needs to protect the rights of everyone, including Antus and his gang."

"And?" asked Plato again.

"And ... and it needs to be strong enough to send a message that we, this community, will not tolerate violations of the law. That will hopefully reduce the chance that others will ignore the law in the future."

"And?" asked Plato, this time with a big smile on his face as he turned and looked into Justine's eyes.

"And it needs to be just and fair. By that I mean it needs to reasonably accomplish what we have just discussed but it shouldn't be more severe than necessary."

"And?"

"I don't know," said Justine.

"And it should only be imposed on the guilty individuals?" Plato's question was not rhetorical, and he was expecting more than a yes or no answer.

Justine appeared confused. Suddenly her expression changed as she understood. "And what I impose should be appropriate for the actions of each individual. I don't have to impose the same sentence for everyone. I can impose individual sentences provided they accomplish what the law intended. No sentence should be cruel, no sentence should be vengeful. Each sentence should be just."

Plato put his wing around Justine and hugged her. He stepped back and took a long look at her, his eyes appearing to tear up. "You're something special, Justine. I'll see you tomorrow. I'll be by your side when you impose justice."

"Thank you, Plato. Thank you for everything you've done for me and for all of us. I'll do my best tomorrow. I'll try to live up to your expectations."

"You've already exceeded my expectations. Good-bye."

"Good-bye, Plato."

Chapter 35

Hardy woke after a sound sleep. He stood and walked around in an effort to clear his head. Laslo was still sleeping so Hardy gave him a nudge with his foot. "Wake up. The big trial's today and we can't be late." Laslo just grunted and turned over. "Come on, Laslo. Wake up."

Laslo sat up, rubbed his eyes, and looked at Hardy. "What? What did you say?"

"We need to grab a bite to eat and get going. We don't want to be late for the trial."

"Oh yeah, that is today, isn't it?" Laslo got to his feet and stumbled around the nest. After a few minutes, he seemed to have found his equilibrium. "I hope Justine gives Antus the maximum sentence. If she does, I'll offer to carry it out. He's a mean crow and he deserves to die."

"I'm sure Justine will be fair," replied Hardy. "I don't think you really want to volunteer to execute someone. You saw the battle. Killing is ugly."

"Well, it may be ugly but I can tell you this much: it's really ugly when someone is trying to kill you. I owe Antus and I'd be happy to see him dead even if I don't get to do it. There are plenty of others who'd like to see him dead too."

"This is not about getting even. That's not what Justine's job is. Her job is to administer justice. Plato could've had the blue jay killed for what he did but didn't. Plato's decision was fair and just."

"Well, Antus would be in real trouble if I was making the decision. Yes, he would be in trouble. He'd be in real trouble."

"That's why you're not making those kinds of decisions," said Hardy with

195

a slight grin. "Anyway, you punished him pretty good the last time you met. Let's eat and get going."

"Yeah. I guess I did, at that," said Laslo with a giggle.

The boys ate a quick breakfast. Mother was asleep. They decided not to wake her and off they flew to the trial location. As Hardy and Laslo neared the tree where the trial was to be held, they were shocked by the size of the assembled crowd. Hundreds of birds of every kind were there. A corridor between the large groups of birds had been set up in front of the large tree. Justine, Plato, and Alexander were in the tree on a lower limb. The elders from the woodlot and the pine grove stood on the ground directly below the limb all facing down the long corridor that had formed ahead of them. Hardy spotted Paris, motioned to Laslo, and the two landed.

"Good morning, Paris," said Hardy.

"Morning. Good morning, Laslo," said Paris.

"Hi."

"Where should we go?" asked Hardy. "We'd like to be close enough to hear what's said, if possible."

"I kept a place for both of you. Come with me." Paris led them a short distance just past the point where the corridor of birds started. "Hardy, you're right here next to Nestor and, Laslo, you're right next to Hardy. Take care. I've got to go make sure things stay organized and safe."

"Good morning, Hardy. Good morning, Laslo," said Nestor with a large smile. "This is really something, isn't it?"

"Good morning. It sure is. I didn't know there were this many birds in the woodlot."

"Hi, Nestor," said Laslo.

Hardy looked around and noticed Paris giving orders to several birds. Crows and other birds had been assigned security duties. They were aligned along the inner path of the corridor to make sure that no one made any attempts to harm the prisoners who were to pass through the corridor to face Justine.

Alexander stood and motioned with his wings. Paris and all the birds assigned to maintain order called for silence. In an instant, all was quiet and every bird was staring in the direction of the tree. Justine stood and walked down the limb to a point where she was directly in front of the corridor that lay before her.

"It's time to begin. Bring Antus here."

At the far end of the corridor, a group of ten crows moved forward. In the center of the group was Antus. All eyes turned to watch them approach. Birds in the back rows struggled to get a glimpse of Antus.

As the group passed, Antus spoke to Laslo. "You, stinking duck, er es good es dead. It's just eh mitter of time," said Antus, glaring at Laslo.

Laslo chuckled and responded with a short remark. "I'm rilly sceered, Intus."

Antus then spoke to Nestor. "You scriggly, ugly, miserable excuse for eh crow. Duck lover. I'll get you because I'm smirter than you. Just you wit en see." Nestor looked briefly into Antus's eyes, then turned and looked at Justine.

As Antus approached the tree, Justine spoke in a strong voice. "Prisoner, state your name." Antus just stared at her and Plato. Contempt and hate poured from his eyes. "The prisoner's name is Antus," said Justine. "Antus, you are charged with treason, murder, and other high crimes. How do you plead?"

"Treason? I em cherged with treason? You er stinding there with thit duck and you siy I em cherged with treason? Unlike you, thit scriggly brother of yours, Alexinder, en the rest of these cowardly crows, I stood up for crow rights. I em eh hero. I em the only real crow left. I'll drive every bird from this woodlot, especially ducks ... or I'll kill them ill. Thit's whit needs to be done."

"I take it you plead not guilty," responded Justine in her strongest voice.

"Em guilty of nothing. Em proud of everything I've done."

Justine stood silently, staring at Antus for a full minute. Finally she spoke. "Take him over there," said Justine, pointing to a spot off to her left. "And make sure he stays there. Do whatever's necessary to keep him quiet. Anything. Bring out the rest of the prisoners."

Paris turned and gave a command. Two crows immediately went to the end of the corridor and shouted instructions. In a moment the prisoners appeared, walking single file, flanked by guards. It was a motley bunch made up of males and females. Some hung their heads and looked at the ground as they made their way while others stared straight ahead. A few glared at the birds lining the edge of the corridor.

As the prisoners passed by, Hardy noticed a large fat crow. It was the one he had seen flying behind Antus's gang, he thought. It had to be; no other crow was that fat. As the fat crow passed, Hardy noticed what appeared to be a serious injury to the crow's anus. He started to giggle.

"What's so funny?" asked Nestor. "This is no time to be laughing."

"Look at the back end of that fat crow," said Hardy. "Remember what my dad said, 'If we find a fat crow with a blown O-ring we would have our man.' I think that's a blown O-ring." Hardy giggled again and then Nestor and Laslo started giggling.

Suddenly and without any warning, a loud sound split the air like a thunderbolt. "Quaaa-honk!" Hardy and Nestor turned in the direction of the sound just in time to see Laslo collapse onto the ground. Laslo rolled over on his back and appeared to be struggling to get his breath. There was a united gasp from the crowd of birds and a few screams. Hardy started to go to Laslo's aid when that sound, the same sound he had heard just a moment ago, roared out again and echoed across the field.

"Quaa-honk!" The sound came from Laslo. It was as if Laslo was attempting to quack and then his quack turned instantly into what sounded like a honk from a goose.

"Qua-honk! Ha! Ha! Haaa! Honk!" Laslo opened his eyes and looked at Hardy. "Dad said … honk!… Dad said … Ha! Ha! Dad said, 'That spinker won't … that spinker won't be … that spinker won't be spinkering anytime soon.' Qua-honk! Ha! Ha! Haaa! Honk!"

"Make him stop, Hardy," Nestor pleaded.

"Qua-honk!"

"He's not gonna stop. Look at him," said Hardy.

Just then Paris ran up. "What's wrong with him?"

"Qua-honk! Ha! Ha! Haa! Honk."

"He saw something funny. Now he can't stop laughing," said Hardy with a grin. "It was really funny, Paris."

"Qua-honk! That spinker … Ha! Ha! That spinker won't be spinkering … Qua-honk. Ha! Ha! Honk!"

"What did he see? Nothing could be that funny," said Paris.

"The backside of that fat crow," said Hardy. Paris looked in the direction of the crow prisoners.

"Wow. That's an angry anus," said Paris with a grimace.

"Quaaaaaa-hooooonk! Ha! Ha! Angry anus! Ha! Haaaa! Make him stop,

Hardy. Ha! Ha! Honk!" Laslo fell silent momentarily and then started gasping. "Honk!" Gasp. "Honk!" Gasp. "Honk!" Gasp. "Qua-honk! Angry anus! Ha! Ha! Blown O-ring! Honk!"

"Don't say anything else that'll make him laugh," said Nestor.

"I didn't mean to, but that crow's injury's really bad. I think he's ruined his rectum."

"Qua-honk! Ha! Ha! Ruined his rectum! Ha! Ha! Haaa! Honk!"

Nestor and Hardy looked at Paris with frustration on their faces.

"I'm sorry," said Paris. The three just stood there listening to Laslo, contemplating what they should do, when they noticed that every bird present was staring in their direction. Some were visibly disgusted.

"Do something. Make him stop," ordered Paris.

"He's not gonna stop. There's nothing I can do. There's nothing anyone can do."

The three stared down at Laslo, who was barely moving. His legs were outstretched, as were his wings. It was if all his bodily functions had stopped except for those necessary to laugh and remain alive. He was helpless, paralyzed with laughter.

"Qua-honk! Hardy, it's funny. Qua-honk! Ha! Ha! Ha! Haa! Honk!" Laslo raised his head, looked at Hardy, and tried to speak. His mouth started moving, but no sound came out. Laslo appeared to be struggling for air and then suddenly, "Qua-honk! Ha! Ha! Ha! Haaaaa! Honk!"

"What are we gonna do?" asked Nestor. Nestor glanced in the direction of Justine, Alexander, and Plato. Alexander and Plato had a puzzled look on their faces, but Justine looked as angry as Nestor could ever recall her looking.

"This could go on for hours," said Hardy. "Paris, I think you should just get four or five guards and drag him out of here. Tell them to keep dragging him until he's far enough away that none of us can hear him and that ridiculous laughing."

"Qua-honk! Blown O-ring! Ha! Ha! That spinker ... qua-honk!"

"Then what?" asked Paris.

"Just leave him there to laugh it off, I guess," said Hardy. "Maybe leave one or two guards to make sure he's safe until he stops."

Paris called over a group of guards, and they started dragging Laslo away. His legs and wings stayed limp, and his head hung back as if it was too heavy for him to hold up. He offered neither assistance nor resistance. As he was dragged away, his feet left trails in the ground.

"Qua-honk! Ha! Ha! Haaa! Blown O-ring. Qua-honk!"

"I've never seen anything like that," said Paris.

"Nor I," added Nestor. "Does he do that often?"

"No. He's never done that before that I know of. But you never know what Laslo's gonna do. He means well. He just can't help it," chuckled Hardy, shaking his head. "When I think back about how angry my dad was and the way he said that stuff, well, I can understand why Laslo found it so funny." Hardy looked at Nestor and Paris, who were staring at him with surprised looks on their faces. "Trust me. It's really funny."

"Qua-honk! Angry anus! Ruined rectum! Honk!" Laslo's laughter was beginning to fade in the distance.

Paris looked in Alexander's direction, who motioned for him to come forward. Paris went and spoke with Alexander and then returned. "Alexander wants the three of us to join them on that limb. Justine's not very happy."

"Great. This is not going to be pleasant," said Nestor.

"Laslo's not our problem. It's not our fault," said Hardy.

"Tell that to Justine," Nestor replied.

The three flew up and landed on the limb. There was a moment of silence, and then Paris spoke. "We tried, but we couldn't make him stop."

Justine was visibly angry. "What was that all about? This is a serious hearing. We can't have that kind of behavior."

"Laslo saw something funny and started laughing and couldn't stop. I'm sure he didn't want to do anything to upset the hearing, but he couldn't help it." Hardy paused for a moment. "In his defense, I have to say it was really funny."

"Well, I don't find any of this funny, Hardy."

Hardy looked at Alexander, who just looked away. Hardy then looked at Plato, who shrugged and said, "Don't look at me."

"I'm sorry, Justine. It was Laslo. You know how he is. I'll admit that was extreme, even for him. But we couldn't do anything about it."

"What did he find so funny?" asked Justine.

"It was that fat crow. He has a really bad injury to his ... backside. We saw it, and I remembered what my dad said. You remember me telling you what he said? 'If we find a big fat crow with a blown O-ring, we would have our man.' Well, I think that crow has a blown O-ring. The three of us, Nestor, Laslo, and I, all thought it was funny. Laslo just thought it was a lot funnier than we did."

Laslo could be heard faintly in the distance. "Qua-honk! That spinker! Honk!"

Justine frowned at the sound of Laslo and also frowned at Hardy. "That was it? That's what that was all about?" asked Justine.

"Not so loud, Justine," cautioned Plato.

"No, that wasn't all. Laslo remembered our dad saying, 'That spinker won't be spinkering anytime soon.' That's what really got him going, I think." Hardy paused, smiling at the thought.

"That's not funny," said Justine.

"Qua-honk!"

Hardy glanced in the direction of the sound, grinned, and shook his head. "I know this wasn't the right time, but it was Laslo. He couldn't help himself. I've never seen him like that. Here's what you should do. Ask that fat crow to turn around so you can see his injured backside. And then think about my dad being really angry and saying it's a 'blown O-ring' and 'that spinker won't be spinkering anytime soon.' Then maybe you'll understand."

"Go back to your places. We'll talk about this more later. I'm really disappointed in you three."

"We didn't do it. It was Laslo. We were just unfortunate enough to be standing next to him," said Nestor.

"Go," said Justine. The three left the tree and returned to their respective places.

"I apologize for the disruption," said Justine to the crowd. "We'll now proceed."

"You should do more thin apologize. This is eh disgriss. I told ill of you those ducks er no good," yelled Antus.

"Quiet. Quiet or I'll have you removed. Now, we shall proceed."

Antus stared angrily at Justine in response.

"You," said Justine to the first prisoner in line. "You are charged with treason, murder, and high crimes. How do you plead?"

"Guilty and proud of it," responded the crow.

"So you support Antus?"

"Yes. He's our leader."

"Go stand with Antus then." The crow was led over to stand with Antus. Justine then spoke to the next crow.

"You are charged with treason, murder, and high crimes. How do you plead?"

"Not guilty. I didn't want to do those things. But I was afraid of Antus and the others, so I went along with them."

"Coward. Tritor," yelled Antus. Two guards spoke harshly to Antus, and he immediately quieted down.

"Go stand over there," said Justine, pointing to the opposite side of the corridor from where Antus stood. Justine asked each crow in line the same question and directed them to either side based on their responses. The fat crow said he was not guilty, claiming he was too fat to keep up with the others and so never went on any raids.

"Really? Then how do you explain being captured during the battle?" asked Justine.

"I came here the day before. I was going to warn all of you, but I was so exhausted I fell asleep. I woke up during the fighting and surrendered when attacked."

"You fet idiot," yelled Antus. "I will kill you."

"You were seen during the fight by Hector on the other side of the cornfields, and later you were here. I don't see how that would be possible if you were unable to fly the distance. How do you explain that?" asked Justine.

"Someone has mistaken me for another. Or someone is lying."

"You're hard to mistake for any other crow. Turn around."

"Why should I turn around?"

"Do it," commanded Justine. The crow turned around in a complete circle. His injury was serious, so serious it was painful to look at. And it was clearly visible, even from the elevated location where Justine and the others stood. "How did you get that injury?" asked Justine.

"Qua-honk!"

Justine turned and looked in the direction of the somewhat muffled sound. There was Plato with his back turned and his wing over his face. He immediately turned around, coughed, and pretended to be trying to clear his throat. "I'm sorry," said Plato. "Go ahead and proceed."

Justine looked at Plato, cocked her head to one side, and opened her eyes real wide. She then turned back to the crow. "I'm waiting for your answer."

"I ... I just, uh, I was injured during the fighting."

"I don't think so," said Justine. "We both know how you go that injury. Certainly an injury like that wasn't inflicted in any of the fighting." Justine could hear Alexander giggle slightly, struggling not to laugh. She cleared her throat, indicating he'd better stop. He did. "Go stand over there." Justine sent him to the group that had all claimed they were not guilty. All the crows had been questioned and separated based on their responses.

"Bring that group here," said Justine, pointing to the group that had claimed they were not guilty. Justine looked down on them, paused while she stared each directly in the eyes, and then spoke. "Do you renounce all allegiance to Antus? Each of you shall answer, starting with you," said Justine pointing to a crow. Each answered yes. "Are you willing to live among us in peace and not start any more trouble?" Again each answered yes.

"I will not impose a sentence at this time but will hold the right to impose a sentence, if warranted, at a later time. However, I am ordering that you serve under the command of Alexander as he directs. You will each train and participate as you are instructed. Your freedom will be greatly restricted but not taken from you completely. If you want your freedom restored, it will be up to you and your future behavior." Justine paused and looked sternly at each one. "If any of you cause any trouble of any kind, you'll be returned for sentencing. Now go."

"Thank you," the group mumbled. The group turned and began to leave. As Justine watched the fat crow turn and leave, she glanced at Plato, smiled, and shrugged.

"Now, bring Antus and that group here." When the group, a total of seven crows, was assembled in front of her, Justine spoke softly and deliberately. "Each of you, by being captured in the act and also by your own admission, is found guilty of treason, murder, and other crimes. The penalty for these crimes is death."

The crows stood there silently. Some appeared shocked and hung their heads.

Antus stepped forward and yelled, "We er guilty of nothing. We fought for the rights of ill crows. Do whit you wint with us. You er worthless, ill of you er worthless. Stind up for your rights, you cowards!"

"Are you finished, or do you have something else to say to me?" asked Justine.

"I hiv nothing to siy to you. Do whit you wint."

"Do any of you have anything you'd like to say on your behalf before I impose sentence?" None of the crows said anything. Several shook their heads. "Then I will impose my sentence. While the penalty for your crimes is normally death, I have concluded that this is not a normal situation. I believe most of you acted out of concern for correcting what you believed to be an injustice. The methods you used were wrong and in violation of our laws. Therefore, justice must be imposed. Each of you, with the exception of Antus, is banned from our homeland. You will be taken as a group to the edge of the outer frontiers of our homeland. You will be escorted two days' flight and left to fend for yourselves. If you return for any reason, you'll be taken prisoner, brought back, and the appropriate sentence will be imposed." Justine paused and then added, "There will be no exceptions. I wish you all well."

Justine looked at Antus, who stared back. She held his stare for a full thirty seconds and then spoke. "Antus, you are the cause of all the injuries and deaths that have occurred. You led these others in a selfish bid for power. I do not believe for one second that you acted for anyone's benefit other than your own. However, justice demands mercy whenever possible. You'll have an opportunity to continue your life, but not here. You'll be taken alone, in a different direction from the others, and escorted two days' flight from our homeland where you will be left to fend for yourself. If you return for any reason at any time, you will be killed. If you so much as fly through our homeland while traveling to some other location, you will be killed. If you enter our homeland by mistake, you will be killed. You are banished. If you attempt to return, you will be killed on sight. Those instructions will be issued to every member of our army. No matter what happens, there will be no reprieve. You are to never return here. If you do, you will forfeit your life. That is my sentence. Now, take them all away and impose the sentences in the morning."

"You kint send me ehwiy from my home. Ilone? Thit is not eh fier sentence."

"You should have appreciated what you had here. But you chose violence and sought to incite a war. Your action caused a number of crows to lose their lives. You care about no one but yourself. Living alone should suit you well;

you are your only friend. And I don't think you like yourself very much. Take him away."

"I'll be beck one day, en when I do, I will meck sure to kill you." Antus was led away, yelling threats against everyone.

Justine looked up at the assembled birds and spoke in a loud clear voice. "This hearing is concluded. Let's all go in peace and do our best to create a new society where all are treated with equal respect." The crowd let out a loud cheer and then began to leave. Justine turned to Plato, who smiled and nodded his approval.

"Well done. We should take the remainder of the day to rest, and then the three of us, Nestor, Hardy, and the elders from the woodlot and pine grove will assemble here tomorrow. We have a lot to do if we're going to make this new order work. Good day." Plato then flew away.

Justine looked at Alexander and smiled. Alexander smiled back, put his wing around her, and hugged her. They then stood side by side, Alexander's wing still around Justine, and watched as the birds all departed.

Chapter 36

Hardy said good-bye to Nestor and Paris and then left. He flew slowly, thinking about what had taken place. Hardy decided to go to the lake, relax, and reflect on the events of the past weeks. So much had happened so fast he had not had time to fully understand it all.

The lake sparkled ahead in the distance. Hardy circled and made a nice landing in the cool water. There were a number of ducks there, and Hardy searched, looking to see if he recognized anyone. All the ducks were staring at him, but Hardy recognized none of them. Hardy floated effortlessly. He was relaxing for the first time in weeks and was lost in thought.

"Hi, Hardy."

Hardy turned toward the voice. It was the pretty, young duck he had seen at the lake where he had met Laslo weeks earlier. Hardy felt his heart race. "Hi. You know my name?"

The young duck giggled. "Everyone knows your name. You're quite famous now."

"Oh yeah, I guess. I'm sorry, but I don't know your name. What is it?"

"It's Jean."

"I'm very pleased to meet you, Jean. I'm Hardy, uh, right, you know that. I noticed you that day at the lake when Laslo was … telling his stories and acting the fool. I hope you didn't believe all the nonsense he was telling everyone."

"Of course not; we all know Laslo likes to clown around and exaggerate things so he can be the center of attention. He's funny, but we don't believe much of what he says."

"That's a relief," said Hardy.

"I noticed you that day, too. I thought you were cute."

"Really? Thanks. I thought you were the prettiest duck I'd ever seen." Hardy paused briefly. "Oh, and I still think that," he added with a smile.

"Thank you. I wasn't sure if I should speak to you since you seemed to be deep in thought. But I didn't want to miss the chance," said Jean.

"I'm glad you did." Hardy and Jean floated together, talking and laughing for the next hour. Hardy looked up and saw a crow approaching. "There's Nestor. Let's go over to the log and wait for him." The two swam over, and a moment later, Nestor landed.

"Hi, Nestor," said Hardy with a large smile on his face. "This is Jean."

"Hello, Jean. It's a pleasure to meet you."

"Thank you, Nestor, but the pleasure's mine. Hardy's been telling me about you and some of the things that have happened. Thank you for all you did to prevent a war."

"It couldn't have been done without Hardy," replied Nestor. Jean looked at Hardy with admiration and smiled. "Hardy, we're all meeting tomorrow; Plato, Alexander, Justine, and all the elders. We're to meet just after light at the tree where the hearing was held today."

"Okay. Is Justine still angry with us?"

"No, she's over it. She thought it was funny once she had a chance to think about it. Anyway, she knows how Laslo is."

"What was so funny, anyway?" asked Jean.

"I'll tell you some other time after we get to know each other a little better," said Hardy. "It's a little embarrassing."

"Oh, no wonder Laslo thought it was funny." That caused all three of them to giggle.

"I think I should be going home. My parents get worried if I don't check in," said Jean.

"Will I get to see you again? Uh, I mean I would like to see you again."

"I can meet you here. When would you like to meet?" asked Jean.

Hardy turned to Nestor. "What time do you think we'll be done tomorrow?"

"I'm not sure, but I would guess you could get out of there a few hours before dark."

"Can you meet me here late tomorrow afternoon?" asked Hardy. "I'll be

able to give you a time then when we could meet each day if you would like …
sorry if I'm being pushy."

"I can meet you here tomorrow afternoon. And yes, I'd like to spend time
with you every day."

"Great," said Hardy. "I'll see you tomorrow. Oh, I'm sorry. Can I accompany
you home? I need to go, Nestor. I'll see you tomorrow at the meeting."

"Good-bye, Hardy. It was nice to meet you, Jean. Good-bye," said
Nestor.

"Bye, Nestor. I enjoyed meeting you."

Hardy and Jean left. Nestor took a long drink. He looked around the
lake and realized everyone had left. Empty of bird life, the lake had a lonely
and foreboding feeling. It caused Nestor to feel somewhat uncomfortable. He
shivered, though the day was warm, and then left.

Chapter 37

Hardy accompanied Jean home, said good-bye, and then flew to the command post location. He spent the next hour reflecting on the day's events. His thoughts went to Jean constantly, and each time Hardy's heart raced a little. He smiled when he realized his heart was racing. He was feeling pretty good about things.

Just then he heard a voice calling his name. "Hardy," yelled Laslo. "I'll be right there."

Hardy looked and saw Laslo with two crows starting their glide to land in the tree with him. The three landed and walked over to where Hardy was waiting. Laslo just stood there with a silly grin on his face, looking at Hardy.

"I was wondering if you'd stopped laughing yet. You're such a fool. We got in trouble with Justine because of you," said Hardy with a smile.

"Yeah, I finally stopped laughing a little while ago. These are my new friends, Macario and Gil."

"Hi," said Hardy.

"Hi," said Macario and Gil in unison.

"So, I thought you didn't like crows," said Hardy, winking at the two crows.

"No, these guys are great, and they know how to have fun. They helped drag me out of the hearing today and then stayed with me to make sure I was okay until I stopped laughing. They then made the mistake of asking me what was so funny, and I made the mistake of telling them. When I told them, they got to laughing, and that got me started again. You should hear these guys laugh. My ribs hurt."

"Us? We've never heard laughing like that," said Macario. "It was really funny."

"Yeah, and when Laslo told us about that fat crow and his blown O-ring—that was it," added Gil.

"Qua-honk! That was the funniest thing I've ever seen. I told you guys my ribs hurt. Don't even mention anything about that fat crow. Blown O-ring! Qua-honk! Dad was really funny."

"Cack! Cack! Caaaaack! Ca-ca-Cack!" Macario and Gil's laughing caused Hardy to giggle.

"Well, I suspect no one's ever heard laughing like that before. The three of you laughing together must really be something to hear," said Hardy. "Justine and Alexander are not happy with you, Laslo. And I don't think Plato was impressed either. A little self-control would have served you well."

"I couldn't help it. You saw that fat crow. Qua-honk! Ha! Ha! Honk! Anyway, I don't care who liked it and who didn't. It was funny, and that's all I know. I can't hang out with anyone who doesn't think that was funny. Qua-honk! 'Cause it was funny, and you know it."

"Yeah, I thought it was funny. Just be ready the next time you see Justine."

"How upset is she? Is she real angry?"

"No. Nestor said she's over it. He said she actually thought it was funny too when she had a chance to think about it. But she'll probably pretend to be upset with you, so just go along with it. Okay?"

"Sure," said Laslo. "I will. So what else is happening?"

"I'm meeting with Plato, Alexander, Justine, Nestor, and all the elders tomorrow. We're going to try and settle some issues and try to find a way we can all live together in peace. I'm sorry, Laslo, but you weren't invited."

"I'm not invited? Well, there's a surprise. Don't be sorry. You belong there. I don't. If there was ever any question, I think I took care of that beyond any doubt at the hearing today," said Laslo with a big grin.

"Caaack! We agree," said Macario and Gil in unison.

"Well, just be glad you didn't know about 'angry anus' before you got out of there, or you two would be in just as much trouble as me."

"Caaack! Don't say angry anus. Caaaack!" said Macario. Gil just cackled and muffled the sound with his wing as best he could.

"I know I don't have what it takes to be a leader. That sort of thing isn't for me," said Laslo. "I like to have fun. I just do … things. And I'm fine with that. Maybe I don't think as clearly as I should. But, I can still outtalk, outfly, and definitely outlaugh you, Hardy. Don't you ever forget that!"

"No contest with the laughing. You're the all-time champ," said Hardy.

"That's right. Listen, we need to get going. I promised to tell these guys about the fart. You know which one I'm talking about."

"I know the one. Let me warn you, guys. Let him tell you about it but don't let him demonstrate one. He's deadly. I think he killed a buzzard with a fart. It was beyond description."

"Caaaack! I gotta hear that story! Cack!" said Macario.

"Ca-Ca-Caack. Me too," added Gil.

"Are these guys great, or what? We gotta get going."

"Take care, and be careful. Mom's worried about you. You haven't been by to see her. Promise me you'll stop by every day or two so she won't worry."

"Sure, Hardy. I will, maybe tomorrow."

"Good-bye, Macario, Gil. It was nice meeting you. Bye, Laslo."

"See you later," said Laslo.

"Yeah, we'll see you later," said Macario. Gil just nodded.

Laslo, Macario, and Gil flew off, and Hardy could hear Laslo talking, and then they started laughing like three fools, a musical mixture of qua-honks and caaacks. Hardy decided to go home, see Mother, tell her Laslo is okay, and get some needed rest. He wanted to get a good nights' sleep so he could get started early in the morning.

Chapter 38

Hardy awakened early the next morning. He said good-bye to Mother and set off for the meeting. Hardy noticed that it was cooler than normal, and as he flew he enjoyed the change in weather. He also saw the leaves on the trees had turned from green to many beautiful colors. As he neared the assembly location, Hardy noticed a number of birds had already arrived, and he could see others flying in. He was immediately struck by the number, which was larger than he had anticipated.

Hardy arrived and landed in the tree near a number of the crow elders. He didn't know what kind of reception he would get, but the crows immediately greeted him warmly. Hardy returned the greetings and was soon engaged in conversation with several of the crow elders who seemed more than a little interested in him. One offered condolences on the loss of his father, and the others then offered their expressions also. Hardy acknowledged their condolences and thanked them.

"Here comes Alexander," said one of the crows. Surprisingly to Hardy, the crow elders seemed both excited and somewhat awestruck at the sight of Alexander. Alexander landed, and his escort party flew off and landed in a tree some distance away. Alexander greeted everyone simultaneously with a booming "Good morning."

All present responded with a chorus of good mornings. Several of the elders engaged Alexander in conversation, and then Alexander excused himself, walked over, and greeted Hardy. "Good morning, Hardy. It's an exciting day. It wasn't long ago I had real doubts whether we would ever see this day."

"It is exciting. There are more elders than I thought," said Hardy, looking around. More birds had landed, and there was quite a buzz of conversation taking place. "Look, there's Nestor and Justine."

"Justine?" asked Alexander, looking anxiously in the direction Hardy had indicated. Nestor and Justine glided in and landed next to Hardy and Alexander. Greetings were exchanged all around. Hardy noticed that Alexander and Justine quickly got together and were speaking quietly.

Suddenly the buzz of conversations stopped, and all was quiet. Plato was approaching, and the group began to spread out, providing Plato a place to land in the center of the assembly. In a moment Plato landed and began exchanging greetings and nodding toward those farther away, acknowledging their presence. A few minutes passed, and Plato indicated it was time to begin. He asked if he should begin the discussions with his thoughts on how to proceed, and everyone assented.

Plato got right to the point and stated how he thought the initial discussions should proceed. "It's my view that there are several major areas where we must reach agreement. First, the basic structure of governance must be identified and consensus reached. Second, a system of justice must be established that will be fair to all. Third, we need to establish a plan and a schedule for crows to move into the woodlot. And the last major issue is the army or armies. The existing situation with separate armies is troublesome and will not work." Most nodded in agreement that Plato had identified the key issues, and the various comments that followed made it clear those issues would keep them busy for some time. "Well, if all agree, I think we should get started. I suggest we hear proposals for the structure of our government, and we'll work from those proposals."

The group got right to work, and there was spirited debate throughout the day. Plato deftly guided the discussions and kept them on track, focused, and civil. By the end of the day, much had been discussed, but nothing had been agreed to. Plato called an end to the meeting.

"Let's all meet here first thing in the morning, and we'll try to narrow the proposals to something we can all work with and begin to find some areas of agreement. Good evening." Plato immediately flew off, and the others soon followed. Justine and Alexander said good-bye and left together. Nestor asked Hardy to stay and talk more about the ideas that were raised during the day.

"I'm sorry, Nestor, but I can't stay. I promised Jean I would meet her at the lake. I really like her and want to spend more time with her."

"I understand. Good night. I'll see you here tomorrow."

The meetings continued for weeks, and great progress was made. Hardy noticed that Justine and Alexander spent a great deal of time together. Hardy sensed that the two were becoming more than just good friends. Hardy saw Jean every day after the meetings. On the few days when no meetings were held, Hardy and Jean spent the entire day together, alone or with friends. One evening after the day's meeting had ended, Justine, Alexander, Nestor, and Hardy spoke briefly before leaving.

"Hardy, Nestor tells me you've been spending a lot of time with a girl named Jean. When are we going to get to meet her?" asked Justine.

"We can all get together anytime," answered Hardy. "I've told Jean all about you. She says she feels like she knows you. She asked me the other day when she was going to get to meet you all."

"Sounds serious," said Alexander, taking a quick glance at Justine.

"It is. We've decided that we're going to nest together next spring," said Hardy with a wide grin.

"Congratulations," said all three, simultaneously causing the group to break out into laughter.

"Why don't we all get together as soon as these meetings end? Plato said we'd have the day off," suggested Nestor. The group agreed, and after exchanging farewells, they all left. Hardy told Jean the news that evening, and she was excited and asked Hardy to make whatever arrangements were most convenient to the others.

Over the next several days, the meeting moved forward exceptionally well. At the end of the day, Plato announced that he believed no further meetings were necessary. He suggested that everyone go back to their homes, explain what had been agreed to, and determine if the majority would find the arrangements acceptable. If they could implement a government, explained Plato, then the government could resolve the remaining issues needing attention, including any new issues that were sure to arise. The group agreed the time had come to move things forward as Plato suggested.

"So, let me summarize what we have agreed to. If what I state is not the understanding of everyone here, then let's resolve it here and now," said Plato. "I don't want to have to come back here tomorrow and debate this anymore. We've agreed that the government will be led by four guardians, each considered wise and courageous enough to lead and all of whom posses the necessary love of truth and justice to govern effectively. The four guardians must all agree on every action they take. Those guardians will be Alexander, Hardy, Nestor, and me. Is that agreed to by all?" All indicated their concurrence with what Plato had stated.

"There will be twenty elders, ten of whom will be crows. The elders will serve as an oversight body. The crow elders will be selected by the inhabitants of the pine grove and the balance of the elders by the inhabitants of the woodlot. The elders selected must be confirmed by the four guardians." Plato paused briefly and then continued. "The guardians will rule all. However, the elders may overrule the guardians if at least fifteen agree." All nodded in agreement. "It's also been agreed that in the event of the death of any guardian, the replacement will be selected by the remaining guardians. There will be no more than two crow guardians and at least two other noncrow guardians."

"That part may be a problem to get support on," said a sparrow. "I think those living in the woodlot, since there are more birds in the woodlot than there are crows in the pine grove, would like to see a different number of guardians, so the guardians that are noncrow are more in proportion to those that are crows." There was a murmuring among those assembled, and a variety of opinions were expressed.

"We're all aware of that area of concern and have discussed it at length," said Plato. "But we all agreed we would take this back and explain it in detail. Hopefully, it will be acceptable when it is understood that there can be three noncrow guardians, but no less than one will be a crow. However, at present because of the challenges we face, and the individuals we have selected, we believe it is necessary that at least two guardians are crows. Agreed? And we all agreed that we have full confidence that Nestor and Alexander will be impartial and fair to everyone in their decisions. And finally, no action can be taken unless all the guardians concur." The assembly agreed they would take this back and explain it with the goal of having it agreed upon and accepted.

"Justine will be our judge. She will appoint two other minor judges and more if necessary in the future. Justine will be the chief judge and will have the final word on all issues of law. The guardians must approve her appointments. Agreed?" There were no objections.

Plato then proceeded to outline the process that would be followed for crows to move into the woodlot. The crows would wait until spring to move into the woodlot. This would prevent any other birds from being displaced. An area of the woodlot was set aside for crows as most crows preferred to live together. The birds presently living in that area would build new nests elsewhere in the woodlot. Crows could continue to live in the pine grove if they chose, and other birds would be welcomed in the pine grove if they preferred to live there. Any crows that elected to could live wherever they wanted in other parts of the woodlot provided they did not displace or in any way disturb the birds residing there.

Plato then described the changes that were planned for the armies. "The armies are hereby dissolved. They will be replaced by two separate auxiliaries with two distinct functions. One will be the internal auxiliaries, and one will be the external auxiliaries. Paris has been selected as leader of both auxiliary forces. Hector will be placed in charge of the external auxiliaries, and we have yet to select a leader of the internal auxiliaries. Paris will make that selection, and his selection will require agreement from the guardians. The internal auxiliary leader will not be a crow."

"I think we should consider Laslo for the position. He demonstrated great courage during the fight with Antus, and he saved Plato's life. We should give him the job," suggested a robin. "He's earned it."

"Interesting," said Plato. "What do the rest of you think?" There was a spirited discussion. Some opposed the idea, and some supported it. Most were undecided. "What do you think, Hardy? After all, you'll soon be serving as one of the guardians and would have to concur with this if Paris recommends it later. Should we appoint Laslo to the job now and get it over with?"

Hardy looked surprised and a little troubled that Plato asked him for his opinion. After a long pause, Hardy answered. "I oppose the appointment of Laslo. Laslo is a skilled flyer, and he certainly seems to be fearless. But he's not a leader. He doesn't think things through before he acts. He's somewhat narrowed-minded. He can barely manage himself. I don't see how he could manage or lead others. Maybe he can learn, but I don't think he would be a good choice as a leader of the internal auxiliaries."

"Nestor and Alexander, what do you two think?" asked Plato.

The two spoke briefly to one another, and then Alexander answered. "We agree with Hardy. We like Laslo, but he's not a leader."

"I agree also. Hardy and Nestor are already showing why they're good choices to lead us. They're young but have great judgment, and both will become great guardians. And we all know Alexander is an amazing leader. Our futures are in good hands. So, shall we wait for Paris to appoint a leader of the internal auxiliaries?" All agreed, including the robin. "Okay. Paris has instructions to select and train the internal guardians and choose those with great restraint and self-control. We want laws enforced but don't want any intimidation or force used. In the event force becomes necessary, it will be applied with great restraint. The external auxiliaries will be selected by Paris, and he has been instructed to select strong, aggressive birds that will be able to patrol our frontier borders and protect us all from any threats. They will also patrol the area around the woodlot and protect us from hawks and owls. Paris will work closely with the guardians to make sure we can maintain control over the external auxiliaries. We can never allow them to present a threat to us. We will provide the proper training and education so we develop a strong force of auxiliaries that understand their only function is to protect us all. Their education will be extensive and is of vital importance. Future guardians will come from the auxiliaries."

Plato paused, appeared to wobble briefly, and then took several deep breaths before continuing. "The auxiliaries will serve us all, so we must all care for them. The internal auxiliaries may live in the woodlot among us. The external auxiliaries will live separately in an area set aside for them on the east side of the woodlot. All inhabitants of the woodlot are required to provide food and assist with building nests for the auxiliaries. Each inhabitant shall support the auxiliaries by doing what they are most naturally suited and capable of doing."

Plato stopped speaking and looked at all those assembled. Tears formed in his eyes. "Thank you, all of you, for your hard work and for reaching agreement on these issues. There will be great challenges ahead, but I know you'll be able to create a new, stronger, and more just society. All can live together in peace, and all will be better off living together than living apart. I promise." Plato paused and then spoke again. "I *promise*. Thank you."

Over the next five minutes, the assembly departed. Alexander, Hardy, Justine, Nestor, and Plato remained. Plato spoke to the group. "I especially want to thank each of you again for all you've done. I'm so proud to know all of you. This is a historic day, and you four have made it possible. Thank you."

"You are our leader, Plato. You made all of this happen. What we did just created the opportunity. You got it done. We thank you," said Alexander.

Hardy, Nestor, and Justine all nodded in agreement and said, "You did it, Plato." Justine walked over and gave Plato a big hug. Tears formed in her eyes, and she turned, walked back, and stood next to Alexander.

"It's time to go. I'm very tired," said Plato.

"I would like a moment of your time, Plato, if possible, alone," said Alexander.

"Certainly," answered Plato. Nestor and Justine exchanged farewells with Hardy, and Hardy left. Justine motioned to Alexander, and he walked over to her, and they spoke quietly for a moment. Justine then turned back to Nestor.

"I'm going to go see Momma and Poppa. Do you want to go with me, Nessy?" asked Justine.

"I can't," said Nestor. "I need to finish my study of an amazing stream I've located. There are some of the most extraordinary flying creatures you've ever seen there. They have four wings and all varieties of colors. I'll stop by and see Momma and Poppa later. I hope you're still there when I get home so we can talk. Good-bye, everyone." Nestor flew off. Justine said good-bye and also left.

Alexander and Plato stood quietly, looking at each other, each appearing to be waiting for the other to speak first. Finally, Plato broke the silence. "Well, Alexander, it looks like we did it. I can't tell you how much your help has meant to me."

"I have to tell you, when we first talked, I never thought this could happen." Alexander paused briefly, smiled, and shrugged. "I know how Nestor and Justine got involved, but Hardy? How did you find him, and how did you ever arrange for him and Justine to become friends? I'm amazed."

Plato smiled and said, "Oh, it was nothing." He then laughed and shrugged. "Hardy? That was just plain luck. I had no idea he would turn out the way he has. I actually thought Laslo might be the one. He had all the natural ability to do anything he wanted, but he's just too ... intemperate."

"That's putting it mildly," said Alexander.

"Hardy was very perceptive recognizing his brother was not a leader and taking the position he did. I was really impressed with him today."

"Yes, speaking out and not giving his brother that opportunity took guts. But he did the right thing, and he's earned even more trust among the crows because of his actions. So, how did you get Hardy and Justine together?"

"I didn't. The whole thing happened by chance, just like I told you. I'm still amazed at how it worked out. It was just meant to be. Natural destiny, I suspect."

"Really? That's incredible. I thought for sure you'd arranged that somehow. I have a favor to ask you, Plato."

"Anything, just ask."

"I'm going to ask Justine if she'll nest with me next spring."

"Wonderful. Congratulations, though I'm not surprised."

"Don't congratulate me yet. She may not say yes."

"Oh, she will," said Plato with a big grin.

"You think so?"

"No question. So, what's the favor?"

"I can't ask her to nest with me unless I tell her what we've done. She needs to know that I was in this from the beginning and that you and I planned for her and Nestor to help us. I can't keep this deception a secret from her."

"I see," said Plato. "Okay, but only on one condition. You and Justine need to promise no one else is to know of this as long as I'm alive. Once I'm gone you can decide whether to tell Hardy and Nestor and anyone you choose to tell."

"Okay. I'm really worried that she's going to be upset with me for deceiving her. You know her. She'll see what I have done as a lie, and with her sense of what's right and just, she may never want to speak to me again."

"If she gets really upset with you, just ask her this question: is a lie or deception unjust if it is necessary and does good for the majority of the residents of our community? If she can answer that question with certainty, she's smarter than all of us. If she can't, then she should forgive you. Now, you make sure the others don't learn of this until I'm gone. That's one of the last things I'll ever ask of you."

"Deal. Are you feeling okay?" Alexander realized that Plato was not very steady on his feet.

"I'm just very tired. I'm ready for a long sleep. I need to get going. Night's coming soon, and I'm looking forward to a peaceful rest."

"Good-bye, Plato. Thank you."

"Good-bye. And no, thank you. You all have made my life complete."

Plato flew away, and Alexander stood and watched him fade into the evening sky.

Chapter 39

The old duck floated alone in the lake. He had spent the night sleeping while floating among the reeds and cattails. It was now morning, and the first light of day was shining brightly over the horizon. Plato floated among golden leaves that had fallen from the trees and were resting on the surface of the lake. A heavy mist like beautiful clouds rose from the surface of the lake. There was a lovely chill in the air. It would be winter soon.

"Father, the injustice has been ended. All is in place for everyone to live together in peace. Everything is as it should be. I have fulfilled my promise. My work is done. I am finished."

Plato looked up and saw in the mist the brilliant image of his father. His father looked at him with a slight smile on his face and with eyes filled with pride and gratitude. Plato paddled his feet lightly and moved toward his father. The image turned and disappeared into the reeds and cattails. A bright ray of sunlight fell on the lake and then wrapped its loving arms around the woodlot. Frogs and insects were singing their hymns, the music Plato loved so dearly. Plato tucked his head under his wing and followed his father, slowly fading into the reeds and cattails. A gentle breeze moved across the lake and lifted the misty fog toward the heavens.